To Anita Jaeger

Anita, tho b[illegible]

have invested [illegible] songs

to walk in the authority and power in the name of Jesus. the price you have paid will bless many lives.



# One Door Between Us

Tom Donnan

Gazelle
PRESS

Mobile, Alabama

*Although inspired by a true story, the names of characters have been changed. If names in this book correlate to any living or dead person, it is purely coincidental and part of the author's imagination.*

*One Door Between Us*
by Tom Donnan


ISBN 978-1-58169-690-5
For Worldwide Distribution
Printed in the U.S.A.

Gazelle Press
P.O. Box 191540 • Mobile, AL 36619
800-367-8203

# Part I

## The Beginning
## of
## New Life
## in
## Farmington

# One

"Police station, this is Officer Henry. How can I help you?"

"There's a fire at the Pentecostal church on E. Main and Hutton! I live right across the street. I can see flames shooting out of the windows on each side of building!"

Before seeking any more information, Henry reached across the counter to the switch on the wall. A siren, mounted on the top of a ten-foot pole on the roof, shrieked in response. The noise was so loud, it could be heard all across town. Everyone knew immediately there was a fire emergency somewhere.

It was 9:00 p.m. when the siren sounded, and ten men immediately stopped what they were doing. Adrenalin began to rush through their veins. Their wives drew in a deep breath, and concern was suddenly written on their faces. It took a certain kind of man to run into fire danger; courageous or crazy—some days it was hard to tell. The men ran to their cars and raced to the firehouse.

Chief Rogers was worried. "What a terrible time to have a fire!" he said to himself. The new fire hydrants had not yet been completely installed by the utility company so half of the town was without their water. "We may need the reserve tanker." Although the truck was almost too heavy for most of the roads, it was currently filled to the maximum allowance of 8500 gallons. Living closest to the firehouse, the chief arrived first and heard the phone ringing. He ran to the desk, picked up the receiver, and short of breath, he barked, "Chief here, what do you have?"

"It's the Old Pentecostal church on E. Main and Hutton. Call came in from the house across the street. The residents can see flames leaping out of all the windows—both sides of the church!" Officer Henry exclaimed.

"I got it!" The chief sighed and considered the problem—no working hydrants there. If flames were shooting out of the windows on both sides, it was most likely already out of control. Slamming down the receiver, he quickly suited up and ran to the side door. One after another firefighter sprinted through.

They knew the drill. The second guy in raised the garage door and then suited up. The highest-ranking guy would drive the truck. The truck held four men in the cab while four held onto the bar and stepped into the rear of the engine. Although they all enjoyed riding in the back, only concern was written on their faces tonight. In mere minutes from hearing the siren, the fire truck was pulling out with lights flashing and siren blaring. Chief Rogers yelled for the last two men to bring the tanker to the site.

The local power company had donated the tanker truck to the fire department. Several of their buildings were outside of the town limits, beyond even the reach of the planned hydrant system. Being one of the biggest employers, they thought the expenditure was in their best interest. Now that purchase was helping the town, and proving the power company's interest in being a good neighbor to the community.

Half a block away, the firefighters could see the flames shooting out the windows, extending several feet beyond the roofline. Confusion filled the chief's face. *By now, more of this building should be in flames!* he thought. Building fires usually burn with mostly orange flames, but here multiple colors were undulating in the fire. If he stopped to think about, they were actually quite beautiful to see.

A growing crowd had gathered to watch. People were standing on the sidewalks across the street, looking on in horror. Five cars were parked in the church parking lot. A common concern rippled among the onlookers, and they shouted to the firemen, "There are people in there! Hurry!"

Chief grabbed an axe from the front panel of the truck and began barking orders. "Get the two-inch line hooked up and be ready with the four-inch line to connect to the tanker as soon as it gets here."

The fire truck only held one thousand gallons, and that amount would be depleted in under three minutes.

"Gil," he yelled, "get an axe and come with me."

The two men approached the front double doors of the church as the two-inch line was unrolled, attached to the pump fitting, and ready to be turned on.

As he reached for the door handle, the chief carefully touched the metal with his bare hand. *It's not hot!* he thought. He touched the wooden door and found it too was not even warm to the touch. He tried pulling the door handle, and the door began to open easily. He immediately let it shut. *No internal air pressure? What's going on?* his mind screamed.

Both men stiffened up and their training kicked in as they prepared for whatever was on the other side of the door.

"Ready, Gil?" Chief asked.

His partner quickly nodded, and the two men braced for intense heat as they yanked the doors open and cautiously stepped inside.

Outside, the large crowd that had gathered to watch the event unfold shifted positions to see inside when the doors were opened. In a brief moment, they could see smoke hovering within as the two firemen rushed through the door. The two firefighters had expected to see the inside of the building engulfed in flames. Instead, there was only a haze drifting in the air.

"Chief, what's going on? There's no heat—no flames!"

As they walked a few feet down the center aisle and past the rear rows of old wooden pews, their vision improved. Through the haze, they could see a small group of people at the altar. Five church members—four intercessors and their pastor—were kneeling and praying in tongues before God for the souls of men, women, and children in Farmington and beyond.

"Gil, go outside and tell the men to stand down while I talk with the pastor," the chief ordered in a hushed voice.

As the chief continued forward, he could hear them speaking but couldn't make out any words.

He yelled out, "Pastor Smith, are you okay?"

Startled from his intense, travailing prayer, the pastor looked down the aisle to see the fire chief. Only then did he notice the glory cloud in the church. The haze was so thick, he could hardly see fifteen feet in front of him. The presence of God and the love of God filled the atmosphere within the building.

Bewildered and alarmed at hearing the fire chief's voice, Pastor Smith called out, "Chief Rogers, why on earth are you here?"

Pushing open the right-hand door, Gil walked outside to follow the chief's orders. The onlookers now numbered well over a hundred. They had come from all parts of town—some out of concern, while others came out of curiosity simply to gawk.

Yelling toward the fire truck and the other firefighters, he called, "Break it all down, and roll up the hoses. There's no fire here!"

Everyone within hearing was astonished by the announcement. Stan spoke up, "Gil, what do you mean there's no fire? I saw the flames with my own eyes!"

"I'm telling you, there's no fire in the church."

"You have to be kidding me, Gil! I want to see in there for myself."

"Get the hoses rolled and stored, and then go and take a look-see." The firemen pitched in together for a quick cleanup and then hustled to the front door.

"Pastor, tell me what's going on in here. Do you have some kind of incense burning to cause this haze?" The chief's adrenaline rush was beginning to morph into anger. He wanted to understand the circumstances of the reported fire and deal with them in a controlled manner. What he had seen and experienced was eerily beyond the scope of human understanding, and the hairs on the back of his neck were standing up.

The chief continued, "My word, Pastor, I saw flames leaping from the windows! Why isn't there a fire in here?"

A smile came across Pastor Smith's face.

"Chief, it's what we've been praying for! God showed up tonight. For months now we've been meeting on Wednesday nights, praying for revival. No one noticed the haze until you called out, and we had no idea about any flames."

"Pastor, we're here because people reported seeing flames leaping from all the windows. The glow could be seen for a mile. The church looked like it was on fire. I saw the flames myself as we pulled up, and you're telling me that what I saw was the fire of the Holy Ghost?"

"Praise God, Chief, we've gotten our breakthrough! Although I would have liked to have seen the fire with my own eyes."

"What are you talking about?" the chief asked incredulously as the front door flew open, and all the firemen entered to see what should have been a heavily damaged building with their own eyes. After all, fire causes damage, and from the extent of the fire they saw outside, this place should have been a charred mess. Instead, there was no smell of smoke and no burned or charred wood.

They did, however, feel a presence they had never before experienced. To some of them, the presence felt refreshing while others felt an urgent need to exit the building.

# Two

"Ari, honey, don't stand right behind me when I'm doing my hair. I don't want you to get the hair spray in your eyes, darling."

The girl observed this Saturday night ritual of watching her usually reserved mother standing in the bathroom in front of the mirror, teasing her hair to death. Ari thought, *She begins with the makeup, then the dress, and ends with fixing her hair. When it's all done, my mom is beautiful. Saturday night is the only time I see my father wear his cowboy boots and that string and metal thing he calls a tie.*

When the front door bell rang, Sammy and Joey ran for the door ahead of their dad.

"Hi, Sara," Mike said as he stepped around his boys and welcomed the neighbor girl. "Thanks for babysitting the kids tonight."

"I'm glad to do it, sir."

"The games are out. Ari got them out early. Snacks are in the kitchen."

"Okay, where will it be tonight? Clancy's or HWYs (Highways) Lounge?"

"Judy says she's in the mood for country dancing tonight, so it will be HWYs. Telephone number is on the pad next to the phone. Remember, it's loud there. If you have to call, don't be afraid to shout so you can be heard."

Judy came around the corner dressed and ready to twirl. She was wearing a blouse and a three-wide ruffled, country and western dancing skirt made of lightweight cotton material. The blouse was mostly white with a small floral print and poofy shoulders. The full skirt, worn with a stiff petticoat, was a solid red with gold trim at the end of each ruffle. She wore the same size six she had worn ten years ago before having kids. Tied around her neck was a polka-dot red bandana.

Mike commented, "Judy, you know in three shakes of a leg, your neck will be all hot wearing that thing."

"Honey, if you start out right, the night will go right! You know that."

The couple laughed together. Theirs was a déjà vu moment of the best of times. Closing the front door behind them, Mike slipped his arm around Judy's waist as they strolled to the car. It was their Saturday night on the town with fun, dancing, drinking, and friends.

"So, Ari, did you get the next Nancy Drew book you wanted?" Sara asked as they settled down in the living room.

"My mom picked it up at the library for me just this week. I love climbing into bed with my pillows upright to read. I'm supposed to read and fall asleep in fifteen minutes, but I get so involved in the story! Mom always looks in my room and says, 'Lights out, little lady.' My teacher tells me I'm reading well into the fourth grade or maybe even the fifth grade level. All I know is I love to read and get lost in books. I just loved *The Secret of the Old Clock*, and it only took me two days to read *The Hidden Staircase.* I haven't been able to start the third one in her series—*The Bungalow Mystery.*"

Before she could say another word, Sammy came running out of the kitchen with his mouth stuffed with Nabisco ginger snap cookies. "Whoa, little man, where did you get those cookies?" Sara asked. "And where do you think you're going?"

Sammy loved teasing Sara until it was game time. Then he was all serious.

*If the cookies are already open, I want one—well, several,* Ari thought. Looking at Joey, she couldn't decide if her brother had eaten the cookie or was wearing it. The cookies had an orange-tan color, and that color was all around his mouth and on the front of his shirt.

"Yum," Joey happily chortled.

*Some rules go out the door when Mom and Dad are gone!* Ari decided.

Mike and Judy arrived early enough at HWYs to get a table. As planned, three other couples arrived to the sound of loud music and people having a good time. The band was playing "Boot Scootin' Boogie," and Judy looked at Mike. They both got up to take advantage of the best wooden dance floor in town. The hardwood surface was worn smooth and had no sticky spots. Judy had worn her leather shoes with low heels, and Mike had on his cowboy boots. Mike was starting to loosen up after a long week of grueling work. He grabbed Judy, right up under her left arm, and stepped right into their favorite dance—the two-step.

In the Texas two-step, the girl dances backward as the guy leads. Moving counter-clockwise on the dance floor, the two-step was a series of four quick steps followed by two slow ones. Add a twirl in every once and while, and you have the dance down pat. When things get really hopping, they will twirl and then lock their arms around their waists and go sixteen counts forward together. In unison Mike and Judy glided across the dance floor like they owned it. The longer the dance went on, the closer they seemed to dance—two becoming one in motion, reveling in the pure joy of body, music, and dance.

Further into the evening during the band's break, their waitress came over to take their orders. When Mike ordered Boilermakers for all the guys, the look on the wives' faces said it all. The best of the evening was over; it would be downhill from there.

"Mike, please, not this time. Let's just dance the night away. Don't start."

"Don't worry, Jude, we can handle them."

The truth was, he had been craving some hard liquor all night and finally gave in. The waitress returned, balancing a tray with practiced skill. As the men accepted their drinks and downed them without taking a breath, worry showed in all the women's faces. Once the alcohol took over, their husbands would check out. Judy knew there would be more drinks before they would head home.

Mike talked the guys into a game of pool, giving the gals a break from their loud bantering.

Martha said, "Hey, did you hear about the wild fire call last Wednesday night?"

It was the first time Judy had heard of it. After all, they lived in the new annex to the east close to Anamis Elementary School, and the fire call was on the opposite side of town.

Martha picked up the story. "Yeah, the church was on fire; we all saw the flames leaping out the windows and above the roof. Most beautiful fire I ever witnessed. The fire department arrived, stormed the building, and the fire disappeared. I'm telling you as God as my witness, the chief and Gil went in the front door, and the fire went out. Seems it happened during a Wednesday night prayer meeting. Pastor told Chief Rogers that it was the Holy Spirit. Can you imagine that?"

Unexpectedly, Mike returned to the table and said to Judy, "We need to go, Jude." She shot him a look in disbelief until she saw the look on his face.

Turning to Martha, Judy said, "Martha, let's do coffee at Woody's Café after the kids are in school. I'll have Joey with me, but he's no problem. We'll talk more about the fire then."

For obvious reasons, Judy drove home. As she pulled into the drive, she begged, "Mike, please hold it together until we send Sara home." He nodded. Coming through the door together, Mike plopped down on the nearest chair and sighed.

Their practice was to let the kids fall asleep next to the table where they played games. Joey was the first one to go down but not without a fight. Sammy finally gave up at 9:00 and was out like a light. Ari and Sara played one more game of "Go Fish." After that, Sara had suggested the girl rest on the couch.

Judy handed Sara a five dollar bill and asked how the kids were. "Angels, just like angels," she replied.

"Sara, let me watch you walk home." Judy went out front and watched as Sara ran home four doors down. She waved goodbye and went in her front door, and Judy returned inside.

Judy thought, *Ours is a love-hate Saturday night out. When Mike starts drinking, the fun's over for me; however, tonight we did have several great hours of dancing. Gliding across the dance floor is my relief valve. The world disappears while I'm dancing. Then I'm not a mom, and I'm not a wife—I'm his partner and his focus is on me. He's not a bad drinker; he's a need drinker.*

After the kids were finally in bed, Judy removed her makeup, and the house grew quiet. When the last light was switched off, all was well. For a brief minute, Judy reflected on her life. She had watched her parents struggle through World War II, and she remembered hearing her grandparents talk about the Great Depression. *Enduring an occasional night of too much to drink isn't so bad,* she thought as she climbed in bed. *America has survived the Cuban Missile Crisis and even the scar of President Kennedy's assassination with all the uncertainty that came with it. That's all behind us. Mike's work is steady, and although he works a very strenuous job, I never hear him complain. He brings home enough money, and we live comfortably. I love him.*

# Three

Reports had been coming in the last few days from various church members. The phone rang again in the church office.

"Hello."

"Pastor Smith, this is Anna Morgan. I must tell you about the dream that woke me early Thursday morning about 2 a.m. I've never in my life had a dream like this; I felt as if I were living it. I know I was in my bed, Pastor, but I was really watching this dream unfold," she said so fast she could barely get the words out clearly.

"Okay, Anna, okay. Slow down and tell me the details of the dream. What did you see?"

"Pastor, it was just like the Bible story of Jacob's ladder. Over the church, I saw the heavens open and a stairway appeared in the clouds. Angels—hundreds of angels—were descending into the church. Alongside the stairway was a stream of fog. I was wondering what that fog was when, in my thoughts, I saw a word—grace. The color of the 'grace fog' was bright white with beautiful glittering gold color speckles in it. Pastor, angels and grace were entering the church and flowing out the doors and windows into Farmington. I woke up with my heart pounding like it would come right out of my chest. I remembering thinking, *This can't be good for me.* Pastor Smith, what do you think this dream means?"

"I've heard about things like this before but never experienced it for myself. I've studied the Azusa Street Revival—the birthplace of the Pentecostal denomination. I've read about the great men and women of God. Remember, you were in the services, Anna, when we prayed to God to be used by Him to reach our little area of the world. We've been praying for a move of God for many years. Anna, I think that move has begun. I think we're in the beginning season of revival!"

"I tell you what, Pastor. My dream at first scared me to death. I never saw angels before, and these were as white as the high-noon sun. Their wings had beautiful feathers. I thought maybe they were coming to take me home. I've never felt so excited and alive. Come, sweet Jesus, come!"

Up until the time the new bank had been built on Main Street, the cross on top of the steeple at the Baptist church was the highest point in town. The cross could be seen from almost everywhere. For the last three months, weekly prayer meetings were being held, with members asking God to save the lost.

During Sunday's sermon, Pastor Billings announced, "We are concluding our midweek prayer meetings, and we are now entering into the next phase—going door to door. Please sign up on the sheet in the back that details which blocks you will be taking. You know the old saying: 'If they walk and talk, a good Southern Baptist will witness to them and share the love of Jesus Christ!'

"We've studied several important Scriptures, including Ephesians 2:8, John 3:3-8, John 14:6, Romans 3:23, and 6:23, and the clearest statement of salvation by the apostle Paul in Romans 10:9 and 10. If you haven't done this yet, write down the verses on a piece of paper and keep them in your Bible. Better yet, mark them in your Bible. Some of you will be sowing the Word, others will be cultivating the soil, and then you may play a role in harvesting. Strive to live your faith as in 2 Timothy 2:15 and study the Word."

A divine appointment was already in play. Pastor Billings had chosen the area around the new Animas School and the annex.

In the region of the heavenly host, angels were awaiting an assignment. From the direction of the throne room, one word of the Father could be heard, "Farmington!"

Many groups of angels stood with shouts of excitement, and those not chosen were cheering them on, earnestly hoping for their group to be called too. An invasion was about to take place, and angels would be walking the streets.

Again the voice of God rang out, "Go to Pastor Billings. Accompany the church members going door to door. Assist them as they witness of My Son."

# Four

"Jude, can you pour me some more coffee," Mike asked. His nose was buried deep in the Sunday paper. Arielle, who was sitting at the other end of the kitchen table, tipped down the book she was reading just enough to peer over the top. She glanced toward her mother, watching to see how she was going to respond.

Judy stopped washing the breakfast dishes, stepped over to the stove and grabbed the pot, swiveled and warmed up Mike's coffee. As Arielle watched her mother, she rolled her eyes before returning to her story.

Mike drifted into another article and commented, "It says here they started to divert water from the Animas River into the new reservoir as of yesterday, May 2. According to the town, it's currently listed as reservoir number three of four and later to be named Lake Farmington. But I've heard the local boys calling it the Beeline Reservoir because of the Beeline refinery just across from Davis Dam. I wonder which name will stick."

"What I wonder," Judy responded, "is what this will mean for the Butler Reservoir where the town's water comes from now. We're a growing community. Martha told me the other day that Farmington has grown over five hundred percent in just the last ten years. Can you believe it? Our little town is bursting at the seams. Because of the increased demands for water, that reservoir is always running below normal levels. We count on the snow melt from the Rocky Mountains to replenish the water we use. All it would take, Mike, is for one year of low snowfall in the mountains, and we might be on water rationing."

Mike was listening to Judy, but he jumped to another subject. "No wonder we're a growing town—I can't believe how many pages have help-wanted ads. We're a booming town all right. Speaking of work, did I tell you we're starting on boiler number 3 this week? They have the outside structure finished, the iron workers have built the internal skeleton to support it, and I'll be working on the piping and valves system starting tomorrow. The boiler is already in, but all the connections are just beginning." Lowering the paper, he added, "One train after another is bringing in all the material. They pull up to the dock, and the labor gang begins to unload. They're running three shifts a day, can you believe it?"

Dropping the paper on the Formica tabletop, he asked, "Jude, do we still have some of that cherry jelly in the icebox?"

"Yes, I've been saving it for you."

"Would you toast some bread and spread some of that jelly on it for me?"

With a furrowed brow, Arielle lowered her book to watch her mother make the toast. She shook her head, wondering why her mother didn't speak up and say, "You know where the jelly and bread are at." But her mother showed loving appreciation for all the hard and dangerous work Mike did for her and the family. She decided, *Dad is a good provider, and Mom enjoys taking care of all the little things for him. I guess it's her way of pampering him.*

Just as Mike finished his toast, the phone hanging on the wall rang, and Judy passed it over to Mike. One of his co workers was checking in to see whose turn it was to drive in the morning. Four of them rode to work together, taking turns to save money and to free up a car for the rest of the wives to use during the day. Their carpooling means they only had to drive the fourteen miles to Four Corners Generating Station one week out of the month. Being on the permanent day shift had its advantages.

With the ride to work arranged, Mike asked, "Judy, would you hang up the phone for me?"

Ari could not take any more of her mother's waiting on her father and blurted out, "Dad, do you have a broken leg?"

Both of her parents laughed at her question. They knew that, given time, Ari would learn the value about doing things for the other person. Obviously, Mike could do it for himself, but then he knew he would be taking away the gift Judy always lovingly extended to him.

"Sammy, Joey, come in here," Mike yelled out to the boys who were in their room. "I have something to tell you." Joey came out of his bedroom first, but with a slight shove Sammy reached the kitchen first. "Today, we're going hiking along the river! We'll be leaving in an hour, so get yourselves ready. You too, Ari."

Farmington was nestled among mild hills and river valleys. Hearing that the family was going on a hike meant packing a picnic basket, filling the jug with Kool-Aid, and gathering other picnic essentials.

After they pulled off E. Main Street and onto a dirt road, the drive to the parking area was short. From there, a well-worn path led to the river. Upon immediately exiting the car, they enjoyed the sweet scent of the trees growing on both sides of the stream. Judy loved taking these family outings and seeing the children having fun. As they approached the picnic area, she extended her hand to Mike and gently squeezed his arm. He turned to see her soft smile. *If he has a hangover from too much drinking last night, he's hiding it well,* she thought.

Being typical boys, Sammy and Joey ran towards the river's edge. Joey couldn't out run his brother, so he positioned himself to get out of the car first. As fast as his little legs could move him, he ran. In a mere few strides, Sammy overtook him and gave him a bump for good measure. Adventure and being on the hunt pumped in their veins. Snails, frogs, and fish were just a few they sought to catch. Judy relished them being all boy. Like a hunting dog that has spotted its prey, Sammy slowly got into position to spring into action. Getting wet was a small price to pay for the victor.

"Arielle!" her mother called. "Make sure your brothers don't fall in the river!"

Whatever Sammy got into, Joey was right behind him so Ari immediately ran after them. By the time she reached the pair of explorers, they were on their knees, hands in the water, trying to scoop up something. Sammy showed everyone a snail he had plucked from the river and shoved it in Joey's face.

Mike interrupted them. "Kids, here's the plan. We'll take a walk on the river path, so stay close and don't go too far ahead."

For the most part, Farmington was in an arid place located in northwest New Mexico. Hiking alongside the river always brought the parents teachable moments to share with their kids as well as a review of the rules. One of their favorite activities was a strenuous hike up Hillside Trail. Getting to the trail meant crossing a pedestrian bridge and taking switchbacks that snaked their way up to the plateau. From that vantage point, the hikers could see all of Farmington.

Ari remembered her father telling them recently that while the astronauts circled the globe, they could see two man-made creations from space—the Great Wall of China and the steam plume from the Four Corners Generating Station. Once on an adventure up Hillside Trail, the children had to see for themselves. Sure enough, if you looked in the direction of the Four Corners, the only place in America where four state boundary lines met—Arizona, Colorado, New Mexico, and Utah—you could see the steam coming out of the chimneys.

Today's hike was mild in comparison to Hillside Trail. The Animas River Hiking Trail was wide enough for two people to walk side by side. Judy and Mike held hands as they walked together, and their three children led the way. As Judy walked, she couldn't help but think how blessed the family was. *Life is good! We're all healthy, Mike has a good paying job, and he has work for years to come. In all of my life, I have never felt this safe and secure.*

She watched the boys run ahead once again to their favorite spot—the river's edge. They had obviously spotted something that wiggled and squirmed. Being competitive, they both reached into the water. Joey, shy to pain, jumped back at the first sign of danger from the crawfish. Clearly the creature was not pleased by their intrusion into his life and opened its pinchers wide, so Joey had pulled his hand out of the water. Sammy, having learned from his father, grabbed it from behind on its back and plucked it from the water, very proud of his catch. Looking right into his brother's eyes, the alpha male rose up inside of him. He thrust the crawfish, pinchers fully extended, towards Joey's face. They all knew what was coming next.

Joey yelled at the top of his voice, "MOM!" Sammy had those pinchers an inch from Joey's nose, telling him it wouldn't hurt much. After they finally got Joey settled back down again, they continued the hike.

Today's leisurely hike was more about experiencing nature than about a physical challenge to meet. Judy stopped to look at the flowers—the way they were made, their color, shapes and sizes—right down to the tiniest of them. As far as she was concerned, a flower was nature in its entire splendor.

At one spot on the path, the hiker would be ten feet above the river—a perfect place for a good view of the stream building islands and later eroding them away. As the river's water level receded, shallow places became islands even in the middle of the stream. With each rainfall, everything changed and would be rearranged. The molding of the landscape by the water was a continuous work of art. With no rain for days, the water level remained low. In spring after a good snowfall in the Rockies, water always flowed. The main channel of the river ran deep and fast on the far side. Mike kept an eye out for a small island they could explore. On their way back from the hike, Mike spotted a bed of river rock, lying high and dry. They only had to walk through six-inch deep water to reach it.

One family tradition was to enjoy a rock-skipping contest. Sammy's idea of skipping stones was throwing rocks into the water and watching the splash. The bigger the rock—the bigger the splash!

"Hey!" Dad called. "Let's see who can skip a rock the farthest." Shoes and socks came flying off, and the scramble was on for the perfect skipping stone.

Ari was the first to throw and watched the stone make four skips. Joey just couldn't get the hang of skipping rocks yet. His landed in one plop. Determined to be the winner, Sammy chose fat, oval stones but they only did one skip at best.

Mike bent down, looked over the rocks, picked up a three inch, round one that was only a quarter of an inch thick. Kneeling down, he showed the children how to hold it.

"Place the edge of stone at the tip of your index finger like this. Then put your thumb on the opposite side and squeeze slightly. Now bend over at the waist to get down low over the water with your left leg next to the water. Pull back your arm like you're going to pitch a ball on the side—not overhand. Throw as hard as you can, snapping your wrist, and let it fly."

He stood, bent over, wound up, and let his stone fly. Sailing right above the water for ten feet, riding on the air, the stone barely hit the surface for the first skip. "One, two, three, four, five, six…" they counted in unison. With each skip across the surface of the water, the stone traveled less and less until on the seventh skip, it sank to the river bed. When their arms began to ache from the competition, the family hiked back to the picnic area to claim a table under a tree and in the shade.

By the time the picnic basket was empty, their thirst had been quenched, their stomachs were full, their muscles were tired, and the time had come to head home. Today had been one of making memories for a lifetime. Tomorrow was a school day, so the kids needed to get home. Judy walked over to Mike, wrapped her arms around his waist, and whispered something in his ear. They both smiled knowingly, and the family loaded into the car.

Beyond the veil of human sight, an angel was vigilant in watching over this family. Knowing they were destined to be touched by God, his duty was to see them get there. Today was a day of no concerns—no enemies to ward off. Their lives were safe in his care. The atmosphere of God was flowing across this county. To see 2 Chronicles 7:14 come to Farmington had been placed upon the hearts of the Baptist and Pentecostal pastors. Their prayers were being heard. God was healing their land, and the salvation of the lost was imminent.

A wonderful day had ended. Arielle rested in bed, riveted to the last few pages of her exciting book. The irises of her eyes widened as she read how the car exploded and how quickly the ambulance and the police arrived. First aid was administered to Stumpy, Alma, and the other man. Arielle paid careful attention to how the injured were medically treated. The bad guy was caught; the stolen money and securities were found in the bottom of a suitcase. The crime was solved, and Nancy's friend Laura met her guardians for the first time. Taking a deep breath, Arielle exhaled and slowly closed the book. She placed it on the nightstand, reached up and turned off the lights. To enjoy one of the first warm spring nights, she had opened her window, allowing the mild breeze to flow freely into her room. With her hands clasped behind her head, she rested quietly on her bed, recapping the exciting Nancy Drew story in her mind.

Through the window in the distance, she heard the long, slow whistle blow of a train. The sound rolled through the air like thunder. Each engineer had his own style, and tonight, the sound was a slow building whistle with a powerful whoop at the end. She listened to the whistle, not knowing it belonged to the end of an era. This was the last summer the steam engines would be used because they were all being replaced by the more efficient diesel engines.

Returning to her thoughts, Ari pondered how brave Nancy Drew was in her great adventures. The girls at school were telling her about another mystery series called the *Hardy Boys*. She loved a good mystery and learning how all the pieces fit together in the end. As she drifted off to sleep, the house had grown quiet though the windows were open. The cool night air drifted in.

Piercing the darkness with laughter, Mike commented, "Judy, did you see Sammy and Joey trying to skip large round rocks?"

"Ya know Mike, we could have named the boys Pete and Re-Pete." Another round of laughter filled the air.

# FIVE

Walking in the front door of Woody's Café, Judy looked around. Martha had already chosen a window table for them and waved for Judy to come and be seated. Woody's was a small local diner built before the boom, and many of the locals loved to frequent the café. The tables were arranged in an "L" design, and most of them had been situated along the front windows. At a window table, the patron could look out onto Main Street. For those wanting to see what was happening in town, a window table in Woody's Café was their first choice.

Every good diner of that day had a counter and stools, and Woody's was no different. In the morning, the counter would be filled with men on their way to work, grabbing what was called "Coffee and..."—coffee and breakfast or coffee and a sweet roll. Flirtatious words to the waitress often flowed across the counter. Of course, she knew everyone's first name—"Hon." Those who chose to sit at the counter had their backs to the windows and tables. Usually a person coming in solo looked for an open stool at the counter and a friend to talk with—in that order.

At ten o'clock in the morning, most of the workers had already gone, and some of the day timers had shuffled in. Joey had grown enough to sit in the booth on a booster seat next to his mother and be able to color on the tabletop. The two friends settled in. The first order of business was getting out crayons and coloring book to entertain Joey. Then the serious conversation could begin.

"What ya ordering, gals?" the waitress asked. Martha had a taste for their legendary French toast and of course, coffee. Judy asked for chocolate milk and a homemade blueberry muffin for Joey and coffee and raisin toast for herself.

"Judy, you eat like a bird," Martha noted.

"I had breakfast with the family this morning. I can't keep wearing a size six if I overeat."

"Speaking of your size, where on earth did you get that red dancing dress? You and Mike were burning up the dance floor on Saturday night."

"Tell you the truth, I almost bought a pattern and material. But as I was thumbing through the catalog, I saw the dress and mail ordered it. With raising three kids and even with my loving to sew, I still felt I didn't have the time to make it myself. I did add the gold ribbon on the edge of each ruffle to add a little extra something. Do you think it was too much?"

"It was perfect! That's all I got to say, perfect!"

Right then the door opened, and a man walked in. He looked up and down the counter, which was completely open. The girls could not believe his gall when he chose the stool right across from them. Martha rolled her eyes at his sitting so close to them, placed her hand up to her mouth, leaned forward and whispered, "Can you believe this guy?"

Ding, Ding, Ding! The cook rang the bell on the counter in the food window to let the waitress know that an order of food was ready. She quickly brought their order, which looked enticing. Powdered sugared, stuffed French toast with strawberries would soon be oozing with maple syrup and two scoops of butter.

Joey didn't need any invitation; he pushed the coloring book away and eyed his muffin. Buttering each slice of her French toast, Martha poured maple syrup over them. Turning to Joey, she asked, "Hey, little man, are you going to be able to eat that entire muffin?" Joey merely nodded while taking his first bite.

Now that the food had arrived, Judy directed the conversation to the topic she had been waiting patiently to discuss. "Martha, start from the beginning. Tell me all about the fire at the Pentecostal church."

The waitress poured a warm-up for the man sitting at the counter as he decided to order a sweet roll. He picked up the newspaper the café provided for their customers and opened it up. He was in his own world, or so they thought.

Martha leaned forward and began to tell about the hottest topic in town, emphasizing her words with hand gestures. "When I got to the church, I couldn't believe it when I saw flames shooting out the windows. They were the prettiest flames I've ever laid eyes on. Waiting for help to arrive seemed like hours. Judy, I watched in horror because people were in there! By the time the fire truck got there, a hundred people were watching in front of the church. The firemen had set up the hoses, and the pumper truck was ready to go when the power company tanker truck arrived. Chief and Gil had axes in their hands running for the front door, and girl, you know how those men love to swing those things. I swear, half the fun of being in the department is so they can break stuff. Well, anyway, they paused at the front door and then went in. You could see smoke from floor to ceiling. I watched as the doors closed behind them. You know, I've heard smoke can suffocate people. Honestly, we all expected to hear the worst. Then almost immediately Gil came back out. I believe that the man looked absolutely disappointed he couldn't break anything. He called to the others to pack up. Can you believe it?"

"Pack up? I thought you said the building was on fire."

"It was. Flames were leaping up three feet above the roof; the brightness caused a glow you could see down the block. Now here's the oddest thing. When Chief and Gil went in, the fire shooting from all the windows went out. Poof, out! I found out that Pastor Smith told Chief Rogers it was a fire of the Holy Ghost. Yes, you heard me right—a fire of the Holy Ghost. I would laugh except there was no damage—not a charred piece of wood anywhere. The windows didn't break from the fires. Nothing."

"Look at the hair on my arms, Martha." Judy motioned.

"Exactly, Judy. It's spooky."

The man at the counter set down his paper, folded it neatly, and swiveled on his stool to face the women. Without an "excuse me," he interrupted their conversation.

"I've heard of incidents like that before. In the Bible on the day of Pentecost, the Holy Ghost roared into Jerusalem. The noise was so loud, people came from all around. It rushed into a room where all the disciples and followers of Jesus were staying. As the wind burst into the room, one hundred and twenty people had tongues of fire above their heads. What followed next was an explosion of evangelism. Thousands upon thousands were saved." He paused as the stunned women looked at each other.

"In Los Angeles during the first decade of this century," he continued, "a little church in the poor part of town also had fire burning out of their windows. News of the incident spread like crazy. People from all across the nation went to that little church and caught the fire. It was the birth of the Pentecostal denomination."

He stopped speaking, made a quarter turn on his stool, placed some money on the counter, and stood up. Judy and Martha watched the man's stone-blank expression. He walked to the front door and left the café. Both gals leaned over to see where he was going…only he had disappeared. Martha jumped out of her seat and ran outside. Through the window, Judy watched her looking up the and down the now-empty street.

When she returned to her seat, Martha asked, "Judy, what just happened?"

Speechless and stunned, the two sat silently in thought until Joey slurped his straw in a futile attempt to get the last of the chocolate milk.

Though they were still spooked, Judy gathered her thoughts and offered, "Ya know, Martha, my grandmother used to talk about a Scripture that says we could entertain angels and not know it. But that man disappeared. As you said, Martha, 'Poof,' and he was gone."

The phone in the church office rang. "Hello, this is Pastor Smith."

"Pastor, this is Anna Morgan. I had another vivid dream last night. Can you please tell me what's going on?"

"I'm not yet sure, Anna. However, we do have a passage in the book of Joel that says in the last days we would have Holy Ghost dreams and visions. I'm beginning to wonder, Anna, if the Holy Ghost is giving you these dreams. What did you see in your dream this morning?"

"Pastor, I saw angels following people as they walked through town. They had that glittery gold fog I told you about before. This time, the fog was more like clouds that moved with them. I watched as the cloud would come upon people, and they would cry. Then the dream ended. What do you think this means?"

"At this time, I don't have a clue; however, I have learned hindsight can be a great teacher. We must ask the Holy Ghost to show us its meaning. As you pray, Anna, ask God to show you the meaning of the fog clouds."

"Okay, Pastor, I can do that. Are we having our weekly prayer meeting this Wednesday?"

"No, I believe the time has come to begin a midweek worship service and open up the altar for prayer."

As their conversation ended, Pastor Smith's thoughts turned to prayer. "Father God, please show me how to lead the people into what is next. I have read about the day of Pentecost and the action of the Holy Ghost. How do I learn to line up with His actions as He moves into our services? Please, Lord, show me all I need to know so that this season of revival will glorify You."

After leaving the café, Judy drove to Animas School with Joey to pick up Sammy from his morning kindergarten class. Most of the mothers waited right outside the front door on the days when the weather permits. Today, they all were enjoying the warm sunshine.

Still thinking about what had just happened, Judy couldn't bring herself to mention it. It's one of those things you simply don't talk about! After all, she had sworn Martha to secrecy. Not wanting to talk to anyone, she and Joey waited on the fringe of the group. Judy realized she was still shaken by her experience. *This has to be supernatural,* she thought. She also knew a thing like that could stir up the worst in people. She held her experience inside, pondering it in her mind. Chills rushed over her as she tried to process what she had seen and heard. *What did he mean about the fire and evangelism? What church was birthed, and how did people carry the fire? It's like a riddle; it's not clear, but I'm sure it has meaning. But what?*

# Six

Pastor Billings and his wife Betty prayed, "Father God, we pray to You this night that You will have mercy on the souls of men. Send Your Holy Spirit and Your grace before us, O God. Prepare our way tonight as we go door to door, sharing Your Word. Bring repentance of sin to their hearts, Father God. In Jesus' name we pray. Amen."

The couple walked out the door of their home and took a short drive to the new annex in town. Walking up the concrete sidewalk, they turned toward the first house on their list; no one was home. As they continued down the block, wonder and expectation filled their hearts. Together, under the prayer covering, they trusted God for souls. They knew that sometimes they only planted the seed of the Word of God in people's hearts. The soil in which the seed was planted needed to be cultivated or watered, encouraging a person forward toward salvation. Then would come the times of harvest when a person invited Jesus into his or her heart and life. The germination of the seed took place, the Holy Spirit entered the spirit, and new life sprouted. Whatever happened tonight, the work was all for the cause of Christ.

Because of the warm spring evening, the front door was open. A sweet-smelling breeze was flowing through the screen door. The irises were flowering, and their fragrance, one of Judy's favorite aromas, rode on the wind. Supper was over, the cleanup was finished, and helping Ari with her homework was next on the agenda.

Their protecting angel began to smile as he stepped through the screen door and walked to the sidewalk. Coming down the block was Pastor Billings with several angels on assignment following him. The glory cloud of God's mercy and grace was over them. The light of the gospel and the glory of Christ went with this group, dispelling any spiritual darkness. No verbal words were exchanged between the angels, but a conversation seemed to be in progress.

As Pastor Billings and his wife walked to the door and rang the bell, three wide-eyed children raced for the door.

"Mom! Dad! Some people are here!" Ari yelled toward the kitchen.

Mike and Judy both stood and their eyes locked for barely a second as they instinctively knew what the other was thinking: *What now?* Lately, the only people who seemed to come to their door were church people. Tonight would likely be the same. Their upbringing had taught them to be polite to ministers; after all, they carried the responsibilities of God on their shoulders and deserved respect.

When they answered the door, the pastor greeted them, "Howdy, folks, I'm Pastor Billings and this is my wife, Betty. We're visiting from the First Baptist Church here in Farmington. May we come in?"

Mike opened the screen door and invited the couple inside, "Yes, please come in." Mike led the Billingses into the kitchen as Judy followed. The children knew that all the rules were suspended; company was there!

As the couple sat down, Judy asked, "May I get you anything? Water, soda, or maybe I can put on some coffee?"

Betty answered, "Coffee would be nice," and Mike and the pastor nodded in agreement. After Judy placed the coffeepot on the stove, she joined them at the table.

Mike could hear the children running up and down the hallway. Mike excused himself and went to the children.

"Ari, can you get out the game of Sorry and play with your brothers?"

"Yes, Dad."

An angel leaned over the children as they gathered around the coffee table in the living room. He whispered, "Peace be with you." They turned their attention to playing the game, and he remained with them. This angel had a fondness for children. He had often heard Jesus say that the little ones like these would inherit the kingdom of God. The other angels passed through the wall and into the kitchen; almost instantly a thin grace cloud appeared on the ceiling. The angels could see grace spread out from wall to wall.

Pastor Billings started the conversation with small talk, mentioning the growth rate of Farmington. Everyone felt the awkwardness of the spontaneous visit, but a shift into a feeling of friendliness soon occurred, and their visit became more comfortable.

Making a transition into why they were visiting, Pastor Billings asked if any other churches in town had come by to speak to them.

"Yes they have," Mike answered as the couple nodded their heads.

Without asking which denomination had visited, the pastor continued, "If I may, I'd like to share a verse in the Bible with you."

Mike and Judy glanced at each other. Feeling nervous, Judy left the table to get the coffeepot and cups and brought them to the table with her best cream and sugar containers. After pouring four cups, she set the pot on a potholder.

As Pastor Billings turned to the verse he wanted to share, they all were busy creating their individual version of the perfect cup of coffee.

"Here it is: John 14:6." He turned the Bible toward Mike and Judy and pointed to the verse. "Would you please read it out loud?"

Surprised at his request, together they read, "Jesus saith unto him, I am the way, the truth, and the life: no man cometh unto the Father, but by me." The couple looked up and waited.

"Do you know what that verse means?" Pastor Billings asked.

Judy spoke up and said, "My grandmother talked about Jesus. I think she told me Jesus was saying there is only one God, and that if we want to know Him, we must pass through Jesus to reach Him."

"Yes," the pastor agreed. "The mystery is how that can happen. Let's look at another verse." Taking the Bible back, he flipped through the pages. Betty and Judy exchanged glances as they sipped their coffee. Something was happening; an inner nervousness stirred in the hearts of Mike and Judy. Having never before experienced this type of unrest, and therefore unable to assess it, they remained quiet and focused on the Bible.

"Here it is…John 3:3-8." Turning the Bible toward them again, he pointed to verse three for them to read in unison.

"Jesus answered and said unto him, Verily, verily, I say unto thee, Except a man be born again, he cannot see the kingdom of God. Nicodemus saith unto him, How can a man be born when he is old? can he enter the second time into his mother's womb, and be born? Jesus answered, Verily, verily, I say unto thee, Except a man be born of water and of the Spirit, he cannot enter into the kingdom of God. That which is born of the flesh is flesh; and that which is born of the Spirit is spirit. Marvel not that I said unto thee, Ye must be born again. The wind bloweth where it listeth, and thou hearest the sound thereof, but canst not tell whence it cometh, and whither it goeth: so is every one that is born of the Spirit."

"I just love the promise of these verses; I could preach on them every Sunday," Pastor commented.

Mike looked up at him and asked, "What is being born spiritually all about? I don't understand."

"You see, Mike, God is Spirit, and He wants us to be born spiritually to become His adopted child."

"Pastor, I've heard that all people are God's children," Mike answered with a slight pushback.

"We're all created in the image of God. Before we were born, He knew us. Read verse six again for me."

"That which is born of flesh is flesh and that which is born of the Spirit is spirit."

"Let me explain this verse. We're born of our parents or born of flesh. They brought us into this world. There is a second birth—a spiritual birth that takes place when we seek God with our whole heart, mind, and soul. When we seek Him, He leads us to His plan of salvation through His Son Jesus."

Judy interrupted, "My grandmother would tell me it is a personal relationship with God. How does this affect the spiritual birth you're talking about?" Pastor Billings could tell she genuinely wanted to know the answer.

"Judy, you and Mike are one in marriage. You feel the oneness of two spirits joined to become one. That is what happens when we are born again. At the moment of salvation, the Holy Spirit enters your spirit, and you both become one. The Bible calls this becoming a new creation in Christ Jesus."

Mike asked, "Why is all of this necessary, Pastor? It seems complicated to me."

Pastor could tell Mike was becoming frustrated. "It's all about sin, Mike. God gave us a free will to choose to follow God's ways or go our own way. He longs for those who will freely love Him. Also, heaven is God's home, and since God is pure and holy, no sin is allowed in heaven. That's why God had a plan to save the human race. From Genesis to the book of Revelation, blood has been required for the remission of sins. Before Jesus, blood was shed through an animal sacrifice. Then Jesus came and shed His blood on the cross to pay for our sins once and for all time so we can have a relationship with God through Him and be with Him in heaven forever. When we accept this gift, we're washed in the blood and become saved. We then commit to follow Jesus by laying our lives down and trusting and following Him.

The angels begin to smile, and the grace cloud began to expand across the ceiling. They already knew it would soon fill the room from the top to the bottom. As the grace cloud touched Mike and Judy, their spirits responded. First, their minds opened to new thoughts. As the grace passed over their emotional hearts, the barriers they had erected for self-protection and the years of emotional pain and suffering melted away. Mike and Judy felt their hearts soften in a way they had never before experienced. Letting their hearts be free felt so good.

Judy asked, "Pastor, you say this is a gift. Why exactly is it a gift?"

"It's like this, Judy. In Ephesians 2:8…" Stopping briefly to quickly turn to the reference, he turned the Bible around and pointed to the verse for them to read. "For by grace are ye saved through faith; and that not of yourselves: it is a gift from God."

"You see, Jesus needed to live a sinless life on earth. This verse is saying we can't earn our way to heaven. Only Jesus could earn this gift for us. In our humanness, we would become prideful if we could earn our way to heaven."

The gold sparkles—the knowledge of God—began to fall from its place on the ceiling. The angels' faces began to shine. The knowledge of the glory of God was being grasped as it washed over the hearts and minds of Mike and Judy; they were inwardly beginning to understand. A phrase Judy's grandmother used to say came to her mind. "Pastor, my grandmother would say, 'I am a woman of unclean lips.'"

Pastor Billings explained that Judy's grandmother got a glimpse of the purity of God, and in His reflection, she knew her unworthiness. Now Judy was beginning to see what her grandmother saw. Tears began to flow down her cheeks.

Betty placed her hand on her husband's arm. Harvesting time had come in Mike and Judy's home. She asked, "Do you want to pray to invite Jesus into your heart and commit to following Him?"

Faith had risen; the moment was pregnant, heavy with anticipation. Mike and Judy, with softened hearts and expressions of repentance for their sin, both nodded yes.

Rejoicing inwardly, Pastor Billings said, "Here, Mike and Judy, is a prayer of invitation." Placing a piece of paper in front of them, he instructed, "Pray it together." Under the table, Judy tightly grasped Mike's hand.

Hearing what humans could not, the angels turned in unison to look toward the street. A roaring wind became louder and louder as it approached the house where salvation had come. Above them, the veil between the world and the spiritual realm began to open in a circular fashion. Around the edges and beyond were row after row of angels all singing praises to God for these souls being saved. The angel with the children passed through the wall to join in the atmosphere of heavenly voices and take part in the event. The family's protecting angel had completed his assignment and would now be transitioning into a new role. The wind of the Holy Spirit burst through the screen door and swirled in a fast, tight circle above the heads of the family.

Taking a folded piece of paper from the back of his Bible, Pastor Billings unfolded it and placed it on the table for both of them to read. For them to take steps like this was different; any other night the Billingses would have been on their way before the children had finished their first game of Sorry. Something was happening that neither Mike nor Judy could explain—except they were inwardly being compelled to follow through with the prayer.

They began to read. "Dear Father God, we thank You for Your Son Jesus and the work He did on the cross by shedding His blood to pay the price for all of the sins of mankind. I tell You now, Father, I am a sinner. I am sorry for the pain my sins have cost You. Please forgive me. Now Father, I invite Jesus to come into my heart and into my life, and I want to live for Him. In Jesus' name we pray, amen."

The swirling presence of the Holy Spirit broke off into two smaller streams, entering into their individual hearts. They began to weep openly. The cleansing of their spirits in the blood of Jesus and the presence of the Holy Spirit could not be expressed in human words. They felt new; they felt born again spiritually. The heavenly choir rose an octave in praising God; the beauty of their voices rang throughout the heavens.

The children ran into the kitchen to see why their parents were crying. Instead of seeing a sadness on their faces that usually accompanied tears, they saw expressions of joy. Confused looks came across their faces, and Joey crawled up into his mother's lap. Judy hugged him with a tight squeeze. Arielle and Sammy stood next to their father. They had never seen him this way before and felt somewhat scared. Their young minds wondered what was happening, but only in the days ahead would they learn the answer to that question.

"Pastor," Mike exclaimed, "I've never felt this good!"

In the emotions of the moment, Judy nodded her head in agreement and then added that she felt a fire burning in her heart.

As soon as their emotions calmed, Betty began to share some thoughts of what would be ahead for them. She invited them to church, saying they would need to be fed spiritually and become part of a church family.

"The support of fellow believers will bring strength into your new life in Jesus," she explained.

Pastor also shared a few important details to remember like daily reading the Bible and praying. Judy's mind searched her memories, trying to recall where she had put the Bible her grandmother had given her.

The wind of the Holy Spirit left the house in the same manner He came in. However, He was now in the hearts of Mike and Judy. What would soon be discovered was that Mike was instantly delivered from alcohol. Never again would he be under its control. From this day forward, he would only be under the influence of the Holy Spirit. In heaven, a rather large ledger was opened, and the names of Mike and Judy were entered. The couple were now adopted children, heirs to the kingdom of God.

The Billings left the house with the angels close behind them. The cloud of grace had accomplished its goal and slowly diminished but did not leave the home. As in the biblical story of Zacchaeus, the tax collector, salvation had come to this household. The task of the angel who had been assigned to them was now to become their messenger from God. He would now be delivering dreams, visions, and an inner witness of the goodness of God.

# Seven

The crew with whom Mike worked took their lunch break in the shanty, enjoying a normal day with telling crude jokes and using foul language. Today, listening to their conversations was hard for Mike. He wanted to go outside and eat by himself. This had never happened before! The way Mike talked at home was the way he talked at work, and he hadn't minded the ways the guys talked—until today. Some of the crude jokes were really funny; however, today the joking felt like sandpaper on his skin.

"Come with me," his boss said. "We need to go up top on boiler #2, and I'll show you exactly what needs to be done."

The foreman's asking Mike to accompany him to evaluate a valve job came as a welcome respite. Generating power was all about routing steam according to the drawings, and Mike was one of the foreman's best workers. He always knew he could rely on Mike to get a job done.

Mike grabbed his hard hat, stenciled with Four Corners on the left side, along with his safety glasses. He had opted to have mesh side shields attached to the ear pieces. Most guys used the solid-clear shields. But up top in the heat, the solid ones fogged up while the mesh ones allowed the air to get through.

The two men walked into the main building, took elevator #1 in Building 1 to the top level, the equivalent of twenty stories. The freight elevator, which was large enough to hold a car, had a lifting capacity of twenty thousand pounds. Three sides of the cab were solid metal walls except for the last two feet near the ceiling. That two feet was open mesh to enable the riders to see into the hoistway. The front vertical power gate was composed of a steel frame and a heavy wire mesh.

Due to the weight capacity, the machinery was geared at a lower ratio. Climbing at a rate of three hundred feet a minute took less than a minute to reach the top, unless it stopped to pick up another rider. Mike watched as steel beams, corrugated sheeting, and hoistway doors went by. When the elevator stopped, the bi-parting doors opened, and the steam noise was deafening. Both men automatically reached into their pockets for their ear plugs.

As they stepped out of the elevator, a blast of air easily 110° enveloped them. Huge exhaust fans had been placed on the roof, but even with those on high speed it was hot.

Closing the doors, the foreman yelled, "Mike, follow me."

A layer of dust rested on everything. Touching a handrail or a piece of metal was painful. The brief contact didn't leave a burn, but it hurt. They took the catwalk, snaking around boiler #1 until they were on the far side looking across at boiler #2. Both boilers had been operational for years. Right in front of the men was a catwalk that bridged the span to the other side of the building.

The foreman walked up to it and suddenly stopped. Mike watched as he stood poised and then climbed up the three steps to begin walking the fifty feet to the wall of the second boiler. He made it a point to walk right down the middle of this four-foot-wide walkway. *Why?* Mike wondered. *There are handrails four foot high on each side. Why does he so deliberately walk down the center?*

He knew catwalks have open grating to minimize weight and dirt collection. The walking surface was composed of quarter-inch steel in two-by-four squares and an inch and a half in depth. Plenty of room to see through it! Mike watched as his boss focused his eyes straight ahead and quickly walked to the other side. Mike climbed the three steps, walked halfway, and stopped to take in the sights. The catwalk happened to be the only structure connecting the two buildings. He noted the two hundred feet of openness on either side; then he glanced below through the grating to see the clear view to the ground floor. He chuckled as he finally understood. The foreman had a touch of acrophobia.

Shouting over the noise, the foreman told him, "Mike, here's what I need." He pointed to the relief valve setup where the reheated or superheated steam was routed. "You see how both steam lines have a relief on them? We need to have these safety valves within ten feet of each other in case of an emergency. Steam with this much heat and pressure can't be vented into the building. If the pressure got too high, it would kill anyone in the area."

Mike instantly understood what he was saying. If it needed to pop off pressure steam above safety limits, it would be vented to the roof.

"See the hand valve with a bolted bonnet and rising stem?" he continued. "We need a maximum of ten turns to be fully closed. It needs to be connected right to the relief valve and set for 300 pounds PSI and 110 percent over pressure release. I need you to build this for boiler #3. Can you do this for me?"

"Sure. How much time do I have to finish this job?"

"I need it done in two weeks. Fabricate it, assemble everything, and then come and get me. We can break it down and haul it up to be installed before we work in a surrounding area. We can't put part of the boiler up until this valve is installed. Otherwise, we're holding up the other tradesmen. Got it?"

"Yes, we'll be ready."

Walking to the freight elevator in Building 2 took longer. Mike rightfully surmised that his boss might not want to walk the tightrope a second time. He had experienced enough excitement for one day. Mike didn't have a problem with open spaces; he simply tied off with a safety harness and lanyard when the work was dangerous. But iron workers were crazy guys—a breed of their own. They walked open beams hundreds of feet in the air in winds gusting at thirty miles per hour. Many of them were Indians with no fear of heights. He admired them.

Back down on the ground floor, Mike thought about his lack of enthusiasm about the old lunch-time camaraderie. *What's going on with me? The talk has never bothered me before…why now?* The change he was feeling was like watching the same magnetic polarity pushing away—south to south or north to north repel each other.

He realized their crude talk was now repulsive to him, and he couldn't put his finger on why. *Well, it's Friday, and I'll have the weekend to think it over. A myriad of changes have taken place since Wednesday night and the Billingses' visit,* he thought. *I need to talk to Judy. Instead of going dancing, I'd like to see our entire family go out for dinner at the A&W Root Beer Drive-in and see a movie at the Allen Theater. They're replaying "Journey to the Center of the Earth" with James Mason and Pat Boone doing a great job of acting. The kids will love it.*

# Eight

After World War II, automobiles became an American icon with cars built to suit every personality. Manufacturers were designing new cars from Corvairs to Corvettes with every kind of choice in between—from economy cars to muscle cars. Keeping up with the Joneses spurred on people living the American dream, which resulted in many living beyond their means.

Mike and Judy were common-sense people when it came to their finances. Instead of splurging, they had decided to buy a used Chevy Impala, four doors and family-friendly yet still a bit sporty. The car had a straight six cylinder engine on which a handy mechanic like Mike could easily do minor repair work. From the front grill to the round taillights, it was fun to drive and ride in.

Arielle, Sammy, and Joey were excited to be going to the A&W to eat. They dressed in their best casual clothes. Dad unlocked the car, and the family all jumped in and rolled down the windows. As the car started, the radio came on with the song "Danke Schoen" sung by Wayne Newton. Everyone joined in to sing along while they rode down the street.

Under the canopy at the A&W, Mike put the car in park. A young woman on roller skates came up to the driver's window, performed a little twirl, bent down, and looked in.

"Hi, folks, do you need a menu?"

She wore a white blouse with an A&W logo on it and a black skating skirt. The red bandanna tied around her neck was positioned fashionably to the side. Ari took notice of her outfit and make up while Sammy and Joey anxiously waited to order.

After handing them menus, the girl skated away and rolled up to another car while they made their choices. The kids squeezed together to watch her skate away, thinking skating was the best thing ever. They listened as Mom read them their choices to eat. Dad, Mom, Ari, and Joey wanted a cheeseburger and fries, but Sammy wanted a hotdog and fries.

The girl swooped in from the front and asked, "Ready to order?"

"Yes," Mike said and repeated what everyone had decided, concluding with a frosty mug of root beer for everyone—two large mugs and three junior mugs.

Swoosh, she whirled around and was gone.

Judy wondered, *Root beer instead of real beer? Not a peep out of him about going for a drink. Where's the Mike who craved hard alcohol? I must admit that I like the fact we're doing family things together.* She was certainly not complaining but noticing something was different. *But is it going to last?*

As she wondered about these changes, the radio was softly playing "Mack the Knife," and everyone sang with gusto.

"Roll up your windows a bit for me," the skating waitress said when she returned. Trays were hooked onto the glass windows—one by Mike and one in the rear window by Ari. The mugs stayed on the tray for now. Ari knelt on the seat and handed her brothers their food after they sat back and were still. Mike passed Judy her meal.

The car became quiet as the family enjoyed their meal while they listened to Dean Martin sing "Amore." All three children soon squeezed up to the window, reaching for their frosty mug—a scene sure to cause a disaster. Ari took one swallow of the rich, deep root beer taste. The chill brought out the flavor.

"The best I've ever had," she excitedly told her parents. Sammy belched quietly to contribute his opinion. It was odd, but no one spilled food or drink on their clothes or the car.

A short line awaited them at the ticket window of the Allen Theater. The small town theater was a hub of small town society. The marquee jutted out and hung over the sidewalk like a huge triangle. The lighted sign displayed the names of the movies now playing. From nearly every place on the block, people could read it. For small town children, the experience was grand. Directly above the marquee, the name "Allen," in large red neon letters, was stacked vertically.

Walking into the foyer, the smell of popcorn brought cravings to the moviegoers, and if they were not already full, the kids would have begged for some.

"Main floor or balcony?" Mike asked.

Center row, main floor was everyone's choice. As soon as they found seats, the curtains opened and a Woody the Woodpecker cartoon showed first. Sammy loved slapstick; he laughed so hard he almost seemed to stop breathing. Ari giggled and Joey crawled up on Mike's lap to see better. Mike looked at Judy, and as their eyes met, a look of love was exchanged. In a fleeting thought, Mike wondered, *Is Judy missing her dancing night out and being with the other women?* If she was, he couldn't tell.

On the way home, all the children could talk about was the crystal wall and the dinosaurs. *Journey to the Center of the Earth* was a thriller, and for the next few days, the kids yelled, "Ky-aye" as they ran from one room to another, looking for each other. Ari pondered the great escape of the professor, his nephew, and their guide via the volcano's plume. The exciting story, as thrilling as those in her mystery books, was the end of perfect day.

Another surprise happened that night as Mom and Dad tucked the kids in bed—they prayed together with the children. Praying was new for them, and it felt good.

Just before turning off the light in the bedroom, Mike announced, "We're going to church tomorrow, so sleep tight. And don't let the bedbugs bite!"

Ari wondered, *What are bedbugs anyway?*

# Nine

"Ky-aye!" Judy yelled from the kitchen, and the three kids, laughing and giggling, jumped out of their beds and came running. She had prepared one of the household favorites—French toast straight from the frying pan, sprinkled with powdered sugar and soon to be covered with maple syrup. As long as someone could eat more, she made it. After all, she didn't want any of those tummies making hunger noises while they were attending church. Soon the milk glasses were empty, the plates were clean, and the time had come to get ready.

"Kids, I want you to put on your best clothes, brush your teeth till they're sparkling, and brush your hair till it shines. We're dressing up in our best, and I want you to put on your best behavior."

Ari took in all this fuss and wondered about the changes she was seeing. *I don't know what's happening with my parents. Things are different since Wednesday night. What are the clues, Ari? Focus. Their focus of attention is definitely different. Dad's focus is on Mom, and their focus is on us. Mom seems to be loving Dad's glances, and he hasn't opened one bottle of beer. The common factor is God, but how could He bring about the changes I see happening in just a few days?*

Mike, dressed in a dark blue suit, walked into the kitchen. From the bathroom came the good-natured clamor of Sammy and Joey vying over who would brush their teeth first. They couldn't do it together because the one-step box they had to stand on was only wide enough for one at a time. Without it, they couldn't see themselves in the mirror above the sink.

*What about Dad's Sunday paper?* Ari wondered. Her entire life she had watched her father read the Sunday paper first thing in the morning. Now he had no time for it!

Judy had slipped into the bedroom and changed into her favorite dress with a tie collar that buttoned to the waist. The oyster colored dress gathered nicely around her waist had proven to be quite comfortable for sitting for any length of time. She reached into her jewelry box for a modest string of pearls. Which look did she want today? Grace Kelly? Minnie Pearl? She thought, *If I start right, it will come out right. Today I will go with Grace Kelly.* She decided to wear her hair down and reached up to the closet shelf for a round, white box containing her hat.

"It's time to go!" Mike shouted, and everyone headed to the car. The drive to the church on West Main Street was short. The single-story, white, wooden building with a peaked roof had a spire topped with a cross that could be seen for blocks. The windows were Gothic-period stained glass. Classrooms were located on both sides of the building, and the sanctuary was in the center. As they pulled up to the church, they noticed many families entering the church doors. Judy held hands with Sammy and Joey while Mike held Arielle's. Together, the family climbed the few stairs up and through the open doors into the church.

Just inside the door was the angel assigned to Mike, Judy, and the children. He watched them enter the building with an expression of great joy. He knew today was an important day for the family. As they were talking to the greeter, the angel came up behind the children, and one at a time, he placed his hand on each one's left shoulder and whispered, "Peace be with you." He then left to meet and chat with all the other angels in the building.

The greeter called over several people to help him take Ari, Sammy, and Joey to the proper age-related class. Ari was led to the room where her class would be, introduced to the other class members, and seated behind Susan, the pastor's daughter.

Sammy's class had pictures of Bible characters posted on the walls. Five others were also in his class. Joey's class was more like a reading room where the children sat on chairs exactly their size. The chairs surrounded the person who would be teaching them Bible stories. Nearby were tables where they could draw after the lesson.

Mike and Judy were shown to the adult class they were be attending where the chairs were arranged in a semicircle. From the very beginning, the couple realized they would need to bring a Bible next time since they were the only ones there without one. Thankfully, the class had loaners to assist in helping newcomers feel comfortable while going through the Sunday school lesson.

Neither Mike nor Judy seemed to feel odd about this first-time experience. They had become quite comfortable being in a grace atmosphere. Grace filled this Baptist church, and the result was a feeling like home.

When a bell rang signaling the end of Sunday school, the children were dismissed, and the adults filed out into the foyer. A brief time of scrambling followed as families regrouped and then entered the sanctuary together. Everyone, including crying babies, participated in the service. The family walked down the center aisle and took their seats in a mid-center pew.

If those pews could share the stories of sermons of old, the glory of the Lord would be revealed to man. A harvest of souls was still going on. Their current season of prayer and fasting was seeing fruit. On this day, many new families joined the members. In their new life in Christ, they came to give thanks to Jesus.

The choir entered the altar area to take their position. The choir director, started the service by saying, "Open your hymnals to page 70. We will be singing 'Nothing but the Blood of Jesus,' a hymn penned by a Baptist minister named Robert Lowry." Turning to face the choir, he lifted his hands, swung them forward and down, and the choir, accompanied by the organ, came to life.

What can wash away my sin? Nothing but the blood of Jesus.
What can make me whole again? Nothing but the blood of Jesus.

Ari's analytical mind grappled with everything she was observing. She was still attempting to evaluate the changes happening to her parents. Sammy and Joey were at an age where following their parents was natural, but not so with the older Ari. She had a thirst to know why and how things happened. Contrary to all the previous experiences in her young life, these changes defied logic. Within her heart stirred an awakening to things not yet understood. Keeping her thoughts to herself, she continued to observe her surroundings. To deepen her perplexity, she noticed her parents had tears in their eyes as they sang the hymn.

When Pastor Billings took the podium, the choir was dismissed to find their seats. A holy hush fell, and then with a deep breath and a robust voice, the pastor stated, "Today, we will be reading from 2 Corinthians 5:17." The rustling of pages could be heard as the congregation found the Scripture in the Bible. "Please stand for the reading of the Word of God."

The pews creaked, and the wooden floorboards moaned as the people stood in unison to honor the Word of God. Pastor Billings raised the open Bible high above his head, then slowly lowered it, and began to read, "Therefore, if any man be in Christ, he is a new creature; old things are passed away;" and in a modulated tone, he quoted, "behold..." as he paused to look at the congregation and then concluded, "all things are become new." The pastor slowly lowered the Bible to the surface of the podium. "Please be seated." With both hands grasping the edges of the wooden podium, he leaned forward as he began to speak.

The meaning of the verse suddenly hit Ari! Things were new in her home! Love began welling up in her heart as she thought, *My parents are new in Christ! They must have been washed in the blood of Jesus when they prayed to accept Him the night the Billingses visited. This is the missing clue to the mystery!*

She listened carefully as the pastor spoke from his heart. "In closing..." he said and finished his final sermon point. As the choir filed to the altar, the organist returned to her place and began to play softly.

The angel slipped into position behind Arielle. As the choir began to sing, "Just as I am," the time came to bring sinners home. With a tear in his eye and passion in his voice, Pastor Billings said, "Come! Come just as you are. Christ is waiting for you."

The angel placed his hand on Ari's shoulder and whispered, "It's time for you to become like your given name, Arielle—lioness of God."

With a loud voice, the pastor beckoned again, "Come!"

Arielle felt no nervousness; she knew what she wanted to do. She stood, motioned to her parents to let her pass, stepped into the aisle, and slowly walked forward in front of all the people. It didn't matter to her; she wanted Jesus. As she walking forward, golden sunlight radiated though the church windows. *I want what I see in my parents.* If she had looked behind her, she would have seen her mother raise her hands to her mouth to hide the sobs. She would have also seen the expression of joy on her father's face. All she knew was that, in her heart, she wanted Jesus.

The angels turned their attention toward the front door as they heard the sound of a roaring wind. From off in the distance, the noise grew louder until it burst through the doors of the church. Whirling high in the vaulted ceiling, the wind of the Holy Spirit swirled. As each person who came forward accepted Jesus, a whorl of the wind separated to surround the new believer and enter his or her heart.

Mrs. Billings came to Ari and leaned over to speak softly to her. With the sound of the music emanating throughout the sanctuary, no words could be heard by those seated in the pews. Her parents watched as their daughter nodded in answer to a question. They held hands and watched as their little girl gave her heart to God, and Mrs. Billings led Ari in a prayer.

Another whorl of the Holy Spirit left the swirling wind and entered Arielle's heart. The love of God filled her heart. Purity washed over her as the blood of Jesus cleansed her from all sins. She felt new on the inside. She had also become a new creation in Christ Jesus and understood what had been happening to her parents.

Mrs. Billings hugged Ari and sent her back to her seat. Both her parents stepped into the aisle and leaned down to embrace her. Her mother kissed her on the cheek while Sammy and Joey were trying to figure out what all the fuss was about.

Once again, in the unseen realm, the veil pulled back and a choir of heaven's host praised God for a little girl saved by God's grace. In the weeks that followed, Mike and Judy had the joy of leading their other two little ones to the Lord. Sammy and Joey both made a confession of faith in Jesus Christ. The whole household was now saved.

# TEN

*Farmington Times* front page headline on Sunday, May 11, 1964:
"Local Pentecostal Church on Fire!"

The emergency fire alarm was activated by Officer Henry at 9:02 p.m. on Wednesday May 7. Chief Rogers arrived in the station minutes later to receive the location and fire status. From the first accounts, Chief Rogers expected a total loss of the building. He stated, "Officer Henry relayed the caller's report that flames were leaping out of the windows several feet above the roofline. Fire burns at an amazing rate, so I fully expected to see the building completely engulfed in flames on our arrival."

"What did you see, Chief, when you arrived?" the reporter asked.

"Well, it was still in same condition as the original call reported. Fire never burns that slow."

"How did you respond, Chief?"

"We were ready for anything. All our well-seasoned and experienced firefighters had responded. They jumped into action, the hoses were ready, the pumper truck was up to pressure, and the connecting hoses were waiting on the tanker truck. One of our best response times ever."

"What tipped you off that this was no normal fire?"

"The fire had not spread. It was contained to first reports. Listen, that never happens unless someone was fighting the fire before we arrived. That was not the case at the Old Pentecostal church. I'm a praying man—I would even call myself a man of faith—but the hair on my neck stood up when I entered that building. I knew something else was happening."

"Chief Rogers, what do you mean?"

"I mean, I saw the fire, and then when we rushed into the building, the fire went out, but I felt a presence in the place. Through the haze, I saw Pastor Smith. When I called his name, he and four others rose from kneeling in prayer. He told me what I had seen was the fire of the Holy Ghost."

"Chief, that defies logic."

"I've never seen anything like it, but there were nearly a hundred onlookers. Every eyewitness report was the same. The building was on fire, but it wasn't being consumed by the flames."

*Farmington Times* front page headline, Sunday, May 18, 1964:
"Local Man Cured of Terminal Illness"

As long-time residents of Farmington, Bob Petite and his wife Lilly have lived a quiet life. Bob has been a career drywaller, considered one of the best tapers in his field, and in demand for his expertise. He had a natural instinct for creating a smooth surface and hiding all the joints. Two years ago, Bob was diagnosed with lung cancer due to his prolonged exposure to drywall dust. Sadly, his debilitating condition has been increasingly deteriorating. Bob's doctor recently determined that the cancer had restaged and metastasized throughout his body. With stage four cancer, he wasn't expected to live beyond six months.

On Sunday morning, Bob and Lilly attended the Old Pentecostal Church. Pastor Smith gave an altar call for anyone needing healing. Many people reported a heavy presence in the air—almost electrical. Bob, assisted by Lilly, went forward for prayer.

Bob said, "Pastor Smith and three others surrounded me; a man was behind me. They began to pray, and I heard Pastor Smith raise his voice and say, 'O God, in Jesus' name, release the power of the Holy Spirit to heal Bob. Your Word says by the stripes of Jesus, he is healed.' At that moment, I felt power rush into me and right to my lungs. I thought I was on fire. I felt someone hit me on the back, but no human being did that! I felt like someone knocked the wind out of me. When I took a deep breath, I knew my lungs were healed."

"Bob, have you seen your doctor?"

"Yes, Lilly and I rushed over to him on Monday morning. He listened to my lungs and said he was impressed. He sent me for a blood workup to check the cancer count, but I don't need the report to know that God healed me."

The reporter added, "Bob is not the only person reporting on being healed in the Old Pentecostal Church. Seems like a fire of another sort is burning there. Pastor Smith is on record saying an old time Pentecostal revival has begun that has reached the neighboring city of Aztec. Folks seeking healing are coming to the church services. Pastor Smith is now considering adding more services to accomodate all the people who desire to attend. If this trend of God healing people continues, it will become a Four Corners event."

# ELEVEN

Church attendance was up in Farmington, and barroom participation was down so not everyone was happy with the spiritual changes taking place in town. However, the local Christian bookstore was enjoying an increased number of customers as people came to buy Bibles.

When Judy walked into the store, a little bell rang to announce a customer's entrance. The friendly clerk behind the counter welcomed her. "I think that bell is about to break. It hasn't ever rung this much! God knows we need the business."

Most people don't realize that Christian stores sometimes feel more like they are running a not-for-profit ministry. Often they struggle to keep their doors open. With this new turn of events in town, these stores were beginning to see their accounts run into the black.

"How can I help you today?"

"I'm looking to buy a Bible for my daughter. She's just finishing third grade, and she's a really good reader."

"Well, I can tell you that most preachers in town use the King James version, but I believe it might be a little hard for children. I recommend our Children's Bible." Walking to a display at the front and center of the store, she added, "Seems that we have a lot of people asking for Bibles these days, so we moved the display to the front of the store. On this shelf, we have our Children's Bible. Take your time to look over the choices."

"Thank you," Judy replied. She wondered, *How do I make a choice? I don't know anything about which Bible is the right one.*

Judy offered a quick, innocent prayer and made her selection. Asking God for guidance was all new to her. She couldn't help but notice that God was answering even the simplest of prayers. That God was so visibly active in her life was shocking to her at first. She had never noticed it happen before. Now she was convinced that God listened, and very often, the answer to her prayers was yes. The eyes of her spirit were now seeing, and her spiritual ears were hearing the things of the kingdom of God.

While Judy was at the Christian store, she took some time to shop. Walking up and down each aisle, she noticed all the books, music, plaques, and pictures. *If someone walked into our home, would they know we are following Jesus?* she wondered.

She picked up a book called a journal and noticed all the pages were blank. Judy turned to the cashier and asked, "What is a journal?"

"Well, most people keep one to record their ongoing relationship with the Holy Spirit, sharing times when God answers a prayer or when they experience Him in a new way. You can record the lessons you learn from reading the Bible or after hearing a sermon. Some people write thoughts in their journal they can't share with anyone else. I have had moments that were so personal, so intimate with the Holy Spirit that I didn't want to share them with anyone; it was just me and Him."

"I never thought of it that way," Judy replied. Picking up one, she stepped to the counter and bought Ari her first Bible and a journal. School would be out soon for Sammy, and she need to pick up Joey from a play date down the block. She had barely enough time to get home, wrap both books, and pick up the boys.

Jesus was seemingly on the thoughts of many folks in town, and Judy was eager to share what was happening in her life. This new life was very exciting, and she was looking for opportunities to talk about it.

At home she heard the back door open and close, and shoes hit the floor. Dinner was in the oven. "We're eating at 5:30," Judy called. "Get cleaned up, please."

Three smiling faces ran to give Dad a hug. They represented part of the reason why he went to work every day—to provide for his family. As he welcomed their hugs, he reflected on the joy of family life. He picked up Joey, threw him up and over his shoulder and rubbed his ribs with his chin, shaking his head back and forth and making funny noises. He knew exactly where the little boy's funny bone was located and laughed with him.

Sammy came next, and he squirmed like a worm as he laughed uncontrollably. Because he was a whole lot heavier, Mike, worn out, dropped into a chair and looked at Ari. "What did you learn in school today?"

At his request, she happily filled him in on all the details. Lately she seemed to have a fountain of words for them. As he listened he pondered on the differences in his children. Ari wanted him to understand her. He had always felt she was holding back before, but now those walls were down. He realized their relationship was changing.

Judy interrupted the conversation and asked Ari to set the table. Then she whispered a message to Mike she didn't want little ears to hear. "Mike, I picked up a Bible and a journal for Ari today at the Christian bookstore. When we put the boys in bed tonight, let's go to her room and give them to her."

"It would help her to be ready for Sunday school," Mike said.

"I have such a hunger to know more about God, and I want to foster that desire in Ari as well."

"Good, it's like the great mystery of all time," said Mike. "You read a passage, pinpoint the fact, examine the clues, and then see how it applies to your life. I find myself wanting to know how to live this new life. Seems like every time I turn around, someone is mentioning grace. What in the world is grace? There's so much to learn, and I'm eager to find out and to understand. Jude, what happened to us is making our good life even better. And what in the world are blessings?"

"Exactly, we need to discover everything that the Word of God has for us."

Judy could hardly wait for prayers to be finished. The two littlest children were tucked in and kisses were placed on their foreheads, and their lights were turned off. Mike and Judy walked into Ari's room where she was reading her latest Nancy Drew book.

"Ari, sweetie, we have something for you."

A look of surprise and excitement passed over Ari's face. She ripped into the wrapping to see the Bible. Opening it, she read out loud: "To Arielle from Mom and Dad, May 22, 1964." Below the inscription, they had added Acts 2:2, which would become one of her favorite Scriptures. Ari was not sure why, but her eyes filled with tears. She had never before received a spontaneous gift like this from her parents. Her friend Susan had her own Bible, and she had wished for one too. *How did Mom and Dad know I wanted one?* She opened the journal next, and it brought a confused look to her face.

Judy explained, "Sweetie, it's for you to write down all your thoughts, questions, and feelings about your life with Jesus. You can even write down your thoughts about what you heard on Sunday while it is still fresh on your mind. That would be a first good entry, don't you think?"

Ari had no words for the depth of emotion she felt. She knelt on the bed and tightly hugged her parents. Ari felt closer to her parents than she ever had before.

That night she wrote her first entry: "May 22, 1964, my life is changing. Jesus came into my heart and life on Sunday. The instant I said the prayer, I felt different. I felt good, and I don't know why. No one could see what was happening in me, yet somehow people understood. There is something I have never felt before that I don't understand, but I don't feel alone. It's as if Jesus is here with me."

Reading over her shoulder was her angel. He leaned over to kiss the top of her head and bless her.

# TWELVE

"Pastor Smith, this is Anna Morgan. I had another dream last night."

"Anna, do you know what it says in Amos 3:7?"

"No, Pastor, I don't."

"It says that those who are close to the Lord are those He likes to show what He intends to do. But before I get ahead of myself, what was your dream?"

"Well, I was up late watching television until the station went off the air—you know, when the national anthem is played, and then the test pattern goes on the screen with all that static noise. I pulled out my Bible and read a few verses in the book of Daniel. Pastor, the verse in chapter 12 verse 4 really struck me. It says people were going to and fro, and knowledge increased. I know I'm old when people fly around the world in airplanes. I look at all the knowledge God has given and how scientists have now built the atomic bomb."

"Anna, tell me, what was your dream?" the pastor said trying to get Anna back on track.

"Like I was trying to tell you, after I feel asleep, I saw people in cars coming from Aztec, Shiprock, and even as far as the town of Cuba. They were driving to our little Pentecostal church. They stayed for the service, and when they left, clouds of grace filled with golden glitter sat right above their cars all the way back to their homes. Can you believe that?"

"Anna, do you supposed that maybe the church needs to think about being ready to add services during the week?"

"I'm sure about that, Pastor. Well, then I had a second dream. I saw cars coming from places as far away as Albuquerque. Same thing happened—clouds of grace followed them home; and before the dream ended, I was looking down on Farmington and saw clouds of grace above houses all over the town. What does it all mean, Pastor?"

"Anna, let me pray about the dreams and come see me on Sunday. In the passage in Amos, the Bible says that those close to Jesus...well, He shows them things. Anna, it seems to me like the Lord is excited for you to see what He's doing in our area. I have no doubt in my mind that the Holy Ghost is on the move! Praise God!"

Hanging up the phone, he turned off the lights, left his office, and walked outside to his car. He had only a short drive home. When he pulled his car up on the two ribbons of concrete driveway with grass growing in between them, he noticed a car also pulling up two doors down. *My neighbor is getting home from work too,* he thought.

As he stepped out of the car, he shouted down the way, "Hi, Mike! Having a blessed day?"

"Yes, Pastor! God is good." They both turned and went into their houses for dinner.

# Thirteen

Judy decided that Saturday evening would be "make-your-own-dinner" night. The children loved it when they could make dinner. She already knew if they chose pizza, she would have a huge mess to clean up after all the fun was over. She left the decision of what to make—and whether or not it was nutritional—up to her children. Creative concoctions and weird combinations were all a part of their experimentation. "Make-your-own-dinner" night was how they had come to love peanut butter and marshmallow sandwiches. However, the possibility of a serious indigestion problem for the adults was a possibility, so discretion was advised.

Using the children's creative genius, the final decision was a grilled cheese, cucumber, and mustard sandwich. Once the preparations had been completed and the eating had begun, Mike broke the silence. "After dinner, we'll be having a family devotional time in the living room before we do anything else."

Questioning glances covertly passed among the children. *What's a devotional?* they all wondered. They couldn't help but notice that their parents were staying home on another Saturday—not that they didn't love having them home! Yet another change had taken place in the family's normal routine.

Theirs wasn't a finely decorated living room found in a magazine. However, the room was tastefully done in the style of furniture in the early sixties. Small-town furniture stores had display rooms with the newest models and volumes of catalogs for ordering them. Judy opted for comfort over trends. She loved a feel-good, homey room to comfortably entertain family and friends.

On the interior wall, she had placed a light-brown cloth couch with diagonally recessed buttons accentuating the deep cushions. Two matching high-backed chairs with a dark wood trim outlining the edges of the arms and back of the chairs flanked a dark stained end table with a single drawer and a contemporary lamp with a white shade on top. Directly behind the end table were two colonial style, nine-pane windows with a vertical opening. Positioned in the center of the front wall was a large, single pane glass window with two modern low-backed chairs of complementing colors placed on either side of it.

Under the window was a new color television in a wooden cabinet. The window treatments were pinch-pleat curtains on an easy glide track with a pull string that extended only to the window sill above the television cabinet. A coffee table had been placed in the center of the room for the kids to enjoy the games they loved to play. In this room, a storehouse full of memories was already made and many more would be made in the future.

A sense of awkwardness filled the room as the family assembled. Mike sat in the chair next to the couch, and Judy relaxed on the couch next to him. Joey crawled up in his lap as Sammy and Ari sat cross-legged on the floor.

"Your mom and I were talking lately about prayer. I came across a verse in the Bible that I wanted to share with you." Reaching over to the end table, he picked up his new Bible. He had already placed a bookmark in the passage he wanted to read. He looked at Judy and then said, "It's in Matthew 7:11." Opening the Bible, he placed his finger on the verse and began to read, "If ye then, being evil, know how to give good gifts unto your children, how much more will your Father in heaven give good things to them that ask him."

Mike paused before continuing, "Your mother and I have noticed that when we pray, Father God is answering our prayers. So let's talk about prayer."

Ari, who was sitting crosslegged, shifted her weight and moved her legs to the side as she posed a question. "Dad, what does it mean when it says good gifts?"

"Ari, on Saturday I love to see the look on all your faces when I reach into my pocket and pull out a dollar and one nickel. What happens next?"

Sammy burst out, almost yelling, "We're going to the movies!"

"What else?" Mike asked.

"We get popcorn, a soda drink, and the movie for all of us!" Sammy added.

"That's right! Do you enjoy going to the Allen Theater?"

"Oh, yes," they all chimed in unison.

Judy added, "That's a good gift, children."

Ari's mind automatically jumped to her next question. "What are good gifts that God gives us?"

"We need food, water, a home, a job, and then spiritual things that help us to become more like Jesus."

"But, Dad, we had those things before…"

"You're right, Ari, we did. They were blessings from God because all good things come from Him. Now we are being blessed by the spiritual things we couldn't see or couldn't understand before. However, we're learning more about them every day when we see the answers to our prayers and the blessings in our lives. We're all new to prayer. Your mother and I have noticed God is answering even the simplest of our prayers. This is why we want to encourage you to pray often—not just at dinner or at bedtime. When you think about Jesus or the Holy Spirit, pray. Prayer is just talking to God. Talk to God because He is listening. Then look for your prayers to be answered. Father God wants to give us good gifts, so let's begin to ask Him."

A soft, pleasant smile radiating from her eyes filled Judy's face. *Who is this man? I understand what he's doing, but where did this come from? I know our lives and our backgrounds. Other than my grandmother's influence, this devotional time is coming out of nowhere.*

"I want to bless each one of you by praying over you." Mike wrapped his arm around Joey and began, "Dear Father God, I thank You for Joey. Please bless him with your love and joy and ability to live a little boy's carefree life. Please help him to learn about You." Mike kissed Joey on his forehead and then set him down. Joey went over and snuggled next to his mother.

"Sammy, come and stand right here." The boy quickly stood, went over to his dad, and looked at him. He was totally plugged into his father. Mike placed both of his hands on Sammy's shoulders and prayed, "Dear Father God, this is my son whom I love. Help him to grow up and be a godly man. Bless him and fill him with Your love."

Ari was ready for her blessing and quickly moved to stand in front of her dad. Mike placed his left hand on top of her head and began to pray, "Father God, You know my daughter; she loves to know how things work by following the clues. Help her to know You as You take her down a road of great spiritual adventures now and all her life."

Mike reached over the table, grasped Judy's hand, and prayed, "Father God, this wonderful woman has blessed my life in many ways. I ask, Father, that You would release blessings into her heart and life. She has been my partner and encourager; I thank You, Father, for her. Because of her, I am a better man. Please release an abundance of Your love into her heart. In Jesus' name I pray. Amen."

Tears rolled down Judy's cheeks as a new kind of joy welled up in her heart. The children were wondering what the fuss was all about. How could they know that, in the course of time, she had so longed to hear those words said out loud and not just understood between them.

Clearing his throat, Mike said, "It's a beautiful day, so you kids go outside and play." Off they went, filled with their father's love and esteem. This new section of town was a safe, wonderful place for children to live. This time of the day on a Saturday, half the children on the block were out playing.

In the unseen realm, golden glitter was floating in the air. Angels understood that the knowledge of God was being received. Receiving and accepting knowledge is part of the transformational process into becoming a new creation in Christ Jesus. In the atmosphere of this home, the most precious flowers were growing and blooming to the pleasure and joy of God.

# Fourteen

Although the month of June would soon be arriving, spring was still in full bloom, and the family was in the springtime of their spiritual lives. The joy of discovery permeated their lives.

That Sunday morning, a flurry of activity was happening at the house. In a raised voice, Judy commented, "Mike, I'm afraid I'll need some money and shopping time if we'll be attending church every week. I can't wear the same dress and hat all the time, and the kids will need some new outfits."

"How in the world did you know exactly how I was thinking? I could use a new blue suit myself."

"Oh, stop!" Judy chuckled. "If I thought you were remotely serious for one second, I would tell you a black or a gray suit would be a nice addition to your wardrobe."

"You're right about needing new clothes, and I'm all for your going shopping. Going to church and being part of this church community is wonderful. In fact, church feels a bit like home."

I know what you mean," Judy replied with a smile.

"Let's go!" Mike called, and everyone headed to the car. As he started the car, the radio, that was already tuned to the local Christian station, came to life. The hymn, "The Old Rugged Cross," began playing.

After parking their car, the family climbed the stairs to the church, and the children all hurried forward. Joey, Sammy, and Ari headed toward the children's side of the Sunday school rooms while Mike and Judy said hello to the greeter at the door. They received a warm handshake, a friendly smile, and a heartfelt hello in return. The couple quickly headed to their classroom.

At the conclusion of the service, Pastor Billings was waiting to talk with Mike and Judy. His wasn't an ambush, although the meeting was very intentional. He came right to the point and said, "Mike and Judy, I want you to know that baptism is a very important step for new Christians to take."

Mike spoke first. "What do you mean, Pastor?"

"Jesus Himself submitted to baptism. Being baptized is an important part of a Christian's life because it shows that you are dead to the world and alive in Jesus."

Judy asked, "Pastor, is it only for Mike and me or are the children included in being baptized?"

"Baptism is for all those how have made a confession of faith to Jesus and are saved. In your case, it is for all of you—a family event. I would like to see this happen sooner than later."

Judy's mind was running ahead of their conversation as she asked, "Is this a total water immersion, Pastor? Or is this a little ceremonial sprinkling?"

"We believe in full immersion baptism. In fact, the church has a changing room adjacent to the baptismal tub. You will each wear a heavy gown over the clothes in which you plan to be baptized."

Something akin to horror went through Judy's mind. *Oh, no! My hair will get wet, and my makeup will run!* She asked, "And this baptism takes place during a Sunday service?"

"Baptism is a church-wide celebration, Judy—a welcoming into the family."

Mike spoke up. "Pastor, do we need to take any instruction or a class beforehand?"

"No, we just ask you a few questions before you get dunked."

Judy asked, "Pastor, can we let you know?" A feeling of anxiety washed over her.

"Whenever you're ready, call the church office, and we'll fill the tank and prepare the gowns. We have sizes for everyone."

As they were leaving the church, Judy felt a chill come over her usual joyful demeanor. She thought, *It's hard to look your best when you're dripping wet.*

This adult decision was discussed for several days. Judy always liked to look her best. She could have easily played the role of Donna in *The Donna Reed Show*. Finally, right before they were leaving for the midweek service, Judy said, "Mike, I've prayed about baptism, and I feel it's important to follow through even if we all look funny being wet in front of the whole church. If you feel the same, then tonight, Mike, please let's tell Pastor of our decision."

"Okay, if you're sure, it's fine with me." Even as he agreed with her, he couldn't help but wonder, *This is going to be challenging. Judy's motto of looking good is coming up against a God request—"Be ye baptized." It may start out right, but it will be a real challenge for her if she dips beneath the water.*

Judy suddenly blurted out, "I want to go last! Got it?"

Immediately after the service, Judy ambushed Pastor to tell him their baptism was agreed upon. "We'll all be baptized."

With telling the pastor, she thought perhaps she would feel some relief from her nervousness. She was right and wrong at the same time. Now that their baptism was really going to take place, her stomach had formed a knot. She asked, "Pastor, when will the baptism service happen?"

"Now that you agreed upon doing it, we'll schedule it for this Sunday."

They continued to talk about all the necessary details. One minor consolation for Judy was that baptism took place at the end of the service. *At least I can make a hasty exit home and to a hairdryer.* She still battled her mixed emotions. Spiritually, she was excited to move forward in her faith, and part of that moving forward was being willing to humble herself by not looking her best.

Mike thought about how he always told her she possessed a natural beauty. *Now is definitely not the time to say it again,* he decided. *I'm learning God has a way of setting us up to challenge our comfort zones. I think my dear wife has met her first challenge.*

The boy inside of Mike awakened to seize the moment. He called out, "Hey Jude, we need to remember to bring your camera for a group picture after we've been baptized." Judy quickly shot him a "not funny, Mike" look and sighed.

The five of them, wearing white baptismal gowns, were standing out of view and waiting to take the four steps down into the water. Pastor Billings had decided that Mike would lead the way as an example for the children. The pastor was already in the water, talking to the congregation about the ordinance of baptism. He proudly shared that on this day an entire family was being baptized.

He turned and said, "Mike, come on in the water." As Mike took the first steps, he could see all the people in his peripheral vision and also noticed the water was warm. Standing next to the pastor, he turned to face the church. Pastor asked, "Mike, is there something you would like to say?"

He quietly replied, "No."

"Mike, is Jesus Christ your Savior and Lord?"

"Yes."

"Based upon your profession of faith in the Lord Jesus Christ, I now baptize you in the name of the Father, the Son, and the Holy Spirit." Pastor brought Mike backward and down into the water to be fully covered. As he did so, he said, "Buried in the likeness of His death," and as he lifted Mike, he continued, "and raised in the likeness of His resurrection for you to walk in your new life."

Fully soaked and now standing, Mike wiped the water from his face as the church erupted in applause. Mike remained in the water to help Joey and then Sammy be baptized—a proud moment for him as their father. Judy was full of joy as she watched her family being baptized.

Arielle wanted to be baptized on her own, so Mike helped her into the tank and then stepped out. He turned around to watch his daughter follow in baptism.

"Arielle, would you like to say something first?"

To her parents' surprise, she said yes.

With an expression of joy on her face, she quoted 1 John 4:19, "We love him [Jesus], because he first loved us." After responding to Pastor's questions, Ari grabbed her nose and let him dunk her in the water.

To Ari, her baptism signified an ending of her life before Jesus and now the beginning of a new life with Him. Mike took her hand and led her to the changing rooms. Her saturated baptismal gown was now heavy with rapidly cooling water. She shivered as she stepped into the changing room.

From the side, Mike watched his wife get baptized. She had swept her hair back into a phony tail. Again the church broke into applause afterwards, and Pastor concluded the service by dismissing the church. Their new friends waited to congratulate them. When they came into the church sanctuary, the family received many hugs and pats on the back. If Judy had any odd feelings or hesitation, she didn't show it.

In the background, an unseen angel was praising God for what was happening to his assigned family.

# Fifteen

School was now out for the summer, and everyone settled into a more relaxed routine. Ari had become accustomed to reading her Bible and writing in the journal. In one of her entries, she wrote the date and the following thought: *Every time the church doors are open, we're there hearing sermons, having the Bible explained, and learning about God. Susan has become a very good friend. We spend a lot of time together at church and at school. I like it.*

Family outings were planned weekly, and their Saturday devotional became a way of life. Their front door could have been a revolving one with family and all their friends visiting. On one Thursday night after dinner, the phone rang.

Judy answered it and found the caller was Martha, who asked in a sharp, petulant manner, "Judy, where on earth have you been? The dance floor at HWYs is wondering where you and Mike are at..."

"Martha, everything has changed. I'm still trying to understand what is happening in our lives. We spend a lot of time at church, and now on Saturdays, we plan family activities. Mike does a family devotional after dinner, and before you know it, Saturday is over."

"I have a feeling there is a huge story here, and I'm not hearing it yet. George and I would like to come over Saturday and hear all about this change in your life. Would 7:00 be acceptable?"

"Yes, if you'd like to, bring dessert, and I'll have a snack and some soft drinks." Judy knew once Martha was in motion there was no stopping her.

"My word, Judy! Are you telling me that you both don't drink anymore?"

"It's true—not a drink since the last time at HWYs."

"Now I for sure have to come over. I don't care what he says; I'm dragging George over there too."

"Farmington has a full-fledged maturity ward down there," noted one of the angels. Sitting in a group of twelve, they were talking about the events unfolding, hoping they would become involved in playing a role in seeing a human soul birthed into the kingdom of God. One of an angel's greatest honors was to be a part of that high calling.

They all understood how their assignments from God were given out. In their group, they waited to hear their names called to be sent. Being sent is conditional on the hearts of mankind. Faith moves mountains, and the activation of that faith is another matter for this is the battleground upon earth. To move the heart of God is given to men if their hearts avail themselves of faith. What was happening in Farmington was the beginning of a new move of God. Excitement reigned in heaven.

Hope arose in this group of angels that they would all be called to serve soon. To labor with the Holy Spirit on earth was a great honor. The word was that two groups of Christians had gotten the ear of God in this small town. In the atmosphere of the prince of the world, the question became whether or not they would stay on point or be tricked into failure. In order for the people to release heaven on earth, they had to push against evil's spiritual forces. In direct opposition to the world inflicted with sin and its consequences, the people needed to seek God to intervene. The emotional heart of man activating faith in God is the doorway into our world. Even if people have a little faith, God will act.

God's ways are not the ways of men. When a person is born again spiritually, he begins to have limited spiritual sight and hearing. Being born again is somewhat like standing at the entrance to a huge maze of hedges. When Christians use their heightened senses, the journey begins with their taking a step forward and then examining to see if it is in the right direction. Upon seeing a positive effect, the person continues to advance forward. If the effect is negative, the person needed to take a step or two back and try again.

Despite the fact people cannot see or hear very well especially at first in the spiritual realm, hindsight was usually twenty-twenty. With each step, faith was increased, spurring the new believers onward. Staying on the path in the maze was a challenge for them. The slightest drifting in the wrong direction meant feeling the pricks of the thorny hedge.

The angels discussed the latest happenings in Farmington. Knowing that evil was laying in wait for the first opportunity to pounce, they all cheered on the believers.

Gaining the ear of God was only the beginning point in heaven. Father God has a storehouse of good gifts to release once the doorway is opened for heaven to rush in like a roaring wind. For this reason it was vitally important for people to find their way through the spiritual maze.

The angels continued to discuss the leaders of the town and wondered if they would discover how to release the floodgates of heaven. In Farmington, the two Christian leaders who had set their hearts upon God with determined faith were seeing a breakthrough. In each church two small groups of followers joined in with their pastor to intercede. They made up a remnant, and their goal was to see God release a new wave of the Holy Spirit upon their church and community.

One of these leaders cherished the knowledge and understanding of God through His Word and having an intellectual relationship with Him. The other leader sought the manifest presence of the Holy Spirit. A quandary in heaven was how they could be opposing each other; after all, both were the bride of Christ. This issue was heavy on the hearts of the angels. Would they—could they—come together in unity and open the floodgates?

From the throne room of God, the names of three angels were called out. In their hearts, they knew they were being called to serve. Praise to God erupted in the whole group. The three of them stood, looked at the remaining angels with an expression of joy, and hoped they too would soon be called up to serve. Together they arrived at Jacob's ladder, descending down to the Old Pentecostal Church. This stairway led to their assignment—the friends of Mike and Judy.

The three new angels arrived at Mike's and Judy's home and began to chat with the angel who was already there. They had been praying for the salvation of their friends, and they don't know that God was going to answer their prayers.

The first order of business would mean going to the corresponding friends' homes to begin protecting them for the time of their conversion.

The house was darkened; everyone was in bed. Judy turned to face Mike and casually mentioned the call earlier from Martha.

"Mike, they've been wondering where we've been. They're coming over Saturday evening to talk. What do you think about it?"

"What do we hear all the time at church? Share the gospel; tell others about what Jesus has done for us, right?"

"I'm not concerned about sharing Jesus with Martha or George, but I am quite concerned that I won't know what to say or how to describe what is really happening in our life and with our family."

"They're some of our closest friends. If we see things are going well, we need to be open to praying with them to receive Jesus just like Pastor and Mrs. Billings did with us."

"It would be so much easier if we were having just girl talk. We need a plan."

"How about after snacks and dessert, we send the kids out in front to play, and we concentrate on witnessing to them?"

"Mike, just listen to us! Even our vocabulary is changing."

# SIXTEEN

Mike quietly walked into the kitchen, stepped up right behind Judy and wrapped his arms around her waist. She jumped at his touch but instantly welcomed his embrace in a rush of pleasant emotions. With his left hand, he brushed back her hair and softly and tenderly kissed her neck with an I-love-you caress of his lips. She allowed herself to drift from being chore-orientated to pure enjoyment.

Her thoughts drifted. *Lord, of the many changes we're experiencing, this is a very welcome change. His affection has become spontaneous; I like his thinking about my feminine side. Where is this coming from and will it stay this way?* The house had become too quiet so the children grew curious. They peeked into the kitchen in time to see this demonstration of affection. They did not know they were witnessing the strong mutual love of their parents—the unexpected outcome of their decision and the feeling of security.

"Mike," Judy said when she caught sight of them, "would you please get the kids ready for company? You remember that Martha and George are coming over in a little while, right? I need to get the snacks and drinks ready."

With a new directive from his wife, he became a man on a mission. She turned to look at the kitchen table. In buffet fashion, paper plates, napkins, and plasticware had been attractively placed nearest the door. Potato salad and Hawaiian salad were next. An open place had been reserved for Martha's dessert, and then room for soda, ice, and cups.

*Hmmm, it's lacking something to add color, but it's too late for that now. I could send Mike to the store, but getting the kids ready and occupied is more important for now. It will just have to do the way it is. Lord, please bless us with a special night. Please open the door for us to share You, Jesus, with our friends.*

A new sound could be heard coming through the screen door. The guests had arrived.

Martha called out, "Knock-knock! We're coming in."

When Martha, George, and their two children came into the house, it was instant chaos between handshakes and hugs and the mingling children gathered at the front door.

"Mike," George said, "it seems like a month of Sundays since I've seen you last."

"Yeah, it's been a while, and you're sure a sight for sore eyes."

Ari was listening, watching, and wondering about the visit. The other children were all staring at the dessert pan Martha was holding, hoping that her famous marshmallow brownies would soon be forthcoming. George had a small bouquet of flowers—exactly what Judy needed to add the finishing touch to the table. The kids gathered around the coffee table and played a game while the men sat in the chairs to watch baseball on TV. Judy and Martha finished preparing the light snacks and the dessert on the table in the kitchen.

For some reason, the atmosphere in the kitchen seemed awkward. Two very close friends were trying to feel their way through the obvious changes in their relationship.

Martha finally broke the silence. "Judy, I'm going to burst if I don't find out what's going on with you two."

"Martha, I have tons to tell you, but I believe I can tell you the best when we're cleaning up. Only you have to promise me that you will keep it a secret. I mean it—a secret."

"Really, it's that good?"

"You won't believe it."

Judy turned to call everyone to the kitchen, and the kids were quickly at the door. "Youngest first," Judy ordered, and the rest of the kids lined up accordingly.

"Judy," Martha asked, "have you been brewing that tea in the sun all day?"

"Yes, just the way you like it," she replied. She watched as the children passed one by one through the line. Then came the men and the women would serve themselves last.

George immediately scoped out the drink situation and saw his only choices were tea or soda. *It's true!* George thought. *Mike is on the wagon. This will be a short night for me. I want to get home to watch television with a beer.*

The house briefly grew somewhat quiet as the food was eaten and enjoyed. As always, the brownie pan was soon emptied of every crumb—almost before the adults had theirs!

As Martha looked over the beverage choices, she commented, "I didn't know you could buy A&W Root Beer as a take out."

"We just found out last week when we went there for a family meal. It's become the family's favorite soft drink. Mike picked up a case this morning when the drive-in opened," Judy explained.

"Those skating skirts the girls wear are really short," Martha noted. "You would never get me to work in those skates," she added with a smile.

In the front room, George was talking to Mike. "Do you remember when they put the new phone system in when we were kids?" The girls' conversation about A&W night had prompted a memory almost forgotten. "The roving switchboard supervisors wore skates to get around the room more quickly. Now that we have the rotary phone, that era is over. I, for one, do not miss those party lines. It was hard to make a date with a girl when your neighbor wanted to use the phone."

The girls joined the family in the living room, and small talk carried them through snack time. When everyone had eaten his fill, Martha and Judy went into the kitchen for cleanup. After all, Martha was in a rush to hear the news.

Both of them began doing the dishes; Martha was washing, and Judy was drying. Believing the time had come to share her news, Judy leaned in and started to tell Martha about the changes taking place in her family. Judy glanced at the door, saw that the coast was clear, and knew the time had come for some serious girl talk.

"Martha, last Saturday, Mike started leading our family in a devotional time. He read a Scripture, and we helped the children understand it by giving examples for them to understand. Then Mike prayed for each one."

"Prayed? Where is that coming from?"

"I'm not sure, but that family devotional time is having a positive effect on all of us. When Mike prayed for me, he thanked God for me and that I helped him to be a better man."

Bang!

A yell immediately came from the front room. "Is everything okay in the kitchen?"

"Yes, everything's fine," Judy answered. "The pan Martha was washing slipped from her soapy hands."

Her hands poised in the soapy water, Martha turned to stare at Judy. "He actually said those words?"

Judy slowly nodded her head.

Martha was almost too stunned for words. Finally she uttered, "Whatever you too have…I want it too."

"Martha, it is Jesus in our lives."

Inside their home, grace increased as well as the golden glitter gathering about the ceiling. Knowing the gospel was about to be shared, the two angels began to stir. They each understood their roles. One of them would go outside with the children, and the other would stay with the adults to release strength and boldness when needed.

As the girls returned to the front room, Mike suggested that the children could go outside in the front to play. All six of them—five children and one angel—went out in front to play Simon Says. The angel's job was to bless the children with peace while the adults talked.

For a mere moment, the four adults all looked at each other expectantly until Judy spoke up and began to tell them about the night Pastor and Mrs. Billings had come to visit them. From memory, Mike and Judy shared the Scriptures and told their friends about being born spiritually. Judy shared how it felt when they were washed in the blood of Jesus and cleansed of all their sin, and what it was like to have their souls pure and clean.

"George and Martha, the Holy Spirit entered our hearts and now He helps us to live a better life. Best of all is being totally in love with Jesus!"

Golden glitter began to fall. The veil to the spiritual realm began to pull back and the heavens open as the choir began to praise God. The angels turned their attention to the east. The sound of a roaring wind could be heard. Louder and louder the sound became until it raced into the house and swirled above all of them.

Mike and Judy invited Martha and George to pray the prayer of invitation to Jesus, and they both agreed. Their hearts had been softened, and they felt the need to ask for forgiveness of their sins—something only the Holy Spirit can do. As Mike led them in the prayer, two whorls of the wind broke off and penetrated George and Martha in their emotional hearts. The Holy Spirit had germinated the words of God in the soil of their hearts, and a spiritual birth took place.

That night, George and Martha were born into the kingdom of God and into eternity. The spiritual scales fell off of their eyes, their ears were opened, and their hearts hungered for the things of God. They knew something had happened inside. First would come the Word, then the faith, and then the actions. Tears of joy rolled down their faces as a new relationship began; the four friends now shared the unity of the Holy Spirit. Now they were more than friends; they were all co-heirs to heaven.

George and Martha went with Mike and Judy to church the next morning. Other friends would come into their house and also make a commitment of faith to Jesus. What a summer to remember! Instead of going to HWYs and dancing and drinking, they were now holding Bible studies and attending church.

# SEVENTEEN

The summer of '64 was the best summer Mike and Judy ever remembered. Farmington Lake became a regular cooling-off spot for family fun. The swimming areas were marked off with buoys to indicate the deep water. Judy's cold fried chicken was a lunchtime favorite along with ice-cold lemonade. Before summer's end, Mike would teach Ari to water ski, and she took to the sport like a fish in water. Arielle was very excited to begin fourth grade. Sammy was super-excited too because he was now an official first grader, and Joey would begin kindergarten.

Days of shopping for new school clothes and supplies was ahead for the family. A mother's dream would soon come true—all the children would be in school for the first time. Judy would now have a few hours to schedule tasks that needed to be done, as well as have some time for herself. Shortly before school started, Judy took one child at a time for clothes shopping while Mike watched the other two at home.

A new craze—a trampoline park—had opened on West Main on the outskirts of town. The park had been constructed with nine concrete pits measuring three feet deep by ten feet long by six feet wide. A trampoline mat was stretched across the pit and connected by many springs on all four sides. As a person jumped, the stretching mat would dip down and then quickly propel the child upward.

Though the kids loved jumping on the trampolines, Judy did not care to watch the impulsivity of that activity. Thankfully, Mike enjoyed this father kind of thing. The morning after a trip to the trampoline park during breakfast, the kids mentioned they felt like they were still jumping on the trampoline when they were falling asleep. The three of them giggled and laughed as they discussed the fun they had.

"Funny how each child has his own style when jumping on the mat," Mike said to Judy. "Ari and Sammy were cautious, but I had to rein in Joey for being too reckless. I don't know if he was fearless or completely unaware of what could happen if he missed the mat. In fact, the fun stopped for a while when one of the kids missed their jump. Instead of hitting the mat, his feet hit the springs, and his legs were dangling in the pit. But fun it was!"

"Mike, I'm glad it's you with the children. I don't think I could take it. By the way, tomorrow I'm taking all three children to the pediatrician for their before school checkup. I have the school forms for Sammy and Joey. Ari is already in the system. I have an early appointment, so we should be home about noon. In the evening, I'm going to rush out and get all the last-minute items on the school supply list. Then we'll be all set for the new school year."

"Judy, the way you handle all these details is amazing. If it were me, I would be a mess, and everything else would be a mess."

"Aw, thanks, hon."

The four of them were sitting in the doctor's office, waiting to hear their names called. Leaning over to Sammy and Joey, Judy said, "I'm going to take Ari in first for her exam. She'll need her privacy, Sammy-Joey, so I want you to sit here quietly. You can look at the *Highlights* and *Boys' Life* magazines. I know Sammy that you'll be learning how to read this year, but you can look at the pictures and puzzles. Joey, I know you like the hidden picture puzzle. Do not leave your seat!" she emphasized.

Sammy had that "Aw, Mom" look in his eyes, but he slowly nodded in agreement.

"Judy, you and Arielle can come in now," the receptionist said.

Judy watched Ari get up on the examination table; she knew the routine. Within minutes the doctor knocked on the door and came in. Even though she had been through this before, Ari was a little nervous.

"Well hello, little lady! How are you today?"

"Fine," she said.

"School is right around the corner. Are you excited?"

Ari spoke up. "I'm going into fourth grade."

The doctor looked toward Judy and stated, "Outwardly, Arielle looks good and healthy. Now let's take a good look at her." He looked into Ari's left ear with his otoscope. Next he took out a tongue depressor, and said, "Say ahhh."

"Ahhhhhh."

"Great job, Arielle. Your throat looks good." Stepping around the examination table, he checked her other ear. "That one looks good too."

"Mom," the physician said, "please, give me a hand with this. Lift her blouse in the back. Now, Arielle, take a deep breath." As he moved the stethoscope to several locations to listen to her lungs, he asked her to take deep breaths. He pronounced her lungs to be healthy.

Stepping in front of her, he said, "Mom, please place the stethoscope inside your daughter's blouse for me and cover her heart so I can listen. "She's good," he said. He removed the stethoscope's headset from his ears and draped the instrument around his neck. He looked at Judy. "Well, Mom, your daughter is in perfect health."

"That's wonderful, Doctor. Let me settle her in the lobby and bring in my boys."

Judy stepped back into room with Sammy and Joey and told them to sit on the examination table. For Joey it was a climbing adventure.

"Hi, Joey! You've certainly grown over the last year. Are you going into kindergarten this year?"

"Yes, Doctor."

"Wonderful, that's very exciting to hear. Now let's get a look in your ears." He went through the ear, nose, and throat checks with Joey. "Joey, will you take off your shirt for me?" After the boy quickly slipped it over his head, the doctor said, "Okay, Joey, now take a deep breath." He listened to different places on his chest and then moved behind him, encouraging Joey to take several deep breaths.

He said, "Judy, Joey's ears, nose, and throat are fine. His lungs are clear and sound good."

Stepping in front of Joey, he placed his stethoscope over his heart, repositioned it twice and said in Judy's direction said, "Sounds strong and healthy. Okay Joey, put your shirt back on and sit in the chair while I look at your older brother."

When he went through the same steps with Sammy, everything was routine. Eyes, ears, and throat all looked good.

"Sammy, take off your shirt for me please." He listened to his lungs, and they were good. Stepping in front of Sammy, the doctor placed the stethoscope over his heart and listened. He repositioned it and listened carefully. He placed the stethoscope on the side of his chest and listened. A troubled look crossed his face.

"Judy, please take Joey to the waiting room with Arielle and come back. Then I need you and Sammy to wait a minute." He turned and walked out of the examining room.

"Sammy, stay right there" she told him, and taking Joey by the hand, she walked him to the waiting room where Ari was confused by the turn of events.

"Ari, honey, watch your brother for a minute." She turned and walked back into the exam room with Sammy, now very concerned. This had never, ever, happened before.

He quickly returned with his associate and introduced him to Judy and Sammy. "Judy, I'd like my associate to listen to Sammy's heart."

By now, Judy's heart was in her throat. Worry was written all over her face. She watched the associate place the stethoscope in four different places. He patted Sammy on the shoulder and said, "Sammy, you did a great job!"

He turned to the family doctor and said, "May I talk to you outside?"

Though she could not hear their words, Judy could hear them talking in the hallway through the door. The tone of their voice brought an instant alarm that something was not right.

The family doctor finally returned. "Sammy, please put your shirt back on. Would you mind going to sit with your sister? I need to talk to your mom for a few minutes."

He walked Sammy to the door, patted him on the back as he left, and closed the door. He slowly turned to look at Judy.

"Please sit down, Judy."

*What could possibly be wrong?* her mind screamed. *He's healthy! He runs and plays like all the boys do.*

"I'm very concerned about your son. From what I can hear, I believe there is a regurgitation of blood transferring from one chamber to the other in his heart. I believe Sammy may have Ebstein's anomaly—a rare heart defect present at birth."

While the doctor was explaining what was happening in her son's heart, Judy's body went into adrenaline shock. Her heart began pounding, and her mind shut down. She could hardly hear him speaking.

"I believe I can hear blood flowing backward from the tricuspid valve in Sammy's heart, which is affecting his heart's ejection fraction. A normal heart ejection fraction is above fifty percent. With this reduced amount of blood flow, Sammy runs the risk of congestive heart failure."

Judy placed both hands over her face as tears streamed from her eyes. Her body began trembling. *How can this be? He's my healthy little boy. He runs and plays; this can't be true,* she repeated to herself.

"Judy, we need to get Sammy to the Children's Hospital in Denver as soon as possible for testing. He may need immediate heart surgery. Can you call Mike to come home and help you?"

Judy was speechless.

"Let me get you to the reception desk so they can help you." He helped Judy out of the chair, wrapped his arm around her shoulder, opened the door, and assisted her to the counter. As she walked past the children, they saw her expression. Confused, Ari began to cry upon seeing their mother's stricken demeanor.

"Judy, I'm going to make all the calls right now. They'll be expecting you tomorrow in Denver. If Mike needs to talk to me, have him call my private line in my office."

At the counter the doctor instructed the receptionist to call Mike at his work number. She handed the phone to Judy when it began ringing. "Hello, this is Four Corners, construction department."

"Hello, this is Judy. I have an emergency, and I need to talk with my husband, Mike Holmes."

"It's lunch break, and he's in the shanty. Please hold, and I'll connect you now."

When the phone rang, Mike answered it on the second ring.

"Mike!" Judy cried, "The doctor said Sammy is ill. You need to come home right now. We need to get him to Denver tomorrow."

Stunned beyond words, Mike did not question her; he knew immediately from the sound of Judy's voice that this matter was gravely serious. He made arrangements to leave work, and his boss volunteered to drive him home. It seemed like he was breaking every speed limit on the way, and Mike did not care.

Once Judy regained her composure, the nurse gave her the okay to take the kids and drive them home.

Pastor Smith closed the office door to head home for lunch. He drove the short distance home and pulled up to the curb. In front of him, two cars made hasty stops in front of his neighbor's house two doors down. He had seen enough in pastoring to know something serious was going on. *Something life-threatening is happening!* he decided. All thoughts of lunch left his mind as he sprinted toward Mike's and Judy's house.

Mike and Judy arrived home at the same time. Judy fell into Mike's arms as he asked, "What's happening?" He stared beyond her head in stunned silence as he held her close. Mike tried to send the children into the house ahead of them. Not sure exactly what was happening, the trio stood staring at them.

"Mike! Judy! What's going on? Is there an emergency?" Pastor Smith called to them.

Trying to be strong and stifling sobs, they sent the children to stay in Ari's bedroom while they tried to regain control. All the children were crying without knowing why. Their mother had never acted this way before, and that alone was enough for them to cry.

Judy finally answered Pastor Smith, "Yes."

They all went into the house where Mike and Pastor Smith listened as Judy tearfully described Ebstein's anomaly.

Pastor Smith said, "We're going to take care of this right now. May I pray with Sammy?"

Even though they were new to prayer in an hour of crisis, they responded with a firm yes and called the children to the living room.

"Sammy," Judy said, "Pastor Smith wants to pray with you." As he stepped toward Sammy, the pastor placed his right hand on top of Sammy's head and his left over his heart.

Right behind Pastor Smith was a large angel created by Father God to release healings. Placing his hand upon Pastor Smith and upon Sammy, virtue was being released as they prayed. As soon as the pastor began to say the words, the spiritual gate was opened, and power flowed from the spiritual realm into Sammy's physical heart. The Holy Spirit within Sammy responded, and love welled up in his heart. The angel assigned to the family stood very still, knowing God was at work. Things would be okay. In fact, this family was about to have a course correction.

He began praying in his usual Pentecostal flair: "In the name of Jesus, we say to this heart, be made whole. We ask all the functions of this heart to be normal and perfect. We thank You, Father God, for this boy's healing."

He began to raise his voice in making a decree and proclamation in the authority of Jesus. "By the stripes of Jesus, this boy is healed!" Pastor Smith lifted his hands from the boy, and Sammy staggered a bit with a dazed look.

"Pastor Smith, we thank you for praying with Sammy. We need to pack now and get ready to leave tomorrow," Judy said.

The pastor quickly left, went home, called the church prayer line, and placed Sammy's name on the prayer chain.

The stricken family felt as if life should stop. Tragedy had never before touched this home. Mike took Judy's hands and said, "Let's slow down for just a minute. Let's pray for all the details needed to get Sammy to Denver."

In the depth of their hearts, as never before, they pleaded with God for their son. In these moments they were experiencing a deep pain. Hurting for their child would be the deepest pain they would ever come to know. They shrugged off the questions and the pain and got busy with making the necessary arrangements.

# Eighteen

It was a warm morning with a cloudless sky when they arrived at Four Corners Regional Airport right outside Farmington. Mike, Judy, and Sammy had tickets on a Douglas DC 3 aircraft going to Denver. Upon arrival at the airline ticket counter, they checked in two small bags and received their boarding passes. Time seemed to be passing extremely slowly for the parents of the sick child. Seated in the waiting area, Sammy swung his legs back and forth as his parents sat in silence while contemplating the events to take place at the hospital. This would be the first airplane ride for all of them.

Judy had been greatly relieved to have her sister and brother-in-law come to take care of the other two while they would be gone. The couple had driven all night from Dallas. Mike and Judy knew that Ari and Joey would be in good hands and in their own familiar surroundings.

The concourse's overhead speakers crackled to life with boarding instructions for the flight going to Denver that was now boarding at Gate Two. Judy picked up her purse, grabbed Sammy's hand, and they headed to the door where Mike handed the gate attendant the boarding passes. The three of them walked through the door onto the tarmac for a short walk to the plane. The staircase had already been lowered and was resting on the asphalt.

At the bottom of the stairs a stewardess awaited the passengers. She greeted them, saying, "Welcome to our flight going to Denver. Please watch your step." Judy went first, Sammy followed, and then Mike. Once inside the plane, Judy saw their seats—20, 21, and 22—were right inside the doorway. They were in the last row; one would be seated on the right side, and two would be seated on the left. Sammy wanted the window seat; with the dire news they had received, they wanted to allow him to enjoy anything he wanted. Judy sat next to him, and Mike was across the aisle.

The ground crew lifted the stairway, part of the plane's fuselage, as the stewardess locked the handle in place to close the door. She then walked along the aisle, checking the passengers' seatbelts. As the engines started, she went through the emergency procedures and then took her seat. The ground crew pulled the wheel chokes and walked to the wing tips. The engines revved, and the plane began to move forward. Sammy's face was glued to the window. Moving down the taxiway to the end of runway number seven, the pilot stopped and waited for clearance from the tower.

Upon being cleared for departure, the engines powered up, entered the runway, and went to full throttle. In mere moments, Sammy was traveling faster than he had ever gone before. As the plane lifted off, the ground began to recede, and he could see the horizon. In a few minutes the plane was at a cruising altitude of 10,000 feet, traveling at a speed of 150 knots. In an excited voice, Sammy kept pointing at objects far below the plane. Even in the midst of this crisis, the flight was a pleasant experience for Sammy.

As the plane descended into Stapleton International Airport, both Sammy and Mike were glued to the window. They could see the tall buildings in the downtown area. Denver's airport was huge compared to Four Corners. Theirs was a picture perfect landing—an uneventful flight for these first-time flyers. Two bangs sounded on the plane's door, signaling for the stewardess to unlock the door and give it a shove so the ground crew could lower it down to the tarmac. Within the terminal door was an area to claim passenger baggage. They lingered there for a few minutes to retrieve their bags. Right outside the terminal, a man was holding a card with their names on it. The hospital had sent a car for them. God was blessing them with His favor in all the details.

Urgency filled the air surrounding this family as they entered the hospital. Judy and Sammy were whisked away as Mike began to fill out the medical and insurance forms. In the pre-op waiting area, Sammy was prepared for the first of three procedures. Up to now, this unexpected trip had all been an adventure. However, with all the fussing going on around him, he became very concerned and looked at this mother with questioning eyes. Fear swept across his face as he wondered why his parents were allowing this. *Why is this happening? I don't feel sick! I want to go home.*

Mike was brought to the pre-op room to be with Judy and Sammy. Seeing his son wearing a hospital gown and pajama bottoms sitting in the hospital bed tore at his heart. Mike was not often on the verge of tears. However, seeing his son in the bed cracked his tough interior and melted his heart, although outwardly he was being strong for them.

A doctor entered the room and introduced himself as Sammy's pediatric cardiologist. He asked Mike and Judy to step right outside the room where they could talk.

With loving eyes, Judy said to Sammy, "We'll be right outside the door, sweetie. We're not going anywhere."

Once in the hallway, the doctors explained what was about to happen. "Based on the report from your son's pediatrician, we're moving forward to confirm he has Ebstein's anomaly. We start with an echocardiogram of the heart. This noninvasive procedure will enable us to see how Sammy's heart is functioning. In this procedure we can see the blood flow regurgitation rate and how it affects his ejection fraction. After the echocardiogram, he'll have chest x-rays. When we review the results, we'll perform an angiogram by injecting a fluid called a contrast in the artery in his left leg. The contrast will enable us to see the flow of blood in real time. This procedure will give us the precise location of the defect. Depending on the severity, we'll either recommend ongoing treatments or we'll perform emergency heart surgery to repair the problem."

Judy and Mike were distraught at the cardiologists explanation. Their minds fought off denial. *This is real! We're standing here totally unprepared for a traumatic event like this! God, help us now in this hour of need!*

Every now and then, Judy glanced behind to look at Sammy as he rested quietly in the hospital bed. He had a confused look on his face. He was totally ignorant about the procedures that were only moments away from taking place. His life could be about to change forever.

As Sammy watched the adults, the doctor walked away, and his parents returned to his room. Mike walked to one side of the bed, and Judy stayed on the other. "Sammy, your mother and I are going to pray for you." They each took one of his hands, and they joined hands across him. Asking Father God for His provision, help, and favor, Mike and Judy sought God with all they had.

Another person entered the room and greeted them warmly. "Hello, I'm the echo tech here to do a test on Sammy," she said. She looked at Sammy and asked, "Are you Sammy?"

He nodded.

"This test will allow the doctor to see inside your chest. The worst part of this is the jelly that I rub on you will be coooold." The way she said "coool d" was a welcomed ice breaker to the intense mood. "Okay, Sammy, will you please take off your hospital gown, and we'll get started."

He looked to his mom, and she helped him get the gown untied and held it for him while the test was being conducted. Mike was curious and moved over to watch the screen. He saw images and pictures for which he had no references to interpret whether they were good or bad.

Within fifteen minutes, the procedure was over. The echo tech repacked the machine, told Sammy he did a great job, smiled at the parents, and added, "The doctor has placed a rush on this test, and he'll get the results in thirty minutes." They appreciated her thoughtful gentleness toward them as Judy fumbled to get Sammy's gown back on him.

Another tech entered the room almost as soon as first one left. He announced that he was there to take Sammy for a ride in a wheelchair!

"I'm taking him to radiology for chest x-rays. You're both welcome to walk with me, but when we get to the examination room, you'll have to stay in the waiting room. Sammy, think you can jump into this wheelchair for me?"

Sammy hopped out of the hospital bed and into the wheelchair, all ready for a ride. He was more of a little boy right then than a patient in the hospital. In the radiology department, Mike and Judy were shown the waiting room as the tech wheeled Sammy behind closed doors.

Judy sighed and took a deep breath. *Lord, I'm not used to having Sammy out of my sight and not under my control,* she prayed silently. *My maternal instincts are running amuck. Help me keep my balance.*

Sammy was having a full set of chest x-rays done—an AP (anterior/posterior) view and a lateral view. Standing in the background unseen by human eyes was an angel releasing peace and calmness into Sammy's mind. The chest x-rays were not painful, but he had never been without his parents. Soon enough, all the needed images had been made and confirmed, and Sammy was was taken back to his pre-op room.

The family was now playing a waiting game—one that no parents do well. For one of them to be sick was one thing, but their child's being sick was a deep lingering pain. They were exhausted by the suddenness and stress of the whole ordeal.

The phlebotomist entered the room shortly after Sammy returned from radiology. At this points, matters took a more serious turn. He began preparations for the next step in the testing procedure—an angiogram. Up until now, Sammy's tests had been totally painless. Now an IV was being inserted into his forearm with two ports. The insertion of the needle was painful, and Sammy could not hold back his tears. Judy felt like her heart shattered in individual pieces at hearing his cries.

The doctor who would be performing the procedure walked into the room and began to explain what was about to happen, "We will be injecting a contrast into his bloodstream and taking a video of the flow to see exactly where his problem is. Only then will we know for sure what the next step will be—treatment or surgery." Everything had been happening so fast, Mike and Judy barely had time to take it all in and comprehend it all.

As he finished his explanation, a gurney arrived to take Sammy into surgery. Judy leaned over the rail and kissed Sammy, and Mike did the same. As Sammy was wheeled away, both felt as if their hearts were being ripped out of them. Mike wrapped his arm around Judy's shoulder and pulled her close as they walked slowly to the surgical waiting room.

After two long hours of fear and trepidation gripping their hearts, the attending surgeon finally arrived. "Sammy is doing very well and will be in the recovery room for a while." Their expression of tension shifted to one of relief.

The surgeon was carrying a large envelope and said, "Come with me. I have some still-shot x-rays taken of Sammy's heart during the procedure that I want you both to see." He motioned for them to follow him to an illuminated screen. He placed several sheets on the panel for them to look at.

He took a deep breath and began to share the news they had been dreading to hear. "I really don't know where to begin..." He hesitated before he continued. "From what your primary-care pediatrician described, we believed your son to have ASD—Atrial Septal Defect, a condition associated with Ebstein's anomaly. Simply put, ASD is a hole in the wall of the heart where there should be no holes. If the hole is minute enough, in most cases, it can be treated without surgery.

"Now I want you to look at this x-ray, which confirms what the echocardiogram showed as well." He pointed to a raised spot on Sammy's heart of what appeared to be a ripple on its surface. "See this raised ridge of heart tissue right here? That ridge tells me that Sammy had two very large ASDs in his heart. The ridges indicate healed tissue, which also shows me some surgical work far superior than I have ever before seen."

He pointed at another spot on the x-ray. "Now see the length of the ridges? I can tell you if those holes had not been repaired, your son would have died within a month from congestive heart failure."

Turning to face them, he asked, "I want to know exactly what took place between the time you left your doctor's office and today."

Mike was the first to speak. "Wait, doctor. Are you telling us that the ASD, as you called it, is healed?"

"Yes, and it's the best work I've ever seen."

Mike and Judy stared at each other as a rush of thoughts whirled in their minds. Judy began to tell the surgeon about leaving the doctor's office, going straight home, Mike's arriving from work, booking plane tickets, making child-care plans for the children, packing clothes, preparing a last-minute dinner, and taking the flight to Denver the next day.

Mike suddenly interrupted her and said, "Wait, honey, don't you remember Pastor Smith's rushing up to us and asking to pray with Sammy?"

"Yes, he was very insistent."

Mike turned to the surgeon. "He's a Pentecostal pastor in town, and the church has been in revival for the last few months. People are coming from all across the state. Many people are being healed of all kinds of illnesses and terminal ones as well. His church is in the papers and on the radio all over the state."

The doctor listened carefully and finally spoke hesitantly. "If I didn't see those ridge lines on his heart tissue, I'd be thinking your pediatrician made a bad diagnosis. However, I am a God-believing man. I believe God healed your son and that his heart is now normal for a little boy his age."

Judy burst into tears and began sobbing, knowing her little boy was going to be okay and that her Father God had performed a miracle for their precious son.

# Nineteen

A cab pulled up in front of the house. While the cabby was still taking the luggage out of the trunk, the screen door slammed open, and Ari and Joey came running out of the house. In a burst of emotion, they wrapped their arms around their brother and squeezed him until his eyes bulged. Their reaction was a needed release of pent-up feelings and fears, wondering if he were going to be okay.

Judy's sister, Kate, and her husband, James, followed and met them in the front yard. She could not imagine going through this time without her little sister's being her anchor at home. In their wildest dreams, who could have imagined this outcome? No one! The children ran into the house, the two sisters locked arms and strolled in together as the men carried in the luggage. The whole time Mike talked about the DC-3.

Food was on the kitchen table, ready for the weary travelers. Judy's sister had prepared a spread of all the family favorites. Judy thought, *It's good to be home and be a family again. Calamity was on the horizon, and my world was falling apart until Pastor Smith prayed with Sammy and God healed him. Now I have an unquenchable hunger to know more about the Old Pentecostal Church. I need to talk with Mike about this, and we need to find out more about Pastor Smith and God's activity there. I don't ever remember Pastor Billings talking about miracles and healing. We need to find out what he has to say; after all, he is our pastor.*

Mike and Judy began to tell the whole story to Kate and James—the plane ride, the car waiting for them at the airport, the pre-op room, the tests, the technicians, the surgeon, the doctors, etc. "Kate, it wasn't until the IV ports were in Sammy's arm that a wave of full reality swept over me. I was sick to my stomach with fear. When they wheeled him through the surgery doors and out of my sight, it was a horrible first in all of my years being a mother. I pray I will never have it happen again. Knowing that we were not alone—that God's presence was with us—was so comforting, so real, so tangible for us. I don't know how I would have handled all of this without Him."

Kate's brow furrowed as she listened to her sister. *Wow, she's starting to sound like Grandma. We're actually starting to sound like our grandmother. I can see and hear it, living out our grandmother's spiritual heritage.*

Judy continued, "There were so many distraught parents in the hospital with sick children. We left there on a joyous note, but others didn't. Under different circumstances, we would have shared our faith with other parents, but we were in a place of desperation—just like they were."

Sammy remained under the watchful eye of his mother. Though his outcome was unbelievable, the surgeon had placed him under some physical restrictions. She caught his eye and motioned for him to come over to her. In a warm embrace, she reminded him, "Remember what the doctor told you? No roughhousing for a week. Now promise me you're not going to be running around but will take it easy?

"But Mom, everything is going to be all right; the angel told me so."

Stunned, she drew him closer as the others went on to other conversations. "What are you saying, Sammy?"

"He told me everything was going to be okay."

"Are you telling me you saw an angel?"

"Yes, when I was waking up in the recovery room. I opened my eyes, and he was smiling at me. Then he said, 'Everything will be okay.' He stood up and stepped back from the bed, and I couldn't see him then."

"Shhhh, now don't tell anyone else about this until we talk later."

She called Ari over. "Take your brothers into the other room and play Sorry with them while we talk."

Taking Sammy and Joey by the hand, Ari left the kitchen with them.

Kate stood and went to get the coffeepot on the stove to give everyone a warm up. They were just now getting ready to share the good parts of the conversation. As far as they could remember, this type of situation had never happened in their family. They couldn't recall a time when a medical emergency turned out better than before the event happened.

Mike spoke up, "I've heard Pastor Billings say that God's ways are not like our ways; His thoughts are higher than our thoughts. My mind is understanding some of what that means now. When I look at all the factors that fell into place, like the right timing, I am at a loss to explain. For example, getting Judy's call at work when I was in the shanty—I'm only in there thirty minutes of my day. The fact that Judy, Pastor Smith, and I all arrived home at the same time is beyond a reasonable chance. When Pastor Smith, a man who is not even our pastor, insisted on praying for Sammy… at first, I was going to be rude. But then, I submitted to his request. I felt a wind passing over us as he prayed, and I thought it was odd but time was racing too fast to take note of it.

"The plane having seats available at the last minute, the car waiting at the airport to drive us to the hospital, and Sammy's seeing the best pediatrician doctor this side of the Mississippi. I find all these circumstances so mind-boggling because it was against all odds that these things could fall into place in exactly the right order. Do I make any sense?"

Judy sipped her coffee as she gathered her thoughts and added, "When the surgeon came out with the x-rays and placed them on the lighted screen, and I saw a picture of my baby's heart, I stopped breathing. When the doctor pointed at two places in Sammy's heart and told us about the ridge line, he said, "This was where your son's two ASDs were located and now the holes are closed," I almost went into shock. I was expecting bad news—not his explanation of what he believed was the best repair work he had ever seen in all his days of being a heart surgeon."

Taking another sip of coffee, she continued, "I didn't know whether I was going to faint or scream to let out all my emotions."

Kate leaned closer to her sister and placed her hand of comfort on Judy's. They all sat in silence until Mike said, "I don't think my life will ever be the same. I know that I know God is alive and a Healer. I know that He took action for us. I don't know how to put it into words, but I'm humbled by this all."

The family talked and talked the night away—about Grandma's faith and humorous memories from their childhood. Theirs had turned out to be a joyous reunion.

Kate commented, "You know, Sis, this would have been a different night if you and Mike hadn't shared your faith with us months ago. Because of your testimony, James and I were born again and our spiritual eyes and ears have been opened. We can appreciate your openness about God's love for us. Just think, last year at this time our lives were so very different."

James added, "I didn't have a loving dad; he worked hard, went through the war, and became a hardened man. Now being in relationship with God is so strange; He is my loving Father, and in a sense, I feel like He is parenting me—even though I am an adult. I enjoy the feeling; mine was a different type of healing—a different type of miracle."

They all agreed. Salvation had come to their households.

A few nights later, life began returning to normal. Judy was still watchful over her children, vigilant and maybe even a bit overprotective. Ari's light was off; she had finished writing in her journal. The house was dark and quiet.

Both Judy and Mike were resting quietly. Without warning, Judy rolled closer to Mike. Feeling her nearness, he raised his arm so she could snuggle into his arm and against his chest. Then she burst into tears. She tried to be quiet, but soon the sobs became uncontrollable. She could no longer control the feelings she had held tightly in check. She didn't have to be strong now; the trial was over. Sammy and all her babies were well.

She let go and cried in her beloved husband's arms. For maybe the first time in her life, she felt safe enough to let down the walls and release her deepest emotions. She sought comfort and found consolement in her husband's warm embrace.

# Twenty

As was his normal routine, Pastor Billings stood at the doors to say a few words to his flock as they left the midweek service. He always responded to the church members with kind and endearing words that showed his care and concern. "How's work?" or "What's happening at school?"

When Mike and Judy and the children approached the doors to leave, they greeted the pastor and shared their news with him. With Sammy's miraculous healing, they had been displaying a positive attitude. They were becoming the talk of the church. Their testimony of Sammy's healing had been burning through the congregation.

"Mike, Judy, I know it's getting late, but may I have a few minutes with you in my office?" The look on his face was one of dire concern.

They answered, "Yes, of course."

Judy turned to Ari. "Honey, would you please watch the little ones while we go into Pastor's office? We'll be just a few minutes."

Her parents disappeared behind a closed door. At first the waiting was fine until the janitor started turning off all the lights. They were alone in the nearly dark building. *Well,* Ari thought, *it is a church; no need to be afraid.*

Pastor Billings began, "As you know, being your pastor, I must speak to you when there is a spiritual issue or problem."

Mike looked at Judy with a confused look, and both began to wonder where this meeting was going. Already the tone of Pastor's voice was not good. Pastor continued, "I have heard you are telling church members that God healed Sammy?"

Full of love and praise for his Savior, Mike started to share what God had done for his son. However, it soon became evident that Pastor Billings did not see Sammy's healing in the same way.

He started again, "I have heard you're telling people that God healed your son. Now that just cannot be."

All joyous expressions and color faded from their faces. They were devastated to hear him say that, knowing full well that God had indeed healed Sammy.

Mike tried to reason with him. "But, Pastor, what are you saying? I don't understand. You preached on Scripture where Jesus and the apostle healed people."

"Mike, Judy, that was a time of special dispensation. Healing and miracles stopped when the last apostle died."

"But, wait, in the newspaper, there are articles every week about people being healed by God in the Old Pentecostal Church. How can you say healing ended nearly two thousand years ago? There's proof right here in our town."

"I'm your pastor; I have invested in you both and in your children. You know my little girl is very good friends with Arielle. But I must tell you that the miracle you've seen and the ones being talked about at the Pentecostal church are of the devil."

"What?" Mike exclaimed. They both expressed deep shock at what they were hearing from Pastor Billings. They didn't know if they should be angry or sad, but both were greatly dismayed.

Judy spoke up because she remembered something during her time of disbelief. She said, "Pastor Billings, while I was in the pediatrician's office and he was examining Sammy's heart, he had me listen to my own heartbeat through his stethoscope. Then he placed it on Sammy's heart for me to hear the difference. I could heard the backflow of blood. Pastor, I heard it. The surgeon in Denver said he was a God-believing man and knew Sammy's ASD was a miraculous healing. He also said it was the best work he had ever seen. You can't be telling me that our loving heavenly Father didn't heal my son."

"I'm sorry, but I must tell you the truth. Healings and miracles have stopped. If your son has been healed, God didn't do it."

With those words of finality, Mike stood and said, "Pastor, I think it is time for us to go." With bowed heads, they both stepped out of the office and went to the children. They had heard the raised voice of their pastor.

Ari looked at her parents in wonder. *Just a short while ago, we were happy and singing. Now we're being whisked away in a huff. What just happened?* Ari was too afraid to ask.

In the waiting area of heaven's angelic host, expectations dropped. A unity of denominations would not be taking place in Farmington as they had hoped. If unity among the denominations had been realized, many angels would have received assignments on earth to serve. Any angel who has been assigned to serve considered it a privilege.

For Mike and Judy, the time had come for them to find a new church home. New beginnings are often preceded by difficult endings.

In the days that followed, life resumed. The children were now all in school. What a day that was! Joey had been both excited and mortified at the same time. His mother, his best friend, had always been close by. He was not sure if he liked being away from her while at school. Even if he didn't like the separation, he soon realized he really had no choice. Sammy was a typical boy, and he was learning fast in first grade. Arielle was entering a season of change. Being in school she was in her element and was successful in all her subjects. Relationships were another subject altogether.

Martha, Judy, and the other girls who were part of the dancing club made plans to meet at Woody's Café to talk. With their newfound freedom of having the children in school, meeting would become a part of their regular schedule. Their get-together soon morphed into a woman's coffee and Bible study. However, at this first meeting, Judy shared what had happened in Pastor Billings' office.

Martha was the first to arrive, and she waited to get the same booth they were in the last time—front and center. After all, everything that happened on Main Street could be seen from that vantage point. Judy was the next to arrive, and then Beth and Mary came. Voices rose as they inevitably jumped into girl talk.

Beth asked, "Is that the stool?"

Judy shot Martha a look asking, *You told them?*

She responded, "Now look, Judy, it will increase their faith."

Judy's feelings of betrayal softened to agreeing her friend had a point. Martha and Judy both nodded in affirmation.

"You mean…" Mary interrupted, "an angel sat right there?"

Again they solemnly nodded yes. The new girls felt both excitement and a sense of eeriness at the same time. Then it was time to tell them the whole story. Not one of them glanced out the window as Judy shared what had happened. They all leaned in as if to hear better, and when something shocking happened, they shifted backward against the booth seats as if they couldn't believe what they were hearing.

Since they had all been saved in Judy's house, they attended the Baptist church and the same Sunday school class. The ladies of the former Saturday night dancing group were now church-attending believers. This good time in their lives was shattered. They were experiencing something none of them had ever experienced. They had never even heard the term spiritual warfare, and without their awareness, the Enemy had invaded their lives. They were all greatly affected by the strange turn of events.

Beth spoke up. "We all know what it says in Romans 8. 'All things work out for the good of those who love God.' We have to have faith this will work out well."

Judy answered, "I understand that; it is the emotional pain I didn't expect."

Mary added, "How are you going to forgive Pastor for making such a statement? You know forgiveness is important to God, and you all know I am working on forgiving that man in my life." Laughter filled the booth.

Finally Martha could not hold back the question that had been most on her heart. "Are you and Mike thinking of going to the Old Pentecostal Church now?"

"Yes, I admit that the thought is on our minds. We don't feel like we can go back to our old church now. In our hearts and minds, we know God has healed our son. What if we need God to do a miracle again someday, and we stop believing because of what Pastor said. Then what?"

"Any of us may need the healing power of God for our families in the future," Mary agreed.

Martha brought them back around to the subject at hand—which church. She declared, "I'm telling you right now, if you decide to move, I'm talking to George. We're all best friends; it would be nice if we stayed together."

Beth added, "Girls, seems to me like it would be a good idea for all of us to talk to our husbands. We might need a change of churches in our future."

With her pillow resting against the headboard, her light on, and her journal in her lap, Ari made a poignant entry.

*Dear Father God, I have questions today. I know You healed my brother. Why is Pastor Billings saying You didn't? This is a prayer, God, and I am hoping You'll answer me. I want to know. Church feels like my second home. I've felt Your presence with me there too. You see, me and Susan are best friends. What's going to happen now? Why doesn't Pastor believe You still have the power to heal people? I believe You healed Sammy. Tell me, Father, what are the clues to people getting healed? I was there when Pastor Smith prayed for Sammy. What happened that I didn't see? Tell me, please. Amen.*

Standing beside Ari's bed was the family angelic protector/messenger. Ari's future had been revealed to him, and he was very pleased. Soon this family would understand, but for now the change in their lives would be difficult. The angel knew that when God closed one door, He opened another. With a new door comes new lessons. His family was about to embark on a new journey that would enable this little lioness of God to one day step into her destiny.

# Twenty-One

When Judy turned into the A&W, Sammy's eyes grew large. The two of them had been doing clothes shopping the past few hours, and he was glad the ordeal was over. He'd been sitting quietly, but to get a better look, he excitedly knelt on his car seat. Placing his hands on the dashboard, he smiled from ear to ear. Judy parked the car under the overhang out of the afternoon sun. The roller-skating waitress came over to the car, performed her pirouette, and then said, "Hello, do you need a menu?"

"Yes," Judy said. Handing her the menu, the waitress added, "Just so you know, we have the best French fries in the Four Corners. They're cooked fresh. Take your time; I'll be back." *Judy thought, this won't take long; Sammy has his favorites—hotdog, fries, and a root beer.* "What do you think, Sam?

His mom was the only person he allowed to call him Sam. He was Sammy to everyone else. He looked carefully at the menu as if he were reading it, took a deep breath, and said, "Let's see, I think I'll have a hotdog, French fries, and a large root beer."

"Excellent choice! Are you sure you can finish a large root beer?"

"No problem, Mom."

Judy relayed the order to the girl, and she skated away under the watchful eyes of Sammy. He thought roller skating from car to car would be a cool job.

"Sam," Judy said. "Do you remember when you told me you saw an angel after you woke up in the hospital?"

"Yes. He was a tall man like Dad. He smiled at me, and I remember he took my hand. I felt something roll up my arm. I didn't care 'cause I felt okay. Then the nurses saw I was awake and came over. That's when he stepped back, and I couldn't see him anymore."

"What was he wearing?"

"His clothes were white. That's all I can tell you, Mom."

"Tell me again how you knew he was an angel."

Stating it as a matter of fact, he replied, "Because he told me, Mom."

They sat in silence for a moment, and Judy turned on the radio. She moved the dial off the Christian station to the local one. The radio came alive with a Beatles' song, and Sammy started to sing along.

"Sam, where did you learn the words to that song?"

"Oh, the other kids play it on their transistor radios."

She was quite surprised at his nonchalant reply. Historic events seemed to be happening every day. Christian adults tended to see some of them as fearful events that would lead them to believe that the rapture was coming soon. She had been trying to shield the children from the rest of the world outside of Farmington.

Streaking toward them came a girl on skates. Judy rolled the window up to hold the tray. Sammy's face wore a look of pure joy.

"Here's your order," the waitress said as she clipped the tray to the window, handed Judy some napkins, and then skated away.

Sammy opened the glove box door to set his root beer on it. He had his own ready-made little tray. He placed the fries, packaged in their paper holder next to him, and opened the paper wrapper around his hotdog. He waited for his mom to give thanks for the food.

As Judy watched her little boy eat, she thought, *He is surely conquer oriented when it comes to eating. You would think if he didn't eat it fast, it would get away! He takes after his father. Where does he put all that food? Sometimes I wonder if he has a hollow leg that fills as he eats. Of course, that's why we were out shopping. He's in one of those growing spurts.*

Sammy spoke up after taking a long drink of root beer. "Mom, it wasn't the first time I saw the angel."

Judy about dropped her food. Turning toward her son, she asked, "What do you mean?"

"When Pastor Smith was praying for me, I had my eyes closed. But then it was like he shoved me, so I opened my eyes. I saw the angel standing behind him, and then he disappeared."

"Why didn't you tell me before?"

Sammy simply shrugged his shoulders.

Judy paid the bill and silently drove home deep in thought as Sammy listened to the radio. Pulling up to the curb in front of their house, Judy said, "Sammy, let's keep the angel story between you and me for now, okay?

He nodded his head and bounded out the door car, moving on to the next adventure in life.

Thinking back through the events of Sammy's healing, thoughts began running through Judy's mind. Pastor *Billings told us miracles no longer happen, but Sam was definitely healed. I wonder what he would say about him seeing an angel. I don't want to know right now. I have a hard enough time managing the world events taking place and caring for my family. Now I'm experiencing things beyond my world. I cannot make sense of it.*

Comprehending the spiritual realm was so confusing in her mind. Sam had told her about the angel in real experience terms. *I feel this hunger to know more about God and why He is blessing our family in supernatural ways. I can't grasp it; God, please help me.*

# Twenty-Two

The average onlooker would have thought a Christian holiday service was taking place at the church. Those are the times when more people are in attendance at church because of the holidays. They called those times "CNE times—Christmas, New Years or Easter." The parking lot was full, and every available parking spot in the neighborhood was filled until people had to park a block away. Mike, Judy, and the children walked down a new sidewalk toward the church. Once the utility company had finished installing the fire hydrants, the sidewalks had been replaced. They were nervous, but their apprehensive feelings were short-lived.

The greeter held the doors open as people walked up the steps and entered the front doors. Ten feet from the door, they all slowed their pace at feeling a thick spiritual atmosphere—like stepping from the cold outside temperature of winter into a warm, loving home.

As Mike, Judy, and the children entered the church building, they felt a tangible atmosphere of love. Their reaction time was slow, due to a lack of experiencing anything like this before. They barely acknowledged the greeter as they went in. Right inside the sanctuary, their friends had held space for them in the second to last pew. Everyone was smiling; the joy of the Lord was in the house of God.

Judy glanced around and marveled at the beauty of the stained-glass windows. Each window told a story through the creative workmanship invested in them. The rich wood tones of the altar area brought a feeling of warmth. The modest decorations emphasized the focus on things above. The most cherished items were the people themselves—restored jars of clay in the Potter's hands. The once heartbroken, sin-sick souls were about to express adoration to the One who had set them free and restored them; that One was Jesus.

Mike and Judy's experience of belonging to a conservative congregation in their prior church had not prepared them for the freedom in the Holy Ghost about to be unleashed in times of worship. They would soon feel as if they were attending a celebration at a newlyweds' reception.

The organist approached the Hammond organ, sat down on the bench, carefully placing her feet on the foot pedals, and switched on the instrument. She began to play "I Have Decided to Follow Jesus." The church instantly erupted into fluid motion.

Glances were being exchanged in the newcomers' pew. Mike and Judy looked at each other in surprise. Up and down their pew, the looks of surprise passed between the families. Even the children were caught up in the singing with a little bounce to the music. It was so different from the old hymns they were accustomed to singing. Feeling the love of God brought freedom they had not known before.

The organist moved right into another upbeat worship song when Ari noticed a finely dressed woman leave her seat and walk to the front where she started to dance. She skipped and twirled, swayed and hopped, and her face was filled with joy. *How strange!* she thought. People were clapping their hands; others raised them toward the ceiling, swaying them back and forth. By the fourth song, the atmosphere of God was thick and wonderful.

Mike thought, *My soul was meant to be in the loving atmosphere of God.* He had tasted something he liked a lot. Judy looked at Mike and the other men and saw how engaged they were in the service. For a brief moment, she felt like she was back at HWYs on a Saturday night, forgetting the world outside. The exception was the dark atmosphere there whereas here, she was surrounded by the light. She embraced the love of God as she swayed in place. She felt like a little girl standing before her father in the reflection of his attention. *This is unbelievable, and to think I'm in the company of our best friends!*

Now they were all sharing Jesus in their lives together. Once they gathered together around the familiar spirit of alcohol; now they had changed and were sharing in the spiritual influence of the Holy Spirit. Their relationships were growing stronger than ever.

Pastor Smith walked up to the podium and said, "I thought I was going to cast my message aside and let the Holy Ghost have His way. Whew, it is powerful in here today! God is good! Amen?"

The people responded in kind.

He turned the pages in his Bible and announced, "We'll be reading from the book of Luke 7:37-38. All will remain standing for the reading of the Word of God." He grabbed the podium, looked up toward heaven, and slowly lowered his face until in a soft voice he began to read.

"A woman in that town lived a sinful life learned that Jesus was eating at a Pharisee's house, so she came there with an alabaster jar of perfume. As she stood behind him at his feet weeping, she began to wet his feet with her tears. Then she wiped them with her hair, kissed them and poured the perfume on them."

"This is the Word of the Lord." Everyone was seated and silent.

In a loud voice, he stated, "We know, we know, we know why she broke open the costly alabaster jar of perfume. If we were in her place, wouldn't we have done the same?" Toning down for effect, he continued, "We're forgiven sinners washed in the blood of Jesus. We do not have an alabaster jar of costly perfume to give to Him; we do have our hearts of praise. We give to Him our joyous expression for setting us free. Can I get an Amen?"

All through the church came shouts of "Amen" because they too had been washed clean.

"That woman had Jesus in the flesh; we have His presence with us here today." Again shouts of "Amen" could be heard.

"Now let's look at the fourth chapter of book of John where Jesus had returned to Galilee. In verses 43-50 the text tells us there was a problem of unbelief in His town. However, a royal official had heard Jesus was near so he traveled 20 miles to ask Him to return to his home to heal his sick son. Jesus told him that his son would live. The official believed Him and returned home to find his son healed and well upon his arrival."

Pastor Smith looked over the flock and said in a loud commanding manner, "It is a paradox. Those people in Galilee had knowledge of Jesus and His family throughout the years, and they had a hard time believing. Yet a man from 20 miles away had heard the very same reports of the signs and wonders Jesus released by the power of the Holy Ghost and hurried to meet Him for the sake of his ill son."

He paused, shifted his weight, and began anew. "We have people coming to our church from places beyond our county to be in the Sunday service, hoping to receive a healing. We have decided to begin a healing service on Friday nights especially for those desiring a physical, emotional, or spiritual healing. Beginning this coming Friday, our focus will be on seeing God move in healing the masses."

Whispers spread from pew to pew, and people tried to make sense of the change and decide if they wanted to be a part of it. Pastor Smith ignored the whispering and added, "Many of us here are like the woman with the alabaster jar, expressing deep gratitude to Jesus for forgiving us our sins. Others have deep gratitude for the physical healings that have taken place in His name. We have decided to make this available to those who are beyond our little community. I request your prayer and support. In the end, it is all about Jesus and Him being Lord of our lives and church."

Looking into the congregation, he asked the organist to come and play softly. "Anna, would you come and pray with the women? Gil, would you please pray with the men? Mrs. Smith and I will be right up front. If you need a touch from God, come while He is here; don't be shy."

With a loud shout, he beckoned to those in the pews, "Come you who are sick. Come you who are weary." The organist played the song, "I Surrender All" as the people left their seats and came forward for prayer.

Pastor said, "Chief, stand behind them while we pray," and he took up his position. The organist played louder, and the people who were yet seated watched to see what God was about to do.

With a shout, Pastor Smith said, "In the name of Jesus!" and Chief caught a man as he fell backward toward the floor. Mike leaned over and out of his pew to see what was going on. Now the newcomers understood why there was such an open space between the altar and the first pew. It was for all those who would fall under the power and influence of the Holy Spirit.

A brush of angel wings was fanning over the people. The wind of the Holy Spirit swept over them all. A release of the love of God and His compassion rushed over their very hearts. Rays of intensely bright light emanated from heaven and encompassed the church. An intersection of heaven and earth was realized. God knew the hearts of everyone in the service. Even if they didn't go forward, He touched their souls. God was in the house.

Prayer time continued, but Mike, Judy, and their friends left the church. Outside they gathered for only a few minutes. Mike said, "Can you all come over tonight? I need to talk about this. I have never seen a demonstration like this in all of my life. I want to hear what you think. Is this of God?"

A time was set, and they all left the church property for home.

# Twenty-Three

Mike took the liberty of having Sara come to their house to watch the children so the adults could talk. The warm fall evening was a beautiful time for outside games. The kids liked to play Simon Says and Red Light/Green Light." Sara could keep them busy playing games for hours.

Judy prepared snacks, and she hoped the other girls had time to bring their favorites. Sara, Ari, Sammy, and Joey were already playing in the front yard when everyone arrived. Instant chaos ensued. Four cooks were in the kitchen preparing the buffet of snacks, four men were watching sports, and a yard full of children were playing.

Judy called from the kitchen, "Whoever wants coffee or a soft drink come and get it before we start talking." The men immediately filed into the kitchen, chose their favorite, and headed back to the front room. The television had been turned off, two additional chairs were brought in, and all eight adults were ready to talk.

Mike began the conversation. "This morning's service was over the top. Does anyone else think that?"

Martha, who was never shy, spoke up next. "I'm new to all of this, and I have no way of confirming that what was happening was by the Word of God. It was like chaos in there with bodies flying everywhere."

Beth's husband Ron added, "What do we know? Something beyond our world was happening in that church. I don't know what I was feeling, but I felt good inside."

The screen door slammed, and Ari ran to the bathroom. But when she came out, she sat down next to her mother on the floor. Judy leaned over to whisper, "Ari, honey, go out and play with the others."

"No, Mom, I want to hear what everyone thinks was happening in church this morning."

"Okay, but be out of sight."

George was the next to speak. "We've all read the testimonies from the local newspaper. Reading about what's happening in my own hometown on Sunday mornings is one thing. Seeing all the commotion happening while God's miracles are going on is certainly another."

Judy chimed in, "I saw Chief Rogers and Gil up front. Did you see they're a part of the church now? I think if they were skeptical, they wouldn't be there."

Martha noticed that Mary had shifted in her seat. "So, Mary, are you going to say what's on your mind?"

"Well, I guess it's this: I have never felt the kind of love I felt in church today. I will say that I want to go again just to be in that love. Let me learn about the rest."

Mike took a deep breath and offered, "At Pastor Billings' church, the Holy Spirit was there. It seems to me that Pastor Smith goes further and allows the Holy Spirit to move like on the day of Pentecost."

Ron jumped in. "If what I witnessed was the Holy Spirit, I need a whole lot of learning to understand. Look what happened to the apostles. Thousands came to Jesus the day the Holy Spirit showed up."

George added, "Let's say it. One church seems orderly, and today's had a flavor of disorder." On and on the give and take of the conversation continued with statements and questions but no real resolutions.

Ari broke her mother's rule and spoke up. "Excuse me," she said in her little girl's voice among all the adults' chatter. "My brother was healed by God through Pastor Smith's prayer. If he didn't pray for my brother, Sammy would be really sick and might not have lived much longer. I saw God at work today in church. I believe we need to give it some time and experience it more and learn more about the Pentecostal ways."

When Martha commented, "Out of the mouths of babes…," the four couples all laughed together.

Mike summed up the evening's get-together. "I have never felt this good about myself and my life. When I'm in the love we all feel in church, life is better. Let's just trust God is leading us all."

Beth added, "Aren't you all curious? I would like to know why that man fell to the floor, and what happened to him while he was there. I agree we need to be part of this church before we condemn it just because we're scared. I want to know why I felt my emotions stirring in me with feelings that I have not felt since I was a child. Something was happening to me in that atmosphere, and I want to know more."

Finally, they had reached a decision. All four couples agreed unanimously to keep going to the Old Pentecostal Church.

Mike said, "Let me end this evening in a prayer. Dear Heavenly Father, we ask that You would confirm to us what was happening in church today was You. In Jesus' name, Amen."

A group of sweaty kids came bursting through the screen door, eager to have some of the treats they knew were awaiting them. The adults moved on to other topics and they returned to just being friends. Sara stayed for treats with the hope she would learn why none of these couples went to HYWs anymore.

# TWENTY-FOUR

In a flash of light, he arrived and was now standing in their bedroom. He looked at the other angel, and they spoke to one another through their thoughts. "I've come from the throne room. God has heard their prayer requesting confirmation that He's leading them."

"You have a message for which one?"

"For the one who leads this family spiritually."

"Do you have a message for the girl?"

"No, she will soon see her destiny. She will need to learn and experience many things first." He stepped to where Mike was sleeping. He extended his left hand and placed it over his head. A warm glow descended from the palm of his hand to Mike's mind, and he slipped into a dream...

> "No, I haven't seen him today. Did you check with Joel?" Mike looked at his watch, and the time was 2:28 p.m.
>
> "No. Do you know where he is? It's 2:28 now, and it's going to rain. I need to speak to him."
>
> Mike left the office to look for Joel and stepped into a hospital emergency room. He stopped the first person he saw and asked, "Is Joel here?"
>
> "Yes," the person replied. "He's in bay 2 healing someone; you can see him there."
>
> Mike walked down a long corridor flooded with extremely white lights until he found ER bay 2. He walked in, and everything was white. He heard a voice say, "The patient was just healed; now he is saved." Mike pulled aside a curtain and walked into a garden courtyard where it was pouring rain. He saw a man whose back was to him that he thought might be Joel. "Sir, are you Joel?"
>
> "It is the latter rain; step in and get wet." He stepped aside, and Mike could see a path lined with fruit trees on each side. He noticed the stunning beauty of deep colors he had never seen before. The flowering trees were in bloom and bearing fruit. From down the path he could hear the sounds of children playing. Mike stepped into the rain and, within moments, he was soaking wet. The temperature of the rain was refreshing but not cold.

The glow ended, and the angel withdrew his hand. He looked at the other angel, and said, "I'm being sent to a member of the other four families to share the same message. The Lord is bringing them into a great adventure, and they will experience many things."

Hearing this message, the attending angel smiled. With a bright flash, the messenger angel had disappeared.

Mike woke with a start; chills ran over his body in waves. His mind raced. *I've had dreams before—but never like this!* He easily recalled the vivid details and the stunning colors, but the message of the dream was so confusing. He rested quietly in bed and committed to memory everything he could remember—asking for a man named Joel, noticing the time was 2:28 p.m., the hospital emergency room, witnessing an instant healing, stepping into a garden when it was raining, being invited to come into the rain and getting wet, the path, and the indescribable beauty of the fruit trees. Another memory touched his mind: *Why did I hear children laughing?* From within, he felt a quickening of his spirit that his dream meant something. He felt God was giving him a message. *But what is the message?*

During breakfast, Mike told Judy about his dream. This kind of sharing was new for both of them.

"Everyone dreams," Judy responded.

Mike remained adamant that the dream held a message from God. They had no resources and no way to explore the clues.

Judy concluded, "As odd as this suggestion seems, you need to talk to Ari tonight and give her the clues. See what she might say about it. Now don't be distracted at work; keep your focus, Mike."

"You're right, Judy. I will."

A car horn honked outside—Mike's signal that his ride was waiting. He quickly put on his work shoes, grabbed his lunch, kissed Judy, and left by the back door. Judy now had fifteen minutes of solitude before she had to wake the children. She poured a cup of coffee and mulled over the dream. *If Mike's dream is a call to an adventure, where is it leading?* she wondered.

Once the children were off to school, the kitchen cleaned and organized, she poured her second cup of coffee, placed the pot back on the stove, stepped over to the doorway, and reached for the phone to call Martha. Judy quickly came to the point of telling her all about Mike's dream. To her surprise, there was only silence on the other end of the call. "Martha, are you there? Are you listening?"

She finally heard the voice of her friend. "I didn't understand until right now, Judy. I thought I was coming out of a dream. You know I have what seems to be an overlap when I'm dreaming and beginning to wake up. For a moment or two, I seemed to be in both states. I heard a voice while I was asleep that pulled me out of it. The voice specifically said, 'Joel 2:28.'"

Now there was silence on the other end of the phone. Martha said, "Judy, there's no way this is a coincidence."

"I agree, but I'm a bit unnerved. Do you feel the same way?"

"Yes, it makes me wonder if this is how the disciples felt when they were on the stormy sea in the battered boat, afraid it might sink when they awakened Jesus, and He quieted the storm. The Bible says that they were stunned. That's how I feel. But how do we find out about Joel?"

"You think about it, and I will too. We'll talk after lunch. After you have picked up Joey, call me."

Beth was getting ready to read her Bible. For her, the best time was in the morning. In the quiet she could read, think, and pray before heading into her daily list of activities. Everyone else had settled into their day. Ron was at work, and the children were at school. Holding her Bible in her right hand, she rested the spine on the edge of kitchen table just as she lost her balance. Trying to hold on to her full coffee mug, she let the Bible drop to the floor. As she looked down to pick it up, she noticed it had fallen open to the book of Joel. Her eyes were drawn to chapter 2, verse 28, and she read it.

Mary was driving Tim to his workplace because she needed the car. On the way, they listened to a live message on Christian radio. The pastor was talking about the latter rains, the day of Pentecost, and how thousands were saved. He talked about the apostle Peter's quoting the prophet Joel, emphasizing the latter rains of the Holy Spirit. He explained how the Holy Spirit had swept across the crowd and brought them to repentance.

Tim commented, "Hon, it sure sounds like what's happening in Farmington." The couple grasped how the Holy Spirit was sweeping over their community.

In different ways, all four families were convinced beyond a shadow of doubt that God was leading them to be part of Pastor Smith's church. Judy saw Beth at school when they were both picking up their kindergarten students. Beth shared with Judy what had happened during her devotional this morning and how she felt God was telling her that what was happening at church was really Him.

Judy told Beth about Mike's dream and Martha's experience. Together, they said, "We need to call Mary."

Beth, with her child in tow, stopped by Judy's so the two of them could be together when she made the call.

"Wait, what are you saying?" Mary asked.

They told her about the Joel 2:28.

She replied, "Well, Tim and I were in the car this morning listening to one of those radio preachers talk about the latter rain of the Holy Spirit. We could see in our minds how He's sweeping through Farmington, but it didn't occur to us it is a confirmation to what is happening in Pastor Smith's church. It makes sense now after what you've told me. I think we should all plan on being at church on Friday night. What do you think?"

A plan was forged among the women friends.

Mike prayed, "Thank You, Lord, for this food and let it be nourishment to our bodies. In Jesus' name, amen."

The kitchen was filled with the aroma of a hearty meal of mashed potatoes and gravy, white bread and butter, roast pork loin, corn on the cob, and ice-cold milk.

Mike looked at his oldest daughter. "Ari, your mom told me to ask you for help on a dream I had early this morning. She thinks you might help me to understand its meaning."

For Ari, Daddy's asking her for help was a first, and her head was thinking and her heart was racing. The other children kept eating. As he ate, Joey continued to swing his legs under the chair, one of his favorite table activities. All Sammy wanted to do was clean his plate and hope for dessert.

Judy instructed Ari to listen to the clues as her father told her all of the details he could remember. When he was finished, Ari sat in silence as her parents watched her. They could see her eyes were open, staring into space. She thought through her known experiences and all the books she had read. She finally took a deep breath and replied, "Well, Dad, you're in the beginning of the story. You'll have to read the book in order to find the answers."

Mike and Judy each had a pleased look on their faces. In all Mike's life experiences, he had never needed to seek out and learn about dream interpretations. He would soon learn that a good teacher is hindsight, and it would be as good as twenty-twenty vision. The first lesson he had learned was that what was occurring at church was of the Holy Spirit. It might not look pretty, but what he saw was of God, and he realized he wanted to be a part of it.

# TWENTY-FIVE

Laughter was coming from the front room where all three children were engrossed in watching a Saturday morning television program called "Tennessee Tuxedo and His Tales." Watching the antics of the cartoon characters brought them to spontaneous laughter—a sweet sound in light of their recent events. Mike stepped into the front room and said, "After the show is over, get your backpacks and fill your water bottles." They immediately knew what he meant. All three faces beamed with the excited look that Mike was seeking. The family was going hiking!

They watched Tennessee Tuxedo right up to the very last second and then jumped up and ran toward their bedrooms. The race was on. Their closet doors were flung wide as the kids grabbed backpacks, water bottles, walking sticks, hats, and sunglasses. Sammy added his binoculars, which he always brought.

Ari was the first one to the refrigerator. She opened the freezer door and grabbed an ice-cube tray that would fill all their insulated water bottles. Using one hand to hold the tray, she pulled back the handle to break the ice into individual cubes. As always, when her hand came in contact with the ice-cold tray, her skin adhered to the side of the frozen tray so she carefully removed her hand.

Judy had lovingly prepared the family favorites to fill the picnic basket. She had tucked inside cold fried chicken, potato salad, fresh fruit, and raisins. Knowing life is a precious gift from God, they wanted to have family time today as a celebration. Beyond their wildest belief, considering the alternative, they had returned to normal family life. Now five healthy bodies were scrambling in the kitchen all at one time.

"Okay," Mike said to get the children's attention, "we're going to a new place called Angel Peak over near Bloomfield. It's going to be an hour's ride, so get whatever you need to help pass the time. Ari chose her latest Nancy Drew book, Sammy picked out his favorite toy cars, and Joey grabbed his coloring books and crayons. Most of their family excursions were within a thirty-minute drive and didn't require items for distraction. Despite all their preparations, one of the children will inevitably say, "Are we there yet?"

All families live with rules. There are in-house rules—especially for when the phone rings or someone is at the door. There are in-car rules—

except for the times when they were in the hill country. To help the children see better when they were going up and down the hills, all three were allowed to kneel in the back seat with their arms resting on the back of the front bench seat.

They had set off on their day's adventure with much anticipation and just such a stretch was just ahead. As they crested the hill, all three of them yelled, "Push the clutch in!" Mike and Judy laughed because the kids didn't know this car had an automatic transmission. Mike put the gear shift into neutral because it felt the same as pushing in the clutch pedal. All five enjoyed the feeling of acceleration as they coasted down the hill. As the car picked up speed, they felt like they were riding a roller coaster. Tapping the brakes on the ride down along with the natural gravity of going up the next hill slowed the car enough for Mike to slip the gear shift into drive, and on the happy family went. Everyone enjoyed the thrill of their make-believe roller coaster!

Pulling off U.S. Route 550 and onto the service road, they changed from pavement to a flat gravel road. The desert landscape could be seen all around them. An occasional tumbleweed rested alongside the road until the next gust of wind came its way. They passed the Sage picnic area and made their first stop at Cliff's parking area, then Castle Rock, and finally Angel Peak Campground.

At the first stop when the family got out of the car, the kids immediately wanted to rush to the viewing area. Dad spoke up. "Okay, what are the rules?"

They recited together: "Rule number one, stay on the path. Number two, if you hear a rattle, stand still and call Dad. Rule number three, don't pick up any rocks—scorpions and black widows could be under them."

To the left of the picnic table was a narrow path lined with round rock that led to an observation point where they could see Castle Rock and in the background, Angel Peak.

New Mexico's landscape is not everyone's cup of tea. For those who are enthralled with the desert, to them, the scenery holds its own beauty. The family took some time to appreciate the vast valley in front of them. Judy motioned for them all to stand quietly to experience the moment. There was a total absence of sound—no wind, no noises of birds or animals, no people talking. Then off in the distance came a buzzing sound. A few feet away, they spied a fly. The sound of its wings broke the silence. Was the noise eerie or refreshing? Here in this place and time, the sounds of silence reigned. Just like that, the magic was over. The family headed to their next destination—Cliff's pull off.

There was no doubt now—they were now on the plateau. Walking from Cliff's parking area to view the panorama, they could see sheer drop-offs. The deep jutting eroded hills merged with the rolling crevices and then to the valley floor below, filling the horizon. Judy cautioned the children to hold back and not go near the edge.

In her best mothering voice, Judy stressed, "Children, let's go to the fenced area where we can look safely." Sammy immediately whipped off his backpack to get out the binoculars for a better look. Right there in front of them was the splendor of God's creativity. The Four Corners area was teaming with geological variations. Recognizing this as a photographic moment, Judy pulled out the Brownie camera and said, "Smile everyone!"

The family journeyed onward to Castle Peak where they could get a good view of the rock formations. As the edge of the plateau eroded away in the wind and rain, the softer sediments had washed away first, leaving the harder soil behind. In the midst of wavy hills, one unique outcropping of rock had formed that looked much like a castle with towers and turrets, thus the name Castle Peak. As the family stood breathlessly taking in God's creation in the dry desert air underneath the shining sun, clearly the fall season was upon them.

When the family had made their pictorial memories in front of Castle Peak, they headed to Angel Peak Campground and the hiking trail. In the rearview mirror, Mike could see the dust kicking up in the wake of the car. Looking ahead, he caught a glimpse of something on the road. He slowed down and came to a complete stop when he saw what was on the road.

Deciding to make the find into a teaching lesson, he said, "Kids, this is why we're always careful while on desert hikes. Look out the side window and down on the road."

Three bodies squeezed together so they could all see at the same time. There, sunning itself to get warm in this high desert elevation was a five-foot-long rattlesnake.

Ari screamed, and that's when Judy leaned over Mike to take a look at what had caused her to scream. She gasped at the sight of the rattler.

"Cool!" Sammy exclaimed.

"In order to eat, they need to warm up," Mike explained. "Soon that snake will be moving on, looking for a tasty meal." Driving forward carefully to avoid the snake, they were soon on to the next adventure.

Judy opened the car door, swung her legs out, and stood to look in the direction of Angel Peak. She stood still like a statue, looking but not really seeing. She thought, *I was so scared we might never have family outings like this again. This joy I am feeling is so wonderful. Our family is being strengthened and growing under God's guiding hands. In her heart, she whispered, Thank You, God, thank You.*

The other car doors flew open, and the rest of the family gathered near the trunk. As soon as Mike opened it, six arms reached in for backpacks, water bottles, hiking sticks, and hats.

Judy woke from her reverie and called, "Okay, everyone, take time to get a drink before we hike to the point." Zippers were unzipped, bottles were opened, and ice-cold water was enjoyed. With hats on, walking sticks in hand, and a rehashing of the rules, the family of five started out on the hiking path.

The trail Mike had chosen was not one many mothers enjoyed, but many a dad relished. After all, a bit of a thrill was involved in this hike. Mike was used to heights; but Judy was not and was even somewhat fearful. The trail ran on top of a ridge that wound back and forth, sloped up and down, and at best, was only two feet wide. On either side of the path was a downward slope toward the valley below. There really was no great danger; after all, the slope had less than a fifty-percent decline. If people should slip off the beaten path, the decline would be easy enough for them to slow themselves down. However, to Judy and the children, walking it brought a hint of an adrenaline rush.

At the beginning of the trail, Mike stopped and pointed out the observation point to them. Without any enhancement, you could see the light colored ground of the path winding back and forth like a ribbon. He told them to follow him, keep their eyes on the trail, and pay attention and off they went.

The children followed their father in blind faith; as for Judy, she had to allow herself to be challenged. The only sound they heard was that of their feet padding along the dusty path. The hiking sticks provided a third point of contact to help keep the hiker steady should he or she stumble. The kids were naturals at hiking; Judy was a bit of a nervous wreck, but she pressed on.

At the scenic view point, two benches had been provided for people to rest, sit for a while, and take in the sights. In front of them was a vast valley, hundreds of feet deep, and on the other side more than a mile away was the towering rock formation.

"Hey kids," Mike said, "you know how we sometimes look at the clouds and see animals or other things? Well, if you look really hard at the rocks over there…" he pointed in the direction of Angel Peak, "You can see an angel with its wings outspread."

Joey responded, "I see it, Daddy. He's right there! Do you see him?"

"Yes! I sure do."

Sammy pulled out his binoculars to take a look and said, "Looks just like rocks to me."

Arielle, being the artistic one in the family, exclaimed, "Use your imagination, Sammy!"

"Still can't see him," he replied in a matter-of-fact manner.

Judy smiled at the whole exchange between the children. Taking a deep breath, she stared at the view she loved.

Mike had the children stand on the benches to enable them to look back at the winding path they had just walked. "Sometimes, kids, life is like the path we just hiked. It winds back and forth; it slopes down and then slopes up. We've been on a path of life like this one these past few months. Everyone, let's sit down; this is going to be our devotional time today."

Judy and the children sat quietly on the bench seat and focused on him. Mike reached into his backpack and took out his Bible. He had preplanned this moment to make a special memory. He opened the Bible to the book of Acts and read to them about the day of Pentecost. He explained how the wind of the Holy Spirit showed up and changed everything. "Before the Holy Spirit, they had their routine for church."

Judy knew he was simplifying the biblical event for them.

He continued, "When the Holy Spirit showed up, He changed the way church happened. It was like before, you know, when your mom and I went out dancing every Saturday. Then the Holy Spirit showed up, and changes began to happen in our life."

Ari said, "Dad, is it just like when you began our devotional time? That was a change, right?"

"Yes, Ari, and another change is our going to church each Sunday."

Joey added, "Wednesdays too, Daddy."

He smiled. Continuing, he said, "Take a look at Angel Peak. It has also been changing over time and transformed into the beautiful place it is today. I believe God has brought us all through change, and we are being blessed by Him." He looked at Judy to see if she had anything to say, and her body language said no.

"Let me pray for us as a family." Every family member focused his or her heart upon God, and he prayed, "Dear Father, I thank You and praise You for all You have done for us—for healing Sammy; for Arielle and how she sees You working; for Joey and the joy he brings to our family; and for Judy, the center of this family. Help us to be more like You, Father. In Jesus' name, amen."

Eyes opened and began looking for what was next. Judy asked, "Well, is anyone hungry?"

All of the children responded at once, "Me!"

"Okay then, one more picture for the scrapbook before we go! Say 'Cheese.'"

They all cried out, "Cheese!" as Angel Peak loomed over their heads in the background, overshadowing them like a guardian.

The return hike didn't seem as bad, having been conquered once. Reaching the picnic bench without incident, they all sat down. Judy asked for the car keys, opened the trunk, and within minutes, everyone was eating ferociously.

Judy momentarily basked in all the beauty surrounding her. It was a clear blue sky with a near-brisk temperature and the slightest of breeze. For a brief second, she left her role as wife and mother to be just herself.

Arriving home safely ended their perfect day. Everyone was tired from all the activities. The house was now dark, all the lights were off, and four out of five of the inhabitants were asleep.

Mike's mind was clear, without a thought; he was at peace. Just as he was drifting off to sleep, he heard a loud roaring wind above him. Before he had time to analyze it, he heard the sound of a door close gently. At first the sound was the creaking of the hinges and then the door's hitting the jamb. He jumped up and walked out into the hallway. All the bedroom doors were open, and all was in order in the rest of the house. He returned to bed and wondered what had just happened when he had an inner witness of the Holy Spirit—knowing something without hearing the words spoken.

Although he could see nothing, he could hear a quiet voice speak to him, "The season of change your family has come through is now complete. Settle in to a routine, seek God, and guide your family. In the days to come, you will gain authority to trample on scorpions and snakes and break the spider's web in people. Love in Jesus' name."

# Twenty-Six

She stood strong. *They will not see me cry.* Odd how you can find yourself alone and be in a room filled with other children. For weeks now Ari wondered why the other girls and boys were so distant. She would try to talk with them, but they would walk away with smirks on their faces. The girls would turn up their noses at her and then walk away, talking about her while glancing back at her.

Judy noticed Ari was coming home unusually quiet after school. She was growing concerned. *If it's important, surely she will come to me—especially if there is a problem,* she thought. Today, Judy had freshly baked cookies waiting for Ari and Sammy when they came home from school. Rushing in the back door, kicking off their shoes, and plopping their books on the kitchen counter signaled they were glad to be home. The smell of cookies filled the house.

Joey had been patiently waiting for them. Plus, it was almost time for their favorite television program. Judy called, "Get in your spot," and upon hearing those words, they rushed into the front room. Ari pushed the coffee table away from the couch and grabbed a pillow to sit on. Sammy turned on the television as they sang the opening jingle of one of their favorite programs: "M-I-C" pause, "K-E-Y" pause, "M-O-U-S-E, Mickey Mouse."

Judy loved the sound of her children enjoying life. She and Mike were doing a good job of shielding them from the outside world. She placed the plate of cookies on the coffee table for her three babies sitting in a row, not taking their eyes off the television set.

When the program began, a very large curtain was hanging in front of a stage. On the curtain were two large faces of a boy and a girl wearing Mouseketeer ears. About midway up, the curtain was drawn back to reveal the Mouseketeers poised to perform a choreographed tap dance as the music began. Six girls were dressed in white full skirts and a dark short-sleeved blouse and three boys standing in the back were dressed in a Mouseketeer blazer and lighter-colored trousers. Breaking into their hello song, they welcomed all the children watching the show. Ari, Sammy, and Joey fell silent as they ate the last of the cookies. They were totally engaged in the show.

In the kitchen Judy paused in her meal preparation when she heard the closing song. The sweet little Mouseketeers, Cubby and Karen, started the song, "Now it's time to say goodbye to all our company." She moved into the doorway to listen to her children as they san along. The television screen faded to black, and the show was over.

Judy turned off the set. "It's time for homework," she announced. Of course, Joey did not as yet have homework, so it was coloring time for him. For Sammy, it was reading; for Ari, it was studying the multiplication tables. Picking up the cookie dish, Judy returned to put the finishing touches on dinner. Her daughter choosing not to confide in her was upsetting her. *I can't help but wonder what the issue is.*

The next day Judy was sitting down as she sipped her morning coffee. The house was quiet, and she was entangled in her own thoughts. *What is bothering my little girl?* Setting down her mug on the table, she pushed back her chair with the back of her legs and stood up. She looked toward the hallway and thought about walking to the bedrooms. Shaking her head again, she sat back down, and took another sip of her coffee.

"No, I am going to do it," she said out loud to herself. Inside of her was a mother's need to know. Walking down the hallway, she stopped at the entrance of Ari's room and hesitated. *This quietness has gone long enough; I must find out what is happening.*

Normally, Ari kept her journal on the nightstand next to her bed, but it was not there. *Judy,* she said to herself, *do you really want to violate your daughter's privacy?* It didn't take long for her to find the journal in the bottom drawer under Ari's winter clothing. Picking it up, she sat down on the edge of her bed and looked at the front cover. *This isn't what I had in mind when I bought this book for Ari.* She made a deal with herself to only read the entries explaining the problem.

Starting in the back of the journal, the instinctive mother began paging through, looking for the last entry. Going back three weeks she found the beginning of the problem. As she read, she covered her mouth with her left hand. Her eyes widened as tears formed and slowly trickled down her face. Her mind raced over what she had just read. Quickly closing the journal and replacing it exactly where she had found it, she closed the drawer. Judy returned to her now-cold coffee. Lost in thought, she got a warm up. *Okay, it's not serious, but yet very disturbing. I'm going to wait.*

The last week of school had come. By now Ari had gotten used to being ostracized by the other children. As she sat alone during recess, four students—two girls and two boys—approached her. Her one-time best friend Susan turned to talk to the others as if she were not there.

Susan snidely said, "There's that holy-roller Pentecostal girl. They believe in things the Bible says doesn't happen anymore."

One of the boys commented, "I heard those Pentecostals swing from the chandeliers during church."

Ari didn't respond to their remarks. *What are holy rollers and a chandelier?* She was being accused of a behavior of which she had absolutely no knowledge. *Why is Susan being so mean?* Until now Ari had not understood why they were treating her differently, but now she knew it was because she and her family attended Pastor Smith's church.

Susan turned to Ari and confronted her, "You do things of the devil. Your family needs to repent, or you will all go to hell!"

The recess bell rang as Ari tried her best to wipe away the tears before going inside. *I'm so confused. Don't we all know the same God? I love God, and I'm in His presence at church. This does not make sense.*

On the walk home from school, Sammy called after her, "Ari! Ari! Why are you walking so fast?" He was having to run to keep up with her. When they were two houses from home, she broke into a run and headed right in the front door. Dropping her books and beginning to sob, Ari ran to wrap her arms around her mother as Judy came out of the kitchen. She couldn't hold back the tears any longer. Judy sat her down at the kitchen table as she put snacks on a plate and took them to Sammy and Joey while they watched their television show.

When she returned to the kitchen, she drew Ari close and had her sit on her lap. "What's wrong?"

Through her sobs racking her body, she heard the whole story. Oh, how she wanted to call the Billingses and give them a piece of her mind. With her soothing words, she calmed her daughter's hurting heart. A little of her daughter's innocence was now gone.

"Ari, at times people can be cruel, and when it comes from those closest to us—as you and Susan once were—it hurts more deeply. Betrayal and scorn are two of the worst of all human emotions."

Judy struggled to remain empathetic when inwardly she was angry. Now that all the tears had been cried, Judy knew her daughter no longer had to carry this burden. She kissed Ari's cheek, wiped her face with a tissue, and hugged her one more time.

"I'm going to my room, Mom," she finally said.

Judy knew she would be writing in her journal. The sharing between mother and daughter had been good medicine for the soul.

# Twenty-Seven

The phone rang, and Sammy walked over to answer it. He pulled the chair over next to the doorway, climbed up, and picked up the receiver. "Hello?" he said.

"Hello, Sammy, is that you?"

"Yes, it is. May I ask who is calling, please?"

George chuckled and replied, "It's Mr. Fairfax, Sammy. Is your dad home?"

"Yes, he is. Just a minute please." Sammy breathed deeply and yelled, "Dad! It's for you." George could hear the sound of the receiver being dropped on the kitchen counter as Sammy disappeared. He finally heard, "Hello? This is Mike."

"You have a very polite answering service over there, Mike."

Recognizing George's voice, he replied, "We train them well over here," and they both chuckled. The two men had just seen each other, so Mike was wondering why the call.

"Martha and I have been going to the Friday night services. You and Judy really need to come to one of them. It is another type of service. I saw a man from out of town get healed, and no one was praying for him! Pastor and the other members of the prayer team were in other places, and this man was standing in the front. I watched him go forward for prayer. You could tell that he had a bad hip. With each step, he had to lean and force his leg to move. The way he walked looked very painful. Well, Mike, there he's standing, the worship music was playing, and the man flies backward like someone hit him with a Mack truck! He bounced off the floor and was stunned."

"You have to be kidding me, George."

"No, and even stranger, you know how this church is helpful? No one even bothered to help him, they were all so caught up in the moment. Now I was curious, so I watched."

"Big help you were!"

They both laugh. George continued, "I watched him as he got up off the floor and put his weight on that hip. His look of shock was priceless, Mike. The next thing I saw was his stomping on that leg, then he began twirling around, raising his hand, and shouting, "Hallelujah! I'm healed!"

"Whew! Now I am jealous. I would have loved to have seen that."

"My point is this: no one prayed for him, Mike. He was standing alone, and a spiritual force hit him from in front, knocking him backward."

"I have no idea."

"Now, Mike," he said as he lowered his voice to a whisper and continued, "we have been friends for a long time..."

Mike was definitely not the touchy-feely type of guy, and he was beginning to wonder where this conversation was headed.

George started again. "Something happened to me last Friday night that I've been thinking about for days. You've heard people talking about an open heaven?"

"Yes, Pastor and others have mentioned it."

"Well, we all think of it as being a one-way street where the blessings of God come down, where the Holy Spirit and His angels visit us, and where the grace of God is experienced."

"I've heard all that said." Mike was becoming very curious because he had never heard George talk like this before.

"Well, there I was in the pew next to Martha. I started to feel my insides kind of shake when the Holy Spirit comes on you. But then, for lack of a better description, I popped into another realm. I hadn't moved, and yet I was in a different place."

"What are you saying?"

"I'm not sure what I'm saying, and that's my point. Help me out here, Mike. If you can see something here, I surely could use your help. There I was next to Martha, and I popped into the spiritual realm. I saw sparks of light like fireworks coming from people in church. The sparks were above their heads at first. Then they moved toward the altar area and as they got closer, they started to curve upward and were sucked up in some type of wind tunnel and shot toward the sky."

"Wow! George, I'm sorry but I'm not going to be a help to you. I have no clue as to how to explain your experience."

"Best as I can figure, it is like the prayers of people turn into sparks of energy and then they travel into the wind tunnel and shoot upward toward God. Then the praises of the people were also getting swept up. Mike, I think an open heaven flows two ways."

This supposition was about all Mike could handle, so he told George he needed time to think about all of what he had shared. "Hey, buddy, let's call it a night."

*George and I used to talk about engines, welding, fast cars, dance moves, and drinking. Now we're talking about spiritual mechanics that neither one of us understands. How intriguing!*

He began to draw from what he had read in the Bible in an attempt to understand George's experience. However, his thoughts returned to what he understood.

*Could it be like a gasoline engine in the car? When the cylinders fill with gas, an explosion takes place, forcing the piston down. It is a part of creating power leading to motion. Maybe if you there is the right spiritual environment, you create an explosion, release power, and experience forward motion in God's world. But what are the mechanics and parts to understand how this power is working?*

He walked back into the front room with the rest of the family. He was unsure of whether or not he could enjoy the next show—*The Twilight Zone*—he and Judy usually watched after the kids were in bed. Instead, Mike turned to Judy and said, "Judy, I think we need to go to the Friday night service."

# Twenty-Eight

The church was packed, not a seat was available, and people were standing in the back. Gil was leery about this scenario, and in his firefighter's mind, he knew he had to talk with the pastor. *This church is a fireman's nightmare in the waiting, God forbid. If this keeps up, changes are needed for safety reasons.* He and the chief were now on the deacon board; surely they would have some influence.

Pearl, the organist, moved forward, turned on the organ, and let the instrument take its first breath before she began playing. The first song that night was "All Praise and Power in Jesus' Name." Next she played a new song entitled "Come to the River," and it seemed to be an instant favorite. The atmosphere inside the church began to cascade into the presence of the Holy Spirit, and the people were praising God with all their hearts.

Ari asked to sit on the aisle so she could watch better. Joey and Sammy had brought books for when they got bored as most children do. Ari noticed a shift in the room when one person, then another, and a few more rushed out of their seats toward the altar as if their lives depended on it. At the front of the church, they did the strangest thing a full-grown adult would never voluntarily do. They dropped hard at the first step of the altar platform. Some were bent over, others were lying flat on the floor, and yet some were on their knees. The people were wailing and sobbing uncontrollably with no inhibition. Ari thought, *What would make a grown person cry so deeply and so personally in front of a room filled with people?*

The worship was extended on Friday nights, the message was shortened, and the prayer time was opened until the need was met. Her young eyes observed several people who were healed. The oddest occurrence to her was some people being healed when no one was praying for them. Apparently, God simply performed the healing. A miracle like the one that had happened for Sammy was now becoming commonplace.

The service continued long into the evening; however, in the intense love of God, no one wanted to stop the service. Ari moved Sammy and Joey to the open spaces in the last pew where they laid down and drifted asleep. She rested on the floor in her own quiet place and had a one-way conversation with God. *I love Him! I love Jesus, and no matter what anyone says about me, I'm not going to change that.*

As she relaxed on the floor, a sweet presence shared the same space with her. She was in communion with the Holy Spirit. Time passed, and she did not notice until her parents came and got them so they could all go home. The sweet intimacy with the Holy Spirit was something unexplainable, and she did not tell anyone. Only her journal would receive the expressions of her heart. This night was the first of many times she and God would be together. It was life-changing for her. Her destiny was changing. Something was deposited in her heart, mind, and soul that would not ever be quenched.

Standing in the back with the children was their angel. He watched as the presence of the Holy Spirit settled down on Ari. He had looked forward to this time, always wondering if a messenger would release her destiny to her. He had not expected this; she was touched with holiness and set apart for God—by God.

Now the family attended church three nights a week, or in other words, if the doors were open, they were all there. In the community of Farmington an unanswered question lingered in the air about the Old Pentecostal Church. "What would bring people to this place time after time, week after week, and now moving into year after year?"

The only way to answer this question was the glory of God. In this place, those who were coming long term would find out what the apostle Paul meant when he said, "They are moved from glory to glory." In the time ahead, it would be a forward motion in learning of God.

It became clear to Mike that if he lived a long life, he would only learn a speck of the knowledge about God whose creative abilities are truly limitless and humbling at the same time. That God would love him and save him and his family was overwhelming. One day he too would rush forward in the presence of God in total repentance—in humbleness as he saw sin for what it is in the reflection of a pure and holy God. He might not have said the words, but he felt them: "Woe is me, a man of unclean lips." Then he understood the price Jesus had paid for his sins.

# Twenty-Nine

Judy gasped. "Mike, how did you get those bruises on the inside of your legs?" His was a momentary lapse in judgment; he hadn't turned off the light before going to bed. He was counting on having a few more days, and then the bruises would have been gone. He would have had no reason to explain how they had gotten there.

The couple had always had an understanding to share everything between them. But everyone holds back some things for some reason. He had no prepared explanation so he opted for a half-truth. "I was walking into building three the other day when someone called my name. I was in a hurry and instead of stopping, I only turned to see who was calling me. I walked into the end of an I-beam being prepped by the iron workers."

"The bruises look terrible! Do your legs hurt?"

"Honestly, it was a bump and move on. I had no idea they would look like this. My pride hurts more than my legs," he ruefully added.

Judy gave him her "be-more-careful" look and let the incident pass as they settled in for the night.

Folding his left arm under his head, Judy snuggled against his right arm and immediately fell asleep. Taking care of three children and running the home was a full-time job. In her safe environment, sleep came easy.

For Mike, his would be another, near-sleepless night. During the day, there was a constant flow to keep one's mind busy. However, at night there was no escaping the haunting fears that had dogged him since that day. It was not the first incident, but by far it was the worst one. He told himself, *A few more days and I can shake this off and put it behind me.* He knew that when looking in the rearview mirror of life, experiences felt larger when they first happened. Putting one's mind in denial gave one room to put time and distance between them and the issue while moving ahead and leaving it behind. He hoped to deal with it later, if at all.

As morning came and Mike rose, he thought, TGIF. Downstairs he soon heard the car horn honk, took his last sip of coffee, kissed Judy goodbye, grabbed his lunch, and ran out the back door. He had been feeling this morning that the unending flow of strength and energy he had taken for granted all these years was waning, and he was not alone. Easing his sore legs into the back seat of the car, he was greeted by three good mornings and then a silent drive to Four Corners Plant.

Mike had questions about his strength and self-confidence that was shaking his sense of masculinity. As they neared the plant he blurted out, "Am I the only one feeling old today?" Laughter filled the car, as they all admitted to feeling it too. Two decades of working in the trades had taken their toll on a group of men now in their early forties. No, they weren't used up—far from it. However, maybe for the first time they were noticing the downward slide, and it didn't feel good.

A luxury seldom realized, Mike slept in on Saturday morning. The kids were watching cartoons, and Judy was doing laundry—a never-ending cycle in her life. The coffee was hot, and the newspaper just begging to be read was on the kitchen table ready for him. He had formulated a plan.

He heard Judy arranging to go shopping with Martha. He flipped open the newspaper to the Allen's movie schedule, and to his delight, he saw that *Flipper's New Adventures* was showing at three o'clock. He yelled toward the front room. "Hey kids, I have a dollar and a nickel!"—the code phrase for being treated to the movies.

Judy leaned out the laundry room door to give him a look—not "the" look—but the new look. She let it pass. The children came running in to find out which movie they would be seeing that afternoon and then ran outside to play in the meantime.

Soon the whole house was his as Judy was out with Martha. He went into the front room, turned on the sports with no sound, sat down in the corner chair, and let his arms rest. The drapes behind the television had been open so he could see outside.

He was staring straight ahead. A person could have waved his or her hand in front of his face, and he wouldn't have seen it. His attention was only on what was playing over and over in his mind. Like a television program that will not turn off, he had been having flashbacks and body memories that sent chills down his spine. Denial was no help to him; he allowed the flashbacks to replay in his mind.

"Mike," he heard his boss calling, "the anchors on pipe stack B are missing between levels four and five. You breathe on them, and they'll sway. What do you think will happen when they're under full steam pressure? Who ran that stack anyway?" He could still hear his boss's tone in his ears. He ordered, "I want you to weld a bracket to a steel girder midway and mount straps to those pipes. We can't be making serious mistakes like this, Mike. Do you read me?"

Someone might ask, "So what's the big deal?"

Right above level four on this chase are "U" bends. Steam will run too fast if it doesn't have resistance or obstacles. However, when the steam hit the bend, it moved the pipe. Mike hated mistakes. He looked at the drawings, and there were the notes for bracing on a girder ten feet below level five and fifteen feet above level four.

He called John over, and the two of them would fix this mistake. The task was a clear-cut job. Drop a welding cable from the catwalk on five where the pipe chase was anchored down to the steel girder ten feet below. If he'd done it once, he'd done it a hundred times. Going over the stairwell railing, he stepped onto the 12-inch-wide steel I-beam called a girder. He walked out to the pipes and tied off his lanyard for safety.

It was just another day. In less than an hour, the job had been completed. The cable was pulled up, but in his mind's eyes, he saw himself turn to walk back, one foot in front of the other. Only openness was on both sides of the I-beam and it was seventy feet to the ground floor. His right foot clipped the heel of his left boot, and he was instantly thrown off balance. In a split second, he knew he was in trouble. His mind raced in response to the fight-or-flight rush of adrenaline. Self-preservation scenarios rocketed through his brain, and he chose what he thought was his best option. He felt himself lurch forward, kicking both feet to either side of the beam in hopes of straddling it. The inside of his legs felt the pain as his weight shot past the edges of the I-beam. He saw his chest and felt it strike the beam, as the side of his face bounced off it. Hugging the beam, he frantically held on and watched as his hard hat fell seven stories down to the ground floor. What only took a second seemed like an hour. A deep fear for his life filled him. He crawled to the railing and climbed over. Because of his position, no one saw his near catastrophe. Sixty seconds had passed that no one knew about, and he didn't tell. In the shanty, he grabbed another hard hat, and no one was the wiser to his near-death accident.

Motionless in the chair, an hour had passed. His mind replayed the memory over and over. He had close calls before and came back. This one, however, was life-changing. Feeling his age and a lack of youthful agility seemed to be the only answer. The replay loop finally stopped, and tears filled his eyes. *I need…I must have a career change, but this is all I have ever known.* Having this job had brought him esteem as a good provider for his family. Leaving would be hard. His conclusion was to use his BA degree in business. Right here, right now was the beginning of the end of a way of life as he had known it. Thoughts entered his mind on possible ways of making the same salary. Soon he would talk to Judy. No one ever needed to know his secret.

Knowing what he needed to do, Mike began to evaluate his possibilities. In the coming months, he would talk to family and friends about their jobs. The time had come for him to put Matthew 7:7-11 into practice. First, he would pray and ask; he had seen God do miracles. Then, he would seek, knock, and watch what kind of doors would open. He was relying on the faithfulness of God's Word and anticipating the good gifts mentioned in these verses. Together, Judy and he had built a wonderful, comfortable life. God, Mike, and Judy formed a rope of three cords—strong and seldom broken. In the days ahead, they would come to trust God in new ways. They would take one more step to becoming like Romans 8:29—being transformed into the image of God's Son.

# THIRTY

Everyday Mike listened to the people around him. What he was hearing over and over again was that they were scared and concerned. Though Farmington may have felt like it was a world of its own, it was a false sense of security that was crumbling and eroding every day. Newspaper headlines read "34 Dead in Los Angeles Riots," Three Thousand Marines in Vietnam," "Martin Luther King Civil Rights March," "Russia Winning Space Race," "Pop Culture Changing Family Values." Not since the Great War were people so consumed with how world events could affect their lives and families. Young men were signing up to go to war. Others were demonstrating against it in growing numbers. America was being torn apart, and what Mike heard was that people were looking for safety and assurance. Then he saw his open door—the opportunity to change careers.

For several days Mike had been thinking about the conversation looming ever closer in front of him. Thoughts ran through his mind: *I know if I start off with "Judy, we need to talk..." I will scare her. She will want a sit-down at the kitchen table to resolve the issue. Maybe if I wait until a Saturday morning, I can bring up the subject casually by saying I have some new ideas I want to run by her. I'm not the straight forward or blunt type of guy. I remember it took me weeks of beating around the bush until I finally asked her to marry me. Not only that, the woman can see right through me and my motives. Really, Mike, your first step is to fast and pray. It's God's wisdom I need.*

He turned toward the street to see two friends and co laborers were coming to the house. Not since Sammy's miracle did the family's guardian angel have ministering angels come on an assignment from God. They entered the house and said, "To God be the glory!" Together, they will be there with the family to release provisions for all their needs as they transitioned. They continued, "God is answering Mike's prayers and going beyond into more good gifts. He has gotten the ear of God."

Then the guardian angels saw their future for the next ten years and understood. Because Mike and Judy lived a life pleasing to God, He was now bringing them into an ambassador's role to the town.

Together they prepped the house for the conversation. At first grace increased to bring an atmosphere of peace. Wisdom was also released to

Mike. Patience was given to Judy. Even though she had gotten up that morning and seen it as just another day, her intuition was telling her change was coming. In the environment of grace and peace, she would be able to listen and not jump to a conclusion after hearing only half of what Mike had to say. It was time.

*Tom and Jerry, Quick Draw McGraw, Sky King,* and *The Adventures of Lassie* were the children's favorite Saturday morning television shows. It offered almost two hours of uninterrupted time for their parents—except for the kids' occasional need for snacks. Judy poured Mike coffee as he reached for the paper.

Judy spoke up, "Now's a good time to tell me what's on your mind, Mike."

"How many fingers am I holding up behind the newspaper?"

She began laughing at how, out of the blue, he could get her off balance with his sense of humor. She said, "Michael, what are you talking about?" She had a sudden rush of whimsy in her, and it felt good.

"Well, you're reading my mind; I wanted to see if you could do it again."

"Michael J., you know very well you do not have any fingers up behind that newspaper! It's your thumb."

His eyes changed from being crafty to being shocked. "We need to get you a job at the carnival next time it's in town." In their light-hearted moment together, they both laughed.

Mike put down the paper and placed both hands around his coffee cup. "Judy, it's time for a change. I'm not the man I was when you married me." Holding her breath, she allowed him to continue. "Building boilers at the plant is a young man's job. As much as I love the work and the life we live, physically, the job is becoming too challenging."

Judy was good at putting two and two together. After a moment of thought, she asked, "Does this decision have anything to do with your bruises?"

Not wanting to go there, he humbled himself and truthfully answered, "Yes."

"I don't want to know all the details, Mike, but I need know why our lives are going to be turned upside down."

In a rush of feelings—those he hadn't dealt with, including denial—his heart was laid open and his throat caught. Judy thought, *This is bad. I have never seen my confident, strong husband vulnerable to this degree.*

"The bruises were the result of saving myself from falling off a girder."

That confession was all Judy needed to hear for her to embrace a new direction. She had always known the job was dangerous. The handwriting was clearly on the wall; whatever it would require, she would be behind it one hundred percent—even if it meant living a more frugal lifestyle. A change in lifestyle was far better than living life without Mike and rearing children alone.

Leaving her chair, Judy asked Mike to turn his chair to the side so she could sit down on his lap. She wrapped her arms around his neck and pressed her face into it. The only way she cared to express her love for him was a tender kiss.

She whispered in a pleading tone, "I know you have plans, and we need to talk about them. First, let me deal with this. Okay, Mike?" He nodded as she wiped the tears from his eyes. A lover's worst fear is losing the object of his or her love. She was feeling it, and for the moment, she was pushing down the knowledge of the near miss. Her little babies were in the next room, and there was no need to alarm them. Within her woman's heart, tenderness toward Mike welled up. She was intent on spoiling him forever.

# Thirty-One

An angel stepped up to Judy's side of the bed. Placing his hand above her head, he released a dream to her. . .

Waves of chills passed over her body as her spirit began to see. She was looking down on a large group of people. As she watched them, she saw Mike and herself walk up to them. Scores of people came to embrace them and shared stories of how the couple had blessed their lives and how they had helped them to invite Jesus into their hearts. A little child walked up to them as their mother told how he had been healed by God as they had prayed for him. Yet another person told how he wanted to end his life if it had not been for Mike's taking the time to share the love of God. Over and over again, people who shared their testimonies gave the credit to the labors of Mike and Judy for the kingdom of God. Darkness began enveloping the scene from the outer edges, and Judy felt an invisible force pulling her backward.

Like a movie playing on a giant screen, she watched Mike working in an office on E. Main Street. The front of the store had wall-to-wall pane glass windows. She could see two desks and two chairs. As she watched, she heard the telephone ring. At that moment, she realized she was the third person, and she watched herself answer the phone.

She heard her voice answer, "Hello, Insurance Agency, how can I help you?" She then opened a notebook to record the caller's information. She replied, "Mike is with a client right now, and he will call you back as soon as he can." Darkness swept in again, and the screen faded to black. Again the feeling of being pulled from behind overwhelmed her, and she was moving again.

Lying on a desk was the rental agreement papers. The family was now renting a four-bedroom house not far from the Old Pentecostal Church. The children, now all in their teen years, helped to bring in boxes and furniture. Everyone was excited to be in their new home. Judy saw the strength and security her children had in the midst of upward change. The light dimmed again, and Judy moved away.

The house was empty as she walked through it one last time savoring the memories. Her two youngest had slept in this room. In that room she had told bedtime stories, calmed fears, and wiped away tears. She moved into Ari's room, and in her mind's eye, she could see her sitting at her desk, writing in her journal. She turned slightly, and images of the times Ari read while lying in bed filtered through her mind. All those Nancy Drew books had taught her to look for the clues to follow.

She moved into the master bedroom where years of safety and love had been experienced and lingered there a little longer. Walking into the front room she saw the family having their devotionals and how Mike had taken time to pray with them one by one. She slipped into the heart of the home, her kitchen, where they had gathered for her meals and had shared the happenings of the day. Sammy had told his silly jokes, and Joey would sit at the table and color endlessly. She relived how she and Mike had been saved by the grace of God at the kitchen table. Together, she and Mike had signed the papers, selling the house so they could buy an insurance agency. In her heart, she thought, *I'd go anywhere with him. We built a life together; we will build a future for our children.* She stopped at the bathroom door, looked into the mirror, and remembered the night she had sprayed hairspray in Ari's face when she had been getting ready for a night of dancing. She laughed at the thought of how far they had come and how much their lives had changed in this home.

The angel stepped away from Judy as she stirred awake. From the corner of the room, he watched her as she grabbed her robe and walked through the darkened house, looking into each room. The beginning of her saying goodbye had come. The clock had started, and time was counting down. Living in this house had been the best years of her life. Day in and day out, she had taken care of the family God has blessed her with. Her love and her influence invested in her children had happened within these walls. The heartfelt memories of all the family and friends who had gathered in this house flooded her. How strong the bond had become between the two of them as they had built and lived this wonderful life. Judy flipped the light switch in the kitchen and started the coffee a little early.

When the alarm went off, Mike was already up and smelled the coffee. He walked into the kitchen and said, "You're up early this morning."

"Oh, I was thinking, Mike, what do you think about going into the insurance business?" she asked. Nearly dropping his coffee cup in his lap, he replied, “That’s my plan. Judy, do you know people are looking for reassurance in our mixed up, chaotic world. What better way to bring it to them but through selling insurance. Bad things happen in life. If things fall apart, insurance will give them the comfort that everything will be okay.” He paused in thought and then continued, “For this to work, honey, you’ll need to get a job. In the beginning I won’t be earning enough to provide for us. Once you get a job, I’ll ask Phil if his offer is still good to work with him. It will give us a chance to see if it will work. If God blesses us, I’m hoping we’ll be able to open our own agency right here in town.”

“I see you’ve been giving this a lot of thought.”

“No, Jude, I’ve been doing a lot more than thinking. I’ve fasted and prayed. I want God to go before us, and I want to know we will be okay.”

“What do you want for breakfast? Your favorite?” she asked.

In the next ten years, many changes occurred. Judy took a job taking portraits in a photography studio. She discovered she had a natural talent for it and soon became the customers’ choice for taking family pictures. Mike left the power plant and worked in insurance. After undergoing training in his new field, his living out his faith before others was blessed by God and financially he did really well. The house was sold for its equity so they could buy an agency. As they approached the glass door to their new office and agency, Mike missed a step, clipped the heel of his shoe, and fell forward. A moment of déjà vu gripped him as he grabbed the door handle to keep from falling.

As a result of making this new job work, the family would move into several rental properties. Building their lives on the solid foundation, the rock of Jesus Christ, had brought strength and stability to the children throughout this decade of change. They had watched their parents work together and persevere to provide for them, all the while making God-based choices. They had watched how they had worshipped at church, living out their faith by investing in people who came into their lives.

Their church continued to grow and see the Lord manifest His power in ways that continually kept people amazed. People were growing in their knowledge of God and their lives reflected it. God was indeed doing a great work in Farmington, and Mike and Judy were happy to have a part.

Mike became known in town for being a man others could work with. Whatever the problem, he would take the time to meet with his clients and figure out a way to help them be covered by insurance. His impact within the Indian community was now well renowned. He had gained their respect by living out his faith, being honest and trustworthy.

Not only had Mike and Judy started and established a spiritual heritage for their family, they were leaving a spiritual inheritance for generations to come. Together they had reaped a harvest in the mission field of Farmington, New Mexico. Now the time had come to let their firstborn child learn to stand on her own.

Ari was enrolled in a Christian college in Springfield, Missouri, and had selected nursing as her major. Going to college would be her first time living away from home. Now her time to fly had come. All the things she and her family had experienced over the years were mere preparation for what was to come in her life.

A new chapter began to be written that day.

# Part II

# Arielle's New Life

# Thirty-Two

As Judy drove away after depositing Ari at college, both of them could feel their heartstrings being broken. The thousand-mile drive home was going to be a long one. She prayed, *Lord, I place Ari in Your hands. Please guide and protect her. Please keep her feet on the pathway to reaching her goals, serving You as a nurse.*

The inevitable tears began to well up, and she brushed them away. Pleasant pictures of the different stages of Ari's life drifted thought her mind. Wonderful, fond memories of her little girl filled the mother's heart. Even though Judy had known this day was coming, she had filled her mind with all the details for the trip and paperwork for the college, she had no time for reflection.

Right now she felt the separation. In her role as a mother, she had covered her children under an emotional umbrella and had kept them safe. For the first time ever, her little girl was on her own outside of her protection and care. Questions arose. *Did I really prepare her for life? Is this college the best first step?* She thought, *Ari is a sweet, good girl, strong-willed but submissive. I thought I was ready for her to begin her grown-up life. She's like a racehorse at the gate; I'm the one lagging behind.*

In her mother's heart of faith, she had the assurance that God was in control, and knowing this helped her heart be at peace. The future might be unknown to her, but she knew the God who knows the future. Judy was moving through another stage in her life—just as Arielle was entering her own new one.

The campus was teeming with parents and students. Watching her mother drive away brought emotions twofold. Ari felt the pulling away and being apart from her family for the first time. She was surprised, though, her sense of loss of family came secondary to her thrill of the new academic life she loved. Excelling as a student throughout high school, she looked forward to learning more.

Her heart was filled with hope and joy as she turned from watching her mother's car disappear to walking across campus toward her dorm. She felt safe in the structured campus life, while enjoying the freedom of being on her own. Since Sammy's illness, she had been wondering about how things go wrong in our bodies and why. Her first year, though, would be filled with general electives in the nursing degree program—not as exciting as the internships she would be doing later.

Ari was thinking about the details of the campus as she walked across the quadrangle, a crisscrossing of sidewalks and lawns going from one building to another. To her right was the dining hall; to the left were the distinctive academic buildings. Behind her was the activity center where her PE classes would be. Reaching for the door handle, she opened the door and walked in Scott Hall. Being new was nerve–racking, but from the beginning, she had felt a sense of belonging and that God had brought her to this place.

The dorm parents lived on the first floor. Mailboxes were conveniently located at the doorway. Off to the side were the quads—code named for where the fun happened—she took note of it. Oh, yes, and there were boys! This year, the first floor was a guy's floor. The other two floors were designated for the girls. The freshmen had been assigned to the top floor, now her new home. On this day, she bounded up the stairs in no time.

Since the college was a Pentecostal school of higher learning, Christian symbols were displayed everywhere. A sense of Christian values was the standard, and being with like-minded people was comforting. Talking about Jesus and sharing the wonders of a manifest God permeated discussions. Ari already had a rich experiential background. Although miracles had often happened at her church, she would soon learn that the church in Farmington was not the norm.

Stepping into her temporary home, she took in the layout of the room again. On the left were bunk beds, and right past them were two closets. At the end of the room was one window. To her right were two desks with chairs that had a division in the middle. Above each desk was a corkboard for tacking up notes and reminders—also a good place for pictures from home. Each desk had a directional lamp that was shining downward to confine its glow for those with late-night studies. On the wall across from the closets was a mirror for all the touchups a girl might need.

Ari, being the first to settle in the room, had chosen the bottom bunk. Her roommate, Carol, would have chosen the top bunk anyway, so it all worked out with no conflict or ill feelings. Reaching for the papers on her desk, she was overwhelmed with anxiety. She started to run a timeline through her mind as to which class was first and in what building when Carol came in talking a mile a minute.

"Well, my parents are gone, so now what do we do?" she asked.

Wondering if this quick attachment was going to be good, Ari answered, "I need to walk through my schedule for tomorrow to see where the classrooms are located and how long it takes to get there. Are you up for a walk?"

The adventure was new for both of them. Going building by building, they first familiarized themselves with where their classes would be located and finally ended up in the chapel. Once inside, they walked to the front. At the altar steps, Ari turned to look around and commented, "Carol, you could fit ten of my churches in here. It was small, but God was there. His sweet presence was everywhere. I hope to see miracles happen here like I saw at home."

"Miracles? You mean healings, deliverance, and things like that?"

"Yes, I never tired of seeing people coming in sick and leaving well."

"That only happened occasionally in my church. We had times in the Spirit and wonderful teachings but not too many miracles."

"My brother was healed of a serious heart deformity. To me that is the best one. Without God healing him, Sammy would have died."

Ari motioned for Carol to sit with her in one of the pews, and she shared the whole story. Carol's eyes widened as Ari told her the details of the x-rays and results from the angiogram and how a surgeon at the best pediatric hospital in the region only confirmed that God does His best work when He heals someone.

As Ari relayed the story to Carol, she felt like she too was at the hospital. This wasn't a story she would read in a book; it was a living one she had experienced. Ari added, "That was when I knew I wanted to be a nurse."

When the girls got up to leave, Carol said, "I'm hungry, Ari. Let's go to the dining hall and then let's check out the quad in Scott." Ari noticed a sparkle in Carol's eyes that hinted at what she wanted to see.

The next day Ari was up early before her alarm went off. She got in and out of the bathroom before many of the girls on the floor were even up. In her mind, she already had the clothes picked out for her day—a below-the-knee dress with a little tie string around her waist. Next she put on ankle-high bobby socks and comfortable shoes. One last look in the mirror gave her confidence that everything was covered.

In the dining hall, she looked at all the choices for breakfast and readily decided that Mom's home cooking was not on the menu. She decided to try the French toast with bacon, juice, and milk. Finishing the meal, she headed toward her first class.

"Good morning, class," the instructor greeted them. Ari took note of his punctuality and his starting right on time and not a minute past. "I'm handing out your syllabus for my class. Please take a minute to look it over." Papers shuffled as twenty-five copies changed hands.

"On the board is our starting point for what you will learn in the next thirteen weeks." He continued to tell them the grade details, how the midterm and final grade would be thirty percent of their grade, and his expectations for them to pass. Ari swallowed hard at the number of requirements and headed off to her next class.

Walking in the doors of Scott, she saw the tables were set up for book orders to be picked up. She now had enough books to weigh her down. *Praise God I only have to walk up two floors.* Opening the door to 303, her room, reminded her of the Bible verse in the book of John: "Ye must be born again." She would have a full night ahead of her as she prepared for tomorrow's classes.

"Whew," Carol greeted her as she plopped her books down on the desk and went off on a diatribe about her classes. Ari was quickly learning that Carol was one of those girls who had reams to say—like her mother's friend Martha. The very first day of classes would be the beginning of one of her many late nights of both listening and studying.

She had forgotten all about them. Stepping into college life had occupied all her thoughts until this morning. While showering, she noticed another—no, wait, three new ones. Deep concern swept over her as she had thought they had been contained. Now she had an outbreak as the what ifs swept through her mind. With each new outbreak, it would just be a matter of time before people would notice. Would it change their outlook towards her? She was beginning her prime of life. She knew she could only cover up so much before people changed their minds about her. She feared she could go from being attractive to repulsive in the worst-case scenario. Now added to all of her current demands was this new burden she was carrying that no one knew anything about. *If Carol knew, would she be so friendly?*

Bursting into the room, Carol shouted, "Ari, you're famous! You're on the front page of the *Lance*. See? Look right here!" She excitedly pointed to a picture on the front page. During the new students' orientation, a newspaper photographer had taken several shots.

There she was, and in a moment of spontaneous reflex, she rubbed her finger over her chin, feeling for the spot.

Carol continued, "I've heard if you want to know what was happening on campus, you have to read the *Lance*. Page two has fun facts about the word Lance. It's a boy's name meaning 'servant,' and it's also a spear."

# Thirty-Three

Two matters were clear: this was not a high school, and chapel was her favorite time of the day. Ari had breezed through high school, achieving good grades. Now each semester felt like she was being pushed to learn a condensed year's worth of knowledge in high school into one semester in college.

Her respite from the classes happened in chapel. Here she would get lost in the worship and praise. Her spirits were lifted as attending chapel lightened her load. During her inner reflections of connecting with God, she poured out her concerns. Her prayers were becoming deeper and more heartfelt. She shied away from the quad, focusing instead on her studies and spending time in prayer.

Walking back from the dining hall to the dorm, desperation welled up in her heart. There must be an answer to my problem. *No, I'm not going to call Mom. I'm here living on my own. The time has come to live on my own faith—not that of Mom or Dad's—mine. I've seen God heal Sammy. I've seen hundreds healed at church. If God can heal them, He can surely heal me.*

Back in her room, she opened her Bible for verses on healing. The first one she came across was Isaiah 53:5-6 where it talks about being healed by His stripes. Over the days ahead, she compiled quite a list of Scriptures on healing.

Nearly six weeks passed before the students had a break in their schedules. Friday was an institute day; classes did not meet so most of the student body planned to go home for the three-day weekend. Going home was not an option for Arielle since Farmington was so far away, and she forged ahead with her plan. Starting Friday morning, she would begin a three-day fast and a Bible study on healing. Until then she would cover up and hole up in her room and keep studying.

A mass exodus took place on campus Thursday night. Carol and hundreds of others said goodbye and headed home to be spoiled by parents. Mouths salivated for Mom's home cooking, and the students carried bags of laundry, hoping she might volunteer to do them. By Friday morning the campus was like a ghost town. Only a handful of students were to be seen, and the dining hall was on skeleton crew.

Bottled water was on her menu for the next three days. Leaving the dining hall with plenty of bottled water, she returned to her room. Only one other girl remained behind on her floor. Closing the door behind her, Ari settled in. She took her Bible off the desk and spread out her notes on the floor. Sitting cross-legged, she whispered, "It's You and me, God, for the next three days, except Sunday church." She mumbled a short prayer. "Holy Spirit, please guide me."

An image of the man at church who was healed of an injured back entered her mind. She had watched how the power of God had hit him, and he went flying backward to the floor. He was stunned, but when he stood, his back was healed and he danced right there in the aisle. Ari had thought, *Isn't God good? He healed and changed that man's life just like Sammy's. If God did it for them, He will do it for me.*

Ari picked up a piece of paper on which was written Matthew 4:23, a verse which said that Jesus healed every type of disease and every affliction. Reaching for another paper, she read, "Heal the sick in it, and say to them, the kingdom of God has come near to you" (Luke 10:9). Ari thought, *Lord, I know the kingdom of God is here on the campus and that You heal illnesses; I've seen it. How do I get Your healing for myself?*

In the dermatologist's office, she had learned she had contracted a virus. The manifestation of this virus was flat warts growing on the skin. Ranging from mild to severe, the virus took on a life of its own. Some cases ran their course, but even with treatment, some scarring would occur. At first she had only three warts—one on her ankle and one just below her knee. She could easily cover these spots with clothes. However, when one appeared on her face, she knew the time had come to see the doctor.

The doctor explained that the treatment was burning it off with liquid nitrogen. Right there in the office, the doctor reappeared with a little cup and a Q-tip. The doctor gently dabbed the wart with the Q-tip, freezing it. The now frozen wart would fall off in a few days. The treatment hurt, and a small scar was left behind on her chin. But then, the warts began showing up all over her body, and the three became twenty. *Where will this stop? Will I get more of them on my face?*

At the age of eighteen, the thought of her face being scarred from having warts burned off sent pangs of fears deep into her heart. In her desperation, she sought God and meditated on the more than forty Scriptures on healing. Ari understood the power in praising Him. She took time to praise God for who He is. In her prayer closet/room, time went by. Once she entered His presence, the time passed quickly.

Retiring for the night, Ari prayed and fell asleep wondering if God had heard her heartfelt cries, seen her tears, or felt her concerns.

He was sitting cross-legged on the floor, having watched Ari traversing her spiritual maze during her fast. He knew she had all the pieces she needed to reach the ear of God. Right now, the pieces formed only a jumbled mess. Having faith for someone else's healing was one matter, having the faith that healing would happen for her needed to become personal.

He decided to speak up, hoping Ari was tuned into that soft voice heard within her heart. "Arielle, you are a lioness of God; read the Scriptures out loud. Faith comes by hearing the Word. Read them not as text in a story; read them as proclamations."

He had watched her earlier that day as she had reached for another paper, and began to read it out loud with conviction. Smiling, he watched her as she read Luke 17:19, and then he said, "Rise and go, your faith has made you well."

Watching Arielle focus her thoughts and heart on God, he witnessed her emotional heart of faith come alive. She began to speak her prayer out loud, moving beyond conviction and into faith. The room filled with the sweet fragrance of Arielle's prayer. In an instant, her prayer shot upward on its way to the throne room. As her guardian angel, he was pleased. She had just learned an important lesson about living the life of faith. He thought, *This is huge.*

On Sunday afternoon, students began to return, and the once-quiet dorm once again took on life and noise. Carol returned and talked about her entire weekend. Then Monday morning came, the time to get ready for classes. Dressed for the day, Ari was standing in front of the mirror in her room, ready to apply makeup to cover the scar on her chin, as well as the new wart that had appeared on her cheek. As she was about to rub a little skin tone foundation on her face, she dropped her makeup on the floor. She pushed down her socks and lifted her skirt to see her knee. She pulled up her blouse to look at her stomach. They're all gone—really gone. Her hands began to tremble. Tears welled up in her eyes. She had been healed!

During the night, God had healed and removed her warts. Great gratitude toward Father God welled up in her heart. She first expressed a form of relief and then joy. God had removed the warts, and He had healed her of the virus. Other than the one reminder—the small scar on her chin—no one would ever know. She thought, *I've got to call Mom!*

# Thirty-Four

Arielle had a plan for her life. She stayed true to her calling. However, change was coming in the wind, and she knew it. She had been studying her curriculum and the college's accredited programs, but they were not lining up. The guidance counselor was very reassuring they would reach full accreditation in their nursing program in time for her to receive the credits for her degree. However, because of her conservative nature, she would rather be sure than take a chance.

In her mind she asked her questions, and several possibilities came up. She could leave the safety of the Assemblies of God college for a state-operated university. After weighing all her options, she chose to attend Women's University in Texas to earn her degree. Wasting no time, she enrolled in summer classes. After completing her first year of college, she looked back with the realization of how much she'd grown. Now the time had to come to get acquainted with a new school and campus.

Living on campus there was a total culture shock. The church had been a huge part of her life. Now she lived within a campus society that had little to do with church. The dress code was not the same. Many things were different; for instance, the classroom sizes had grown from classes of twenty-five to three hundred students meeting in a large auditorium. What was once a small intimate setting for learning had now changed to a sea of students.

Unwavering in her faith to follow Jesus, she did take notice of the new world around her and made modest adjustments. The world had opened before her in ways she had never before experienced. The challenges of her class schedule left little time for her to drift off course.

Living in Denton, Texas, did have some perks. Several of her friends had boats on the nearby lakes. She never refused an invitation to go water skiing. Her first experience at the sport had come years earlier on Farmington Lake. Her spindly legs had wobbled to get up and on top of the water. Before long she had learned how to pop up and land squarely on the top of the water. Now at Lake Lewisville in Texas, she felt freedom. The dominant sound in her ears was the passing wind roaring by. Hearing the sounds of her skis slapping on the water was thrilling as she leaned into a slalom turn. The spray of water on her face was refreshing and fun.

The student body as a whole looked forward to Career Day, bringing dreams of their future and lots of free stuff with food being the favorite. Tote bags and an assortment of books were also available. On a lark, Ari stepped up to the Army recruitment booth and engaged in conversation with the Army nurses. She was intrigued, and they could tell. She was offered a free dinner at a high-end restaurant, and she accepted.

Ari listened to the nurses as they opened her mind to continuing studies and furthering her march toward earning a master's degree. Despite the military structure and her life not really being her own to live, she embraced the thought; no, she welcomed the new challenges. Joining the armed forces would be her own Nancy Drew adventure. Arielle soon graduated from Women's University with a bachelor's degree in science in the nursing program.

A Bible verse that described Arielle's life was Jeremiah 29:11, which says, "I know the plans I have you declares the Lord. Plans to prosper you and not harm you, plans to give you a hope and a future."

Those around Arielle may have thought she looked like a trailblazer in her family. Stepping out in faith and going down new paths were what she had watched her parents model for her. They trusted God and moved forward in life. But to say her family and friends were surprised when she joined the Army and entered their nursing program was an understatement.

The rank of captain had a nice ring to it—one that echoed responsibility. Her choice was not to sign an educational package committing her to a six-year plan. In her heart she wanted the freedom to change direction. Her first stop was San Antonio, Texas, where all types of medical forms and regulations needed to be read and learned.

In the occasional times off, she took in some sightseeing deep in the heart of Texas. What could be more Texan and more inspiring than the Alamo? People had sacrificed and struggled to gain independence to become the Lone Star State. Inspiring in another way was the famous San Antonio River Walk, a place with secluded walkways and restaurants nestled alongside the river. Everyone loved this feel-good place.

In the blink of an eye, Arielle was off to her first assignment. Focusing on earning her master's degree, she elected to enter coronary intensive care and emergency room training. Tacoma, Washington, was her next stop. Going on the road meant needing a new car. She traded in her faithful used-up car, which had seen its best days, for a new one. Together, she and her car took to the road on a new adventure. Her quarters on the Tacoma base consisted of a modest apartment, and one of its best features was free room cleaning.

Arielle thrived in coronary ICU. Helping heart patients became a labor of love. Her patients were mostly older men, with an occasional woman or child. Instead of being the helpless girl of her youth as she was during Sammy's crisis, she now played an active role in caring for the sick. In her year of service, she did not encounter one child with Ebstein's anomaly, the rare illness that had affected her life's decisions.

Coming full circle, Arielle's next assignment was in Denver, Colorado, where it all began. Over the next six months, she would complete her ICU training. She hadn't actually traveled to the Children's Hospital in Denver with her parents and brother, but on this assignment, the hospital was nearby. Upon stepping into this ICU, Arielle was in her element. When nursing those with coronary illnesses, she understood how quickly things could happen. One day, everything was fine, and the next it felt like the world was going to end. With her early-life experiences, Arielle's compassion ministered to those she was nursing. She understood nursing from the inside out.

As part of following after God, she gave her best in this line of work. Her commanding officers had noticed her heartfelt service. The time had come for her to bring that compassion to a major Army base at Ft. Sill, in central Oklahoma, the land of perpetual thunder.

Ari's training played out best in the surgical intensive care unit, where it was mandatory for her to be on a rotating shift. This schedule would take its toll on her social life. Getting used to midnights and the topsy-turvy sleep cycles was nearly impossible, but the different assignments helped to keep life interesting.

Occasionally, Ari was needed to work a shift in the ER. Active artillery training (the rolling thunder heard daily) took place on base, and injuries and mishaps tended to happen with live ordinance. There was never a dull moment. The first order of business was triage, i.e., assessing the manner of care needed. More severe cases would automatically take priority. Once the doctor entered the bay, she would listen for instruction on the care being prescribed. She started IV lines and administered various medicines to the patients. She saw every kind of injury and illness from the common flu to the loss of a limb. To be instantly ready with any instruments the doctor required was important. Every soldier fell in love with his nurse; it was part of the job. Ari's rank of captain kept them at bay, however, and the occasional "Calm down, soldier" set the tone.

Fort Sill felt like home at last. Without an aha moment or a celebratory event, Arielle had arrived. Years of schooling and hard work had brought her to this time in her life. She had built a life for herself. God was good and His blessings were a daily occurrence.

Fort Sill was such a huge base that there was no way to get around easily on foot. Living in the Chimney Hill portion of the base had its conveniences. The drive to the commissary where Ari did her shopping was short, and she somtimes visited the PX right down the street. A dry cleaner and movie theater were centrally located between Randolph and Macomb Roads. The Cedar Lakes running trail was another thing she enjoyed. Ari loved to go for a run to clear her mind and feel the joy of a heart-pumping exercise. Turning heads for a second look always helped any girl's ego, and plenty of that was happening. One segment of the path lined up alongside the base airport runways. Watching planes do their touch-and-go landings fascinated her.

Working at Reynolds Army Community Hospital was comfortable. The terrain surrounding the base felt more like life in Farmington and brought an air of familiarity. One lesson she learned while being in the Army was the need to either make friends or live a lonely assignment. On base there was no shortage of men, but finding girlfriends was another matter and meant being friendly.

Natalie, Barbra, and Joan were three of the nurses working RACH. Coming from different backgrounds and training, they connected more out of need than familiarity. As much as Ari liked Natalie, she rubbed her wrong when she would step into the role of playing matchmaker. For Natalie, having a friend who was twenty-six and living alone stirred her mind with possible dates. Even though she had been shot down time and time again, Natalie never stopped firing her matchmaking rounds at Ari. Her choice in men cautioned Ari to avoid the offers of blind dates. Finally, in her unrelenting pursuit, Natalie discovered a weak spot.

# Thirty-Five

"We rained down the sound of freedom today, boys," Lance said to his officer buddies, using a common expression artillery officers employed for keeping America safe.

Skip added, "Signal Mountain looked more like the moon than ever before after we put new craters in that mountainside. That 155 howitzer is an earthquake maker. Bet they felt that all the way south of Lawton. Here's to fire and rain!"

The four of them tapped their cold drinks together in celebration. Firing artillery shells down range with precision was cause for celebration. The Officers Club was their relief valve—their watering hole in the heartland of America. They were nearing the end of their advanced officer artillery training. In the next eight weeks, they would be sent out on to their assignments. Lance already knew South Korea was his destination. He would be there for one year, guarding the DMZ.

Turning to Lance in a somewhat private talk, Skip said, "Listen, buddy, you have to give her another chance. You're officer material; you can handle it. So she stood you up once. Natalie told me she had honestly forgotten your date; hers was an innocent mistake. You're right on target here, pal. The shell is about to land and explode into true love. Give her another call and make a date. Trust me! Have I ever guided you off course?"

Lance enjoyed his pal's camaraderie, but he seriously was unsure of the women the guy dated. They were too wild for his conservative Christian background. He had a hard time believing he would be comfortable with this woman. Learning the skills of firing ordinances miles away and striking targets with precision was easier than understanding a woman.

"Skip, listen. I'll give her another call." He was thinking, *I'll say yes just so we can move on to the next subject.*

"Skip, what's the story on your name anyway?" one of the other guys at the table asked. Before he could answer the question, the others saw a good opportunity to enter into a round of bantering. One of the guys shouted, "Because he never skipped a meal."

"I couldn't have said it any better than that," he agreed.

They extended multiple knuckle bumps. Diverting the subject, they came back to cannons, drinking, and women. One of the guys asked, "What's faster on base? The cars or the women?"

That comment was Lance's cue; the time had come to leave. When Lance got up from the table, Skip took one last poke. "You're going to call her, right?"

Lance gave him a look that said it all, grabbed the last fry, and headed for the door.

Sitting crossed-legged on the floor in her quarters, Arielle had her prayer list and Bible in front of her. When things got serious, this was her posture to pursue God. Speaking in a soft voice with her heart focused on Him, she said, "In Psalm 37, You said You will give us the desire of our hearts. Lord, the desire of my heart is for You to place a godly man across my path so that together we can serve you. You say in the Word that it is not good for us to live alone. Please, Lord, answer my prayer."

She remained in prayer for a few minutes to delight herself in the Lord. She thanked Him for all the blessings He had brought into her life. Reaching for her Bible, she began to read in Ephesians chapter five.

The phone rang, and she quickly answered it. Being in the Army means being on call 24/7.

"Hello," she said and then listened.

"Yes, sir, I'll be right in."

Hanging up the phone, she dressed for work; the ER was loaded, and the staff needed help. After a fast drive to RACH, she ran in the door. Seeing her lead nurse, she went directly to her.

"Ari, change of plans," the nurse said. "You're needed in the recovery room. A soldier suffered a serious hand injury in a cannon mishap. He's in recovery now as are others; you're needed up there."

Back in her quarters, the phone rang several times and then went silent. It was three in the morning before she walked in the door, hoping for a few hours of sleep before she started her day shift. Lying on top of her bed, she fell into an exhausted sleep.

Hard knocking sounded on her door. "Who's there?" she muttered still half asleep.

"Ari, you've overslept; it's time for our shift!" Natalie rode with Ari in the mornings they worked together. As shocking as cold water in the face was Ari's thinking she would be late. Opening the door, she told Natalie all about the hand surgery, how the doctor had reattached it, and her praying that it would be useable for the young soldier. After she quickly got herself ready, both girls ran to the car.

Once inside, Natalie casually asked, "Did you happen to get any other calls last night?"

"No, why do you ask? Remember I was working in recovery. Oh, no, Natalie, you didn't?"

"Well, I half expected Lance to call you."

"I'm so incredibly embarrassed that I stood him up! Why would he call again?"

"Believe me, he'll call again. You're a catch, Arielle. So you say yes when he calls you."

Arielle was not quite sure which was more difficult—dealing with demanding patients and doctors all day or dealing with Natalie's matchmaking after work. The situation definitely felt awkward.

At her shift's end, Ari met up with Natalie, and said, "I sure could go for an A&W root beer and cheeseburger."

"You're out of luck, but I will say the PX food court has a mean cheeseburger," Natalie added. After they left the hospital parking lot and made a left turn on to Fort Sill Blvd. to head north, the drive was oddly quiet.

They passed squads of soldiers in formation, singing out their cadence as they ran toward Cedar Lakes trail, completed the loop, and made their way back to the barracks. Their next turn was left onto Macomb St. and down to the PX parking lot. After their orders were in and they were seated at a table, Natalie had to ask, "What's with the A&W? I've never heard you bring that up before."

"I'm a bit homesick."

"Well, being all work and no play will do that to you."

*She has a point,* Ari thought.

Having a full stomach on a short night's sleep made Ari eager to stretch out on the bed when the phone rang.

"Hello," she said.

"Hi, it's Lance. I believe we got our schedules crossed and missed each other the other night. I'm hoping we can make plans again to go out for a meal."

Unsure of what to say or do, Ari paused, although she felt she was pretty much roped into this. With a tone of voice that was a bit standoffish, they made plans for Saturday at 7:00 p.m. Unsure about this blind date, her mind was in a blur. She thought, *Natalie, if this goes badly…well, I'll just say no to any other offers. I'll have to be nice, at least, but I don't want to see it drag on all night. How did I get myself into this? Learning, I know; ICU, I know; nursing, I know, but dating?*

Lying on her bed, her mind raced with thoughts of how Saturday might go. Eventually she fell into a deep sleep.

# Thirty-Six

She chose her favorite solid-blue Sunday dress, though it wasn't her first or second choice because she couldn't make up her mind. She was nervous. She knew the steps: makeup first, dress second, and do hair last. In a flash, she saw her mother getting ready for a Saturday night out dancing. No hairspray tonight! Right on time, three sharp knocks sounded on the door. Lance was standing in the hallway. Taking one last, quick look in the mirror, she reached for the doorknob. Two lives were separated only by one wooden door.

She was ready to say her first words, and they were even poised on the tip of her tongue. Ari had decided to play it cool until she had decided which way the evening would go. Turning the doorknob and swinging the door open wide, she saw Lance for the first time. All her preparations flew out the window! Just when she thought she had it all planned out and would be in control, the sight of him took her breath away. In an awkward moment of trying to regain her composure, she had to fight the butterflies and the rising warmth in her cheeks just to say hello.

A thousand men were on base, and not once had she ever felt like this with any of them. Suddenly this strong, confident woman felt like a school girl.

"Hi! I'm Lance. I'm hoping you're Arielle."

"Yes, let me grab my handbag," she said as she realized she was out of breath. Lance appeared cool under fire. Easily talkative, he could take a commanding role in any conversation. Right now, he was also struggling to find any words that would sound confident. His first thoughts included *she's beautiful, she has poise, and she's a lady.*

Lance was stunned by his first look at Arielle. He had no idea. All his preconceived ideas of how the night was going to go blew up for both of them. He had no doubt that this was no ordinary blind date.

The Officers' Club was crowded, but they were able to get a table right away. The music was loud, so hearing each other would be difficult. Looking into her eyes, suddenly Lance wanted to know everything about this woman. Chemistry was surging through his veins.

"Ari, what led you to join the Army?"

Thankful for an open door to conversation and an easy subject to address, she said, "Texas Women's University had a career day when I met

Army recruiters who were nurses. They invited me and a few other girls out for dinner. I listened to them tell us about the advanced nurses' training, and I was sold. Nursing, especially coronary care and intensive care, has been my passion."

Ari found it incredibly easy to talk about her life with Lance. In a short time, her reservation and reluctant safeguard were gone. They ordered soft drinks, which helped Ari feel more at ease. The food in the club was very good. Ari ordered the Atlantic salmon and Lance a filet mignon.

Using her index finger to brush her hair away from her eyes, she told him about the Washington assignment and the critical-care experiences she had while serving there. She shared about going to Denver to complete her training when she had caught this assignment at Fort Sill. She wasn't ready for Lance's next question.

"How did you decide you wanted to be a nurse?"

Sitting a bit straighter in her seat and instantly feeling vulnerable with the immediate rush of emotions, she thought, *Arielle, do not cry in front of this man. What's with you anyway? You never lose control.*

Taking a breath and leaning forward to be heard better, she said, "It started when my brother became ill. My mother had taken him to the pediatrician for a routine school exam when the discovery was made he had Ebstein's anomaly, a rare heart problem. He would have died, but the Pentecostal pastor next door rushed over to pray for him, and God healed him.

Grateful for the food's arrival, they enjoyed the meal as Ari said to Lance, "Do you know your name means 'servant' and 'spear'?"

"I've never looked it up. That's interesting. How did you learn that?"

"During my freshman year at an Assembly of God college, their student newspaper was called *The Lance*. My roommate Carol read to me what they called 'fun facts' on page two."

In a lighter tone, he said, "So, I am fun facts, a servant, and a spear—sounds about right."

They both smiled. The couple talked for hours, and not once did they talk about cannons or the RACH. Life in the club went on around them, but they were in their own world. The bubble burst when Ari saw the time. Lance's intuition read the scene, and like a gentleman, he quickly brought her back to her quarters.

Standing at the door where it had all begun, life was no longer the same. Now two lives were converging—even though they parted for the night. Two hearts met and meshed. Was it chemistry bringing them together or the providence of God?

# Thirty-Seven

Arielle had lived out the plans she had made for her life. Lying in bed, she thought about Lance. The pleasant euphoria of being with him brought an awareness to feelings and emotions she had never before experienced. She had a mind full of knowledge and realized she was lacking in understanding what had happened tonight. Not part of her planning.

Would she use words like dreamy, handsome, a gentleman, and interesting when she described him to Natalie? Would she have the nerve to tell Natalie what it was like to look into his eyes or about the times she had to look away or be drawn into deep eye contact. *Arielle, you're painting a picture of love at first sight. Are you serious?* At this moment, all she knew was the driving need to see Lance again and soon.

In the morning, the analytical part of Ari's mind kicked in—the self-protection part. Words like infatuation, crush, attraction, passion, intrigue, and puppy love crossed her mind. Being with Lance brought something to her life that enhanced everything. She needed to follow the clues to know where this relationship was leading. Glancing at the clock, she had just enough time to dress and drive into Lawton to attend church.

Worship time had already begun when she entered the sanctuary. Walking midway down the aisle, she chose a spot at the end of a pew. The songs were energetic, and it felt good to be in the house of God. However, her mind and heart were totally preoccupied. Her eyes were open, but her sight was looking within. When worship ended, they all were seated, the church news was shared, and the offering was taken as Ari simply went through the motions.

In the pastor's opening statement, he said, "I am taking a break from the series we're doing in Matthew 5—Jesus' Sermon on the Mount. Yesterday, during my devotional, I felt an urging from the Holy Spirit to speak about relationships. I know we're located in a military town, and our guests from the base move on to other locations. Let's touch on a few points this morning on God's strong and lasting relationships.

"Turn to Genesis 2:18." Rustling could be heard as the congregation turned pages to join in reading the Scripture together. "Please rise for the reading of the Scripture."

Pews creaked and people shuffled as they stood in respect to honor of the Word of God. Ari was still going through the motions, thinking about what had happened last night during dinner. She was there, but she had tuned out the service.

Taking a deep breath, the pastor began, "'It is not good for man to be alone. I will make a mate that is suitable to him.' Please be seated." In unison, except one, they all sat down. Shocked out of her inner thoughts, she heard the pastor read the verse; now he had her full attention. That very Scripture was on a piece of paper that she had spread out on the floor in her quarters. Realizing she was still standing and everyone else had been seated, she sheepishly sat down and totally focused on the message.

"Marriage is when a man and a woman take vows before God and become one. The strength of a marriage is in the foundation of two joining to build a foundation of one. Jesus talked about a strong foundation in Matthew 7 when He said, 'Everyone who hears these words of mine and does them will be like a wise man who built his house upon a rock.' Life will be full of challenges. Our very lives will be shaken at times. If we live by the Word of God, we will have a strong foundation. Jesus will have our backs."

Pausing for a moment, he continued, "When believers in Jesus Christ live life serving God, He will bring a mate across their path. He will confirm to each of them He is with them. Infatuation leads to selfish heart desires. The love of God leads to selflessness and living for the good of the other person."

Ari squirmed in her seat because she had liked what happened last night. But she knew what she had heard from the pastor was God speaking to her. She did not need to rush forward with blinders on but to watch for God's confirmation to her that He was in this. She would need to know this in her heart to feel confident.

"Let's turn to Proverbs 18:22 and read," the pastor said. Somewhat stunned by his choice, Ari recognized another verse she had written on one of her slips of paper she had laid out as she had sought God for guidance. The pastor read, "He who finds a wife finds a good thing and obtains favor from the Lord." Ari now had all she needed. She had definitely heard from the Lord.

Lance was feeling many emotions in his heart. He was not forgetting his deployment to South Korea in a few short weeks. Even though the conflict with North Korea had ended in the fifties, the people lived in a constant state of war readiness. At any given moment, war could break out. Their leadership had been on edge for decades.

America's intelligence agency prided itself on gaining information concerning the country. North Korea was an information blackout. The SR 71 Blackbird aircraft, the fastest in the world, flew reconnaissance over Korea to gain intelligence. In 1981, on its third pass over Korea, they fired a surface-to-air missile at the plane. The missile exploded a short distance away. At their airspeed, it was the equivalent of a two-second separation in the distance—a near miss.

Being an Army captain headed into a hostile area, he knew living out his faith was a vital part of his safety. He had read Psalm 91 many times in his life and firmly believed God had angels surrounding him and that he would be under the protective wing of Father God. Having grown up in Lawton, he was already attending the First Baptist Church. Today, he was distracted during the service; welling up in his heart was the connectedness he felt to Ari. Something about her helped him feel his best. He realized they had only had one meal together, but her acceptance and affirming words strengthened him in ways he had never before experienced. The feelings was good in the manner that God had created him and had wired him to be attracted to women. Now he had a burning desire to know the heart of this woman.

He remembered her saying during their meal together that she would often go for an afternoon run at Cedar Lakes. He devised a plan for a chance meeting with her and set out to accomplish it. On the trail at the north bend alongside of the airport runways, he could see a long distance to the west and the south. He decided he would wait at the stretching apparatus. If she were doing the loop running south or east, he would see her coming. After forty-five minutes passed, he thought perhaps there was a hole in his plan. Then in the distance he spotted a slender female running toward him. His heart stirred as he placed his leg on a post to stretch out his hamstring muscles. He bent down at the waist, leaning forward with his head down, then as he straightened up, he called out, "Ari."

Both of their faces brightened visibly at seeing one another. After some small talk, Lance asked to join her on the run. The fact that both were in shape meant they could talk and run without being out of breath. When the finish line of the loop was in sight, Ari dashed for a strong finish. Lance prided himself on being fit but could only do a close second. Now both were winded but smiling. Metaphorically speaking, the chase was on.

# Thirty-Eight

As Natalie and Ari were doing rounds, checking vitals, changing bandages, and taking temperatures, Natalie shot off one question after another. If there were any juicy details, she wanted to know. Talking over their patients as they went, Ari said, "Well, I've only seen him twice."

"Twice?" Natalie said in the raised voice. "It's Monday, Ari! What do you mean twice?"

Reaching for a blood-pressure cup, she wrapped it around the soldier's arm as he smiled and looked from one nurse to the other. He opened his mouth right in time to have the thermometer inserted under his tongue. Pumping up the cup and placing the stethoscope on his vein, they were silent for a moment.

Natalie said, "It's 110 over 74," and Ari recorded the number on the chart.

Lifting up the sheet to see the bandage on his leg, Ari said, "We need to change this," and they went through the motions of cleaning the wound and applying a new bandage.

"It was a wonderful night, and I never would have expected it. Lance was a gentleman—interesting and funny," she said. "The club was like it usually is on crazy Saturdays, but it was as if we were the only two people there."

Finishing with the bandaging and putting the sheet back in place, Natalie removed the thermometer and said, "He's normal," and Ari made a note in the chart. Then she added, "You're doing fine today, soldier," as they threw the waste in the red-bag container and moved on to the next patient.

Continuing on, Ari said, "I have to confess that Lance is a handsome man."

The reason Natalie was a matchmaker was that she was a hopelessly romantic fanatic. In her mind, she was beginning to think this match was going to be better than she had originally thought.

Ari was filtering through her thoughts about Lance, holding back her heartfelt feelings. She felt that she might have been saying too much, which would be a violation to the two of them. So she told her about the details of their surroundings and kept away from the chemistry.

Natalie asked, "Tell me you wore something that showed off your figure."

Not one to do it on purpose, she said, "Relax, I dressed my best."

Jumping back into the conversation Natalie had to know. "Did it end with a kiss?"

"Sorry, that's classified," she answered with a smile."

"Well, what about Sunday? How did you see him Sunday?"

"I was on my run when I saw him on the trail at Cedar Lakes."

"What?"

"Yes, I was coming up to the northeast bend at the runways, and there he was—leaning forward and stretching out his legs. He shouted, "Ari" with a question in his voice.

"What are the chances?"

"He joined me on the run until I sprinted to the finish line and left him in my dust!"

"Are you playing hard to get, girl?"

"One thing at a time…but then, I was leaning up against my car and we talked for another hour. And then I told him I was a Star Trek fan."

"You what? You told him you like Trekkie movies?"

"Yes, and then he said *The Wrath of Klan* was playing at the Ritz Theatre in Lawton. So…that's where we're going…tonight."

"Ari, you are seeing him three days in a row?" Stunned, Natalie could hardly wait to see where this was going.

At 6:30 p.m. three sharp knocks sounded on Ari's door, and she was ready. Fully excited at seeing him again, she opened the door to Lance wearing blue jeans and a green tapered shirt. Her eyes liked what she saw. Together they walked outside and to a different car—a bright-red 1967 Mustang convertible. As Lance opened the passenger door for Ari, she asked, "I love this car! Is it yours?"

"Yes, I keep it off base at my dad's."

Lance slipped into the driver's seat; they had just enough time to get there before the show started at 7:00 p.m. Feeling the warm air and open sky enhanced the ride. Placing his arm on the car door and passing through Scott gate, Lance gave the guard a salute. The drive to downtown Lawton was short. Lawton's downtown area was three blocks wide by four blocks long, and the Ritz was located in the heart of the town. He pulled into one of the diagonal parking places in the downtown area. When she saw the Ritz movie house, fond memories of the Allen Theater back home flashed through her mind.

Lance put the top up on the convertible and rolled up the windows before he got out and opened her door for her. *I'm glad I wore jeans*, she thought. Movie tickets in hand, Lance opened the door to the Ritz, and the smell of fresh popcorn flooded the two of them. In her mind she saw

Sammy and Joey standing at the glass counter ordering popcorn and drinks. Ari then understood they both had a small-town background.

Lance asked, "Where would you like to sit?"

The house was not full on a Monday, so she said without hesitation, "Center, three quarters of the way up. I feel like I'm in the movie when I sit in that spot."

With a large tub of popcorn and two drinks, they sidestepped their way past people and into her favorite spot. The lights dimmed, and the preview began. Lance tucked away the napkins in his shirt pocket. When he noticed she was looking to wipe her hands, he produced them again. He was thinking about her needs, and she noticed it with a smile.

Once the movie began, Ari was totally engrossed in the storyline until Khan removed the creature from the glass tank, and it crawled into Chekov's ear. She looked over at Lance with a scrunched-up nose. *Now's a good time,* Lance thought as he reached out to take Ari's hand in his. She relinquished her hand to him, and they entwined their fingers.

As they left the Ritz, they were both sharing their own recap of the movie—their favorite lines, scenes, and how the creature had grossed them out. Back in the car with the top down again and riding through Lawton, Lance pointed toward Ari's side of the car to show her where he went to high school. For a few minutes, he became her tour guide from a local's point of view. In the crisp night air, his tour was refreshing but not a good time to have bucket seats!

Back on base, Lance walked Ari to her quarters; both knew they needed to be fresh for the next day. Lance would be in his advanced training class and could not afford to look sleepy, or worse yet, let his eyes close. Reluctantly they called it a night but not before making plans to eat at the PX courtyard on Tuesday.

Time could not pass fast enough as far as Ari and Lance were concerned. At 7:00 p.m. exactly, three sharp knocks sounded again on Ari's door. Together they walked to the car with a repeat of his solicitations the evening at the Ritz. Ari liked how Lance was treating her. At the PX, Lance asked for their order while she held a table. After he carried the tray over to the table, they wasted no time and quickly began conversing. Ari told Lance how she had been there last week with Natalie to get a cheeseburger and how she had wanted an A&W cheeseburger like the ones they had enjoyed as children in Farmington.

Lance dropped his food on his plate and asked, "Are you telling me you like cheeseburgers?"

"Yes, they remind me of home."

"Are you scheduled to be off on Saturday?"

"I am."

"I have a treat for you, little missy," he drawled, using his best John Wayne imitation. "Allow me to take you to the best, most unique, and most remote cheeseburger joint in all of Oklahoma."

Between Tuesday and Saturday, they saw each other as often as they could. For several nights that week, Lance would be firing the Howitzer and raining down the sound of freedom.

Skip was beside himself when he finally caught up with Lance. "Where have you been?"

"I'm spending all my available time with Ari."

"There's an empty seat at the club waiting on you."

"You might have to look for a new fourth pal. I'm in for the full court press."

"Honestly? I have never seen you like this, pal. Is she this special to you?"

"Skip, she's the woman of my dreams. I know, 'How can this be?' Right now we're having the time of our lives. Of course, I'm on the hurry-up program."

"Have you told her yet?"

"No, there's still time."

"Man, you know you're totally preoccupied with this woman."

"Isn't it great?"

Skip had hoped to have Lance meet a nice girl and help Natalie along in her pursuit of seeing a budding romance. However, he hadn't seen being abandoned as part of his plan.

# Thirty-Nine

There is never enough time once you find love. Work schedules, laundry, and shopping still needs to be done. They did whatever they could together—going for a run and grabbing a quick meal—and made short phone calls to keep connected until Saturday.

Right at noon when she heard the three sharp knocks on her door, she was ready. The top on the car was down once again. Ari wore a red scarf tied around her neck, knowing it would catch the wind in the car. Lance opened the car door for her and then he hopped in. They headed north toward Apache Gate up to Route 49 and then turned left toward Wichita Mountain Wildlife Refuge. "If it's okay with you, we'll do a little sightseeing before we eat."

Ari nodded yes and smiled. *Of course, he would have their time all planned out*, she thought.

What a wonderful day to take a drive in a convertible! Opening her purse, she took out her sunglasses. She turned toward Lance and said, "It's so beautiful here. I've lived on base for almost a year and never came out to see this."

"We took many trips out here as a family when I was growing up. If you like hiking, this is definitely the place to go."

Crossing over into the park and driving past the welcome signs, they arrived in less than an hour. "Wichita Mountain Refuge is huge. We're going to start our tour on the road leading up on Mt. Scott." On the right side of the road, they turned and started their ascent.

"Mt. Scott is nearly twenty five hundred feet in height. The mountain was named after Lieutenant-General Winfield Scott. Early in his Army career, he was commissioned as a light artillery captain. He had the longest standing commission with fifty-three years in the Army."

"Do you want a long career in the Army, Lance?" Ari asked.

"No," he admitted and then continued, "I want to pursue other careers and continue my education. Right now I'm planning on finishing my tour and then reassessing my options."

*I hope I'm one of those options,* she thought.

Ari had the best view of the landscape from her side of the car. Beautiful scenery stretched as far as the eye could see. Arriving at the top and pulling into the parking area, they left the car to experience the view.

"Lance, this is so breathtaking here! What's the name of that lake down there?" she inquired.

"It's a manmade body of water named Lake Lawtonka—a great recreation area for boaters and fishing."

"Any waterskiing on that lake?" she asked. It had been years since she had put on skis. Lance went to tell her about the marina, rentals, and times he had spent on the lake. They drifted off to the right and looked toward the base.

"Just a minute," Lance said as he jogged back to the car and grabbed something from the trunk and returned to hand her a pair of binoculars. Anticipating that she might want a closer look at the lake and the base, he had brought them with him.

For several minutes she took in all the details. It crossed her mind how wonderful the day was going and how he thought of so many ways to please her. She wasn't going to tell him it wouldn't take much because of how good she felt just being with him. When you love someone, you want that person to share in all the good things and good times in your life and begin new times with them.

At 2:30 they headed down the mountain and back to Route 49. Lance made a right-hand turn, heading to their next destination. Watching the road and speaking over the wind noise, he asked Ari, "Do you like hiking?"

"I grew up taking family hiking trips; I love them."

"Great, here is where I get you hungry for a cheeseburger later." He pulled into the Bison Trail parking area. "We're going to be here a while, so let's put the top up on the car." Once the car was all secured, he pointed to the trail board to their left. There they studied the map, and Ari noted it was just over a five-mile loop.

Lance commented, "There are at least two important things to watch for on the trail. One, buffaloes always have the right of way!" Ari smiled. He continued, "If they move toward you, give them room. They're not aggressive for the most part, but if you caught one by surprise, it will get your legs moving and your heart pumping for sure," he said in a lighthearted tone.

"What's the second thing?"

"Watch out for rattlesnakes. I've only seen one here but be on the lookout." Ari again flashed back to Angel Peak when the family had spotted the rattler sunning itself on the road.

"Okay, good advice."

This trail was not like those back in Farmington. There were round rocks on the trail that hikers had to either step around or walk on top of them. They were everywhere, making the couple focus on the ground.

Once they rounded the parking area, the plains opened up, and the view was wonderful. Just beyond and below them were spots of scrubs and open grassy areas. Buffalo were spread about—some close and others further away.

"When the buffalo were brought to Wichita, only about fifteen were released. Look at them now!" In the distance were over a hundred animals grazing. Following the well-marked trail was easy, and each turn brought new things to see.

Ari thought, *Lance was right; this is an appetite-building trail.* She thoroughly enjoyed the physical challenge and the familiar feelings relating to her early family life.

Once back at the car, Lance opened the trunk and took out cold bottles of water from the cooler; they needed them. With the top down again, they pulled on to the road heading west until they came to Route 115. Lance made a right hand turn and went north.

Ari was totally relaxed. Not knowing where they were going didn't matter; all that mattered was that she was with Lance. Driving up a slight incline, Lance slowed down, knowing they had almost arrived. He wanted to see Ari's first impression.

"Okay," he said and then continued, "Get ready; it's right around the bend."

Coming into view was a very old, piece-meal building that looked like it was falling apart. The side of building had several different materials; it was a sight. He glanced at Ari, and her face was blank.

"Ari, are you going to say something?"

"What's there to say other than it looks very interesting," she said trying to be nice.

Written on the wall near the glass door was "Meer's Store and Restaurant."

"This place is known by all the locals and half of the base. It's 5:30 p.m., and in an hour people will be waiting outside, forming a line."

After parking the car, the couple walked in together. Lance let Ari go first to see the full effect. On the walls were old license plates, pieces of paper, or notes thumb-tacked on the wall with comments about the food. It was dark inside because of all the dark wood paneling. Tables and plastic chairs were placed everywhere. Ari burst out laughing, and Lance didn't know how to take her response.

"The place is oozing character. I love it, Lance!"

"Wait till you taste the food! I'm not kidding, Ari. It's to die for!"

Once seated at the table, Ari needed a second to realize the old town newsletter on the table was the menu. She smiled. Lance had asked for a table by the window to be able to watch the crowds when they gathered. Ari looked everywhere, taking it all in.

"Ari, let me warn you…unless you want to eat a cow, don't order the seismic burger because it's huge. All the burgers are absolutely delicious." They both ordered cheeseburgers with everything except peppers and a basket of fried okra. Their drinks arrived in a Mason jar with a straw, and Ari chuckled.

When food arrived at the table next to them, Ari's mouth dropped open.

"Oh, Lance, is that the seismic burger?" She discreetly nodded in the direction of the table next to them.

"That's it! You could feed a platoon with that burger! That was the second-best look you had today."

"What was the other one, Lance?"

"When that buffalo popped out of the scrub bushes ten feet away! Your eyes were almost as big as his. I'm sure glad he decided to mosey off away from us."

Ari was at a loss for words. Her eyes were taking in all the unique details of the restaurant that was now alive with people and music. Meer's had an atmosphere of old-time mining from years gone by. People were glad to be there. The food arrived, and even her small burger was large.

Ari felt like a ten year old on Thanksgiving Day when her eyes were too big for her stomach! Taking her first bite said it all.

Lance offered, "I told you it's the best cheeseburger I've ever had. As soon as possible, I'll take you to Dwayne's Drive-in, the second-best cheeseburger place, in Lawton.

Finishing up all she could eat, Ari commented, "I think I needed two trails to get ready for that meal."

On their way out, they noticed some guys were looking at Lance's car. Walking up to the car, one of them asked Lance, "What size engine to do you have in it?"

"It has the 283 cubic inch V8—all the power I need."

He'd heard it all before. Everyone loves a Mustang, and this one was in mint condition.

It was still warm enough to have the top down for the ride back. Lance headed east on NW Meer's Porter Hill Rd. until he reached Route 58, where he turned south toward the base.

Ari never stopped talking about the day. He loved listening to her recapping the day's events. It was what he had hoped for, and seeing her happy brought joy to his heart.

Walking Ari to her quarters, they both knew their relationship had changed and advanced. They were comfortable with each other and enjoyed each other's company. They continued to discover what being on a mountaintop was it like, or was it being on top of the world?

As Ari turned to face Lance, she stood on her toes and the couple kissed goodnight. Closing the door behind her, she leaned against it and said, "Thank You, Lord."

# FORTY

In love, there is a freedom to live life. Lance was learning to become an artillery company commander. He was mastering how to lead the men under his command and work as a staff officer on the battalion level. His job was not just about firing ordnances with precision, but how to direct men and women under his command as well as work with those over him.

Spending time with Arielle was pure bliss. When he was not with her or learning command strategies, he was planning his next outing to please her. Seeing her having fun brought a new and wonderful joy to his life. He already had the next three Saturdays planned out.

During the week he was counting on being close to the base, running the loop with her, and taking walks together. When he was with her, he was not Captain Lance; he was free to be himself, which often allowed the fun-loving boy inside him to run free. When he was with Ari, he was not shouldering the burdens of command; he was more like the local tour guide, knowing all the hot spots.

In their schedules, Wednesday was poised to be a surprise. All the time Lance was listening to Ari talk, he had taken notice of her interests. That was how the Wednesday plans came about. They drove through Bentley's Gate, across Rogers Lane, down Sheridan Road, and into Lawton. Slowing down to turn right, Ari could see where they were headed. She broke into a huge smile as she exclaimed, "It's just like the A&W back home!"

Wayne's Drive–In had two carport rows and new advanced ordering stations. Lance pulled into an open spot near the building so they could watch the waitresses skate. Ari leaned over Lance to read the menu and see all her possibilities. Wayne's was known for their cheeseburgers and thick banana shakes.

Ordering had changed since her Farmington days—at least here in Lawton. You pushed a button on the menu station, talked to a person in Wayne's, placed your order, and then a girl on roller skates brought out your meal. They agreed on two cheeseburgers with everything and two banana shakes. With their order completed, Ari began to tell Lance about their family outings to the A&W and how they all squeezed in the same window to watch the girl bring their food. Lance partway rolled up the window of the car when he saw the girl coming. She said, "Here's your meal, folks," and placed the tray on the window next to Lance.

Wayne's Drive-In was more than just about the food; the place was all about the hot cars—GTOs, Camaros, Chevelles—muscle cars of all shape and sizes and colors came to Wayne's to be viewed. People would get out of their cars to take time to admire vintage beauties. Conversations about factory condition, original parts, and engine sizes were discussed. Lance's car received a lot of looks and questions.

After they had finished eating, they drove around the streets of downtown Lawton, which took all of ten minutes. Lance's plans were working. He was in full pursuit of Ari, and she was enjoying every minute of being the focus of his attention. Doing things with family or friends is one thing; the doing takes on another aspect when it in the midst of an atmosphere of romance.

Ari was wondering how things could get any better until Lance took her to Medicine Park, north of the base. As he parked the car, they could see the place was alive with people on a picture-perfect Saturday. An unusual smell permeated the air—that of moisture and the scents coming from the surrounding trees.

Medicine Park was a collection of unique stores and restaurants nestled alongside Medicine Creek. The construction and décor was unlike anything Ari had ever seen. She had heard people on base talking about this place, but she had never imagined it could be so beautiful. The prominent feature was the use of cobblestones as a construction material for almost everything. The landscaping walls lining the sidewalk along the creek, the fronts of building, and the column supports in the Old Plantation Restaurant were all made with cobblestone.

"Whatever you want to do, just say it," Lance offered. Swimming, canoeing, biking, and shopping were all laid out in an attractive way for the visiting tourists. The couple began at Cobblestone Stone Row, walking among the stores filled with items made by local craftspeople. Drifting down to the creek and walking next to the water reminded Ari so much of San Antonio River Walk, although this was totally different.

They stopped and sat down on a bench and watched the children swimming in the creek and the people strolling by. Lance talked about his times of swimming in the creek with his family there. They walked the bridges over the creek and then crossed onto the island. They strolled about and came up to the old cobblestone-faced cabins now turned into cottage stores.

Eventually they ended up in the Old Plantation Restaurant with its many elegant features. Ritzy in its heyday, the restaurant's menu now lacked the specialized meals like the one they had enjoyed at Meer's. However, the ambience was exceptional, and their mouths could almost taste the brisket being smoked in the kitchen.

"Lance, this is a wonderful place. I would have missed coming here if it weren't for you." Taking his arm, she confessed, "I have fun being with you." Changing the focus, she asked, "I wonder who came up with the idea of using red-and-brown cobblestones in building Medicine Park?"

He knew hers was a rhetorical question so he didn't need to answer it. Lance shared, "Many sinister characters have visited here, but my favorite good guys were Roy Rogers and Dale Evans. I've seen the reruns as a kid and loved their escapades."

Having the hostess seat them at a table for two, they had a wonderful meal as the conclusion of a perfect day.

Meanwhile, Natalie and Skip were growing frantic about their mutual friends' blooming relationship. They knew that Lance and Ari were spending all their free time together, and the rub was that they were not hearing about any of the details. They decided to hatch a plan for a double date at the Patriot Officers' Club. As far as Natalie was concerned, working in different locations at the hospital than Ari was a total miscarriage of romance news. When Natalie saw Ari in the nurses' lounge, she would have enough time for them to plan and meet on Tuesday night. Natalie absolutely wanted the lowdown on all the details she was used to hearing with her other matchmaking successes. Right now she was feeling left out.

The average person would think that being the property of the United States government (until their commission expired) would hinder a budding romance. Lance's creative genius, however, squeaked out every minute they could to be together and not affect their duties.

Everyday life involved seeing squads of soldiers running across base, trucks pulling artillery cannons to the firing lines, and being saluted by the enlisted men and woman. In the midst of a military life was the bubble of two individuals moving forward in the hopes of becoming one. In the back of Lance's mind was his looming deployment. Now that he had found the love of his life, he was leaving the country. He could not imagine being separated from Ari. His heart had found a woman who opened the hidden parts of his soul.

Thursday night, upon entering the Officer Club as a couple, they saw Skip and Natalie.

"Where have you two been?" Skip asked Lance and Ari.

They looked at each other, and Lance let Ari take the lead on telling their story. If they could have, Natalie and Skip would have leaned in to hear better, but neither wanted to be quite that conspicuous.

Ari began, “We’ve been all over—from the top of Mt. Scott to the grassy plains of the Wichita Mountains. Did you know that buffalos are very big when you’re up close to them?”

Natalie’s eyes grew big as she exclaimed, “What?”

“Yes, we were on the hiking trail, and he was ten feet away from us in a patch of scrubs. At that range I discovered they have really big eyes!”

They all laughed. Conversation led to stories of Meer’s, Medicine Park, and Dwayne’s. All Skip and Natalie could do was shake their heads in disbelief. Not in their wildest dreams had they thought this would happen.

Skip asked, “So what’s next on the list, buddy?”

“Charon’s Garden Trail in Wichita—I have the trail plotted out for a day’s hike.”

“Ari,” Skip said, “I hope you have good shoes and strong legs for that trail.”

Ari said, “You know, I had no idea that a broken-down-looking shack could have the best cheeseburgers in the world.”

Guiding the subject away from their future plans because she loved being surprised, she spoke of their experience at Meer’s Restaurant. Describing its character took the better part of an hour.

For Ari and Lance to be seen out as a couple felt good to both of them.

# FORTY-ONE

Charon's Garden Trail started out tame enough. The information on the board at the trailhead stated: "Be sure to follow the trail." From the very beginning, the trail was lined with cobblestones and rocks marking the way. However as they climbed higher, the rocks became bigger and bigger and then huge and looked like they were thrown up against each other. What had started out as an easy walk became one of traversing boulders and squeezing down narrow pathways.

Passersby had scratched their names on the rock's surfaces. They chuckled as they read "Tight Squeeze" and "Fat Man's Misery." In some places they had to duck underneath boulders. Stopping to think about how much one of those huge boulders weighed and the fact that you were walking under them could frighten some hikers but most realized those boulders had been there since the creation of time.

The trail was all about the experience now. They were pitting their physical abilities against it. Lance had filled a backpack with needed supplies—drinking water, snacks, paper towels, band-aids, and binoculars. Charon's Garden Trail was like a rabbit trail for humans with all the ducking, squeezing, and crawling between the rocks. At times they could see the sky, and at other times, they felt like they were in a cave. In some places, the positioning of the boulders seemed like a tunnel that stretched out for many feet. They often had to dodge and weave through the rocks. Never before in Ari's life had she been in such a wild place. She valiantly met the challenge and felt exhilarated.

An opening finally appeared in front of them—the perfect picnic spot that Lance had preplanned. Climbing up a boulder and out into the open, they sat down and looked out over the Wichita Mountains refuge. Seeing the magnificent view was a wonderful experience for Ari.

Hungry from their exertion, Lance opened the backpack. He handed Ari a bottle of water, and she took a long drink. While they were enjoying the food Lance had brought, they enjoyed the scenery.

"Lance, this place is so beautiful. I can feel what it is like being on the mountaintop!" Ari exclaimed.

The wind picked up in waves; not to feel the wind at that height would be rare. Once they finished eating, Lance handed Ari the binoculars so she could view the sweeping valley below them and beyond to Lawton. From their vantage point, they could hear the sounds of freedom as puffs of smoke rose on the hillside of Signal Mountain. On the artillery line, red-and-white striped visitor tents had been set up for spectators and dignitaries. Today they were being given a demonstration of America's best artillery units.

"Ari, it's almost as if you can reach out and touch God up here. This awe-inspiring place has a spiritual atmosphere."

The moment Lance had been planning to take a risk had come. "Ari, may I pray for you?"

Somewhat surprised by his question and feeling vulnerable, nevertheless she said, "Yes."

He gently took her hand in his, and they closed their eyes. "Dear Father God, I want to thank You that You have brought Arielle into my life. She is a blessing to me. I ask that You place Your blessings upon her. May Your favor go before her and fill her with Your love. In Jesus' name. Amen."

Ari's eyes were moist. Something was very personal about prayer. She leaned toward Lance and kissed him tenderly on his cheek as she snuggled closer to him and took in a view she never wanted to forget.

Sitting on a hard rock is a great motivator to moving on. Soon they were forced to return to the trail with its crevices awaiting them. At some point Ari noted, "Lance, the information board warned hikers to stay on the trail. What if there are no markings telling us which way to go?"

"That's the beauty of the federal government. Officials tell you to stay on the marked trail and then don't put up signs." They laughed together over his wry comment. "Don't worry; I'll get you back to the car."

Skip had been right about needing good shoes, and her legs were getting sore. Even though both of them were in good shape, the trail still took its toll on their energy levels. They had been duly warned; after all, the trailhead sign had used the word strenuous.

Being in love and enjoying the atmosphere of romance is a wonderful time of life, and Lance and Ari were making the most of every minute. However, many tasks demanded their attention, which is why this day ended early. Once back in her quarters, she disciplined herself to do paperwork and not rush for the phone. Her plan was to wait until 6:00 when she knew for sure her parents would be home. As planned, she picked up the phone at 6:00, dialed the ten-digit number, and listened to the phone ringing. Soon she heard the voice she loved to hear say, "Hello."

"Hi, Mom, how are you and Dad?"

She could overhear Judy shout saying to Mike, "Honey, Ari's on the phone."

It was like this every time she called home. You would have thought it was a lifetime between calls instead of only a month.

Ari said, "Mom, I have some news…" She paused momentarily to get a hold of herself and then she said, "Mom, I've met someone."

Any onlooker could have heard a pin drop in the kitchen. Judy turned toward the front room and shouted to Mike, "I'll call you when it's your turn to talk with her." Ari now knew that she had her mother's full attention.

"Okay, Ari, tell me everything about the man you've met."

From that point on, it was all girl talk—the emotions and feelings, how he listened to her, how he wanted to know her heart, what he was doing to please her, and how he wanted to make her happy. Ari was gushing with so much information and so many stories that Judy was amazed. Then came the statement that Judy was not yet ready to hear. "Mom, I know he is the right one!"

Judy had thought this day might come, but what mother is ever ready to hear this news especially when hundreds of miles apart? So much had happened without her knowledge. She and Ari shared a very intimate moment. Judy had already lived decades of life; she watched her parents' relationship and other couples she had known.

She replied to her daughter's admission with what only a mother can share; after all, she knew the heart of her daughter. The most important part of Lance's being the right one was having the assurance that they were both connected to God so they would not be unequally yoked as the Bible says. From there Judy shared with her the wisdom she had gained from knowing she had chosen the right one.

Mike had become restless in the front room and wondered what they could be talking about that took an hour. He wanted to hear about what was happening on base—from one veteran to his captain daughter. Before any of their children had been born, Mike had seen combat in Korea. He wanted to hear how Ari was doing at Fort Sill. Finally, his turn came, and Ari told him about Lance and that he was an artillery commander. Mike asked her questions about his unit and what type of cannons they were firing now.

"Dad, the guys call the 155 Howitzer cannon the earthquake maker." Ari told him about Lance's thoughtfulness, about Dwayne's Drive-In, and Lance's car. She even told him the Mustang had a 283 cubic inch motor, further impressing Mike.

Mike would have asked her if this man in her life was treating her well—something every dad would want to know. But he could already tell it in her voice and how she described him.

After the call ended, Mike and Judy talked about how serious their daughter was about Lance. "Mike, I think it sounds like Arielle is in love. She told me all the things they're doing together and her feelings for him. She said Lance is a very romantic man and is sweeping her off her feet."

Mike kept to himself as he took things into consideration. If it were not for how well he knew his daughter, he might have concerns. He knew that Ari would seek God first.

Finding time to be together in the upcoming week would prove challenging for Ari and Lance. He was on the final leg of completing his training. Going for a run was one of the physical disciplines they both made time for in their day. As they were on the loop, Lance said he had an idea for Saturday—a surprise for her. They had been seeing each other for almost a month now, and Lance had not yet run out of surprises!

"I have a special place in Lawton for us on Saturday. I'm sure you'll love it."

Ari enjoyed the thrill of Lance's pursuing her and how he had brought new experiences into her life.

Downtown Lawton was alive on this warm summer evening. Lance pulled into the closest diagonal parking spot he could find. They still had to walk a block to arrive at their destination—LaSill's Ice cream Parlor. As they stepped through the door, it felt like they just traveled backward through a time warp. On the left side of the store was a counter with stools that were all occupied. On the opposite wall were booths with vinyl-covered seats, all of which were taken too.

"Ari, may I suggest you try the rainbow sherbet cone?"

As she looked around, she easily noted it was the popular choice, so she agreed. For fifty miles surrounding Lawton, people would come here for the best rainbow sherbet in Oklahoma.

Running the ice cream parlor was one continuous fluid motion. Ten soda jerks were busy filling orders. Not one of them looked over seventeen years old. When they were at the front of the line, Lance noticed a wrought iron table in front of the window was about to open. Motioning to Ari, she walked up and asked politely if they were leaving. At the moment, it was no time to be shy and the people nodded and soon left the table for Ari.

The soda shop was loud, noisy, and fun. Holding the cones above his head, squeezing through and past people, Lance made his way to Ari. Handing her a cone, he sat down and waited. In his mind he was about to take a picture of Ari's first taste. He was not disappointed; her tongue burst into pure pleasure as each flavor moved across her taste buds, and her face lit up with delight. Her first word, albeit an unintelligible one, was "Uhmmm." No more words were needed, though being ready with a napkin was required. The race was on to eat every bite of the cone or lose it to the napkin as it melted.

Nostalgia oozed in this place. Memories were made here, and for decades, people returned to relive them. Ari, looking at the children and put her napkin up to her mouth to hide her laughter. Some of the children had seemingly lost the battle between eating the cone or wearing the sherbet.

Lance responded to her amusement. "Who knows? This may have been the beginnings of tie-dye clothing right here!"

Once outside, they walked back to the car, hand in hand. Ari commented, "We would call this Main Street back home, except your downtown is several blocks wide. My mother loved to go to Woody's Café, which was located on a bend on Main Street. She and her friend, Martha, always sat at the window table so they could watch what was happening up and down the street. You know, she had an angel story happen in Woody's. I just now remembered it. A man gave them a message, walked out the door, and disappeared."

Lance shot her a look. "Really?"

Lance discreetly took notice of a store across the street as they neared the car. Backing out, he made a turn at the end of the block and headed toward Bentley Gate. There were now on Cache Road headed west. He casually glanced to his left at a new store in town, doing reconnaissance for their next visit there.

Back at Ari's quarters, Lance became somewhat nervous, but it was not noticeable outwardly. As they approached her door, opening it was when they usually parted ways. On this night Lance asked Ari if he could come in for just a moment. Normally the answer would have been no, but she totally trusted Lance and knew he was a gentleman.

Her quarters were very modest with not much room. She was about to pull out the chair when Lance took her hands in his hands. With an expression of love and concern, he looked into her eyes and said, "Arielle, I love you."

It is one thing when it is understood; it is another thing to hear someone speak the words. These were the words Ari wanted to hear from Lance. Her heart leaped within her for she too loved Lance and was about to say so when he began to say more. "Will you marry me?"

Without a doubt, Lance was the love of her life. Her mother had asked her, "Can you imagine yourself living without Lance?" She had decided she couldn't. Immediately she answered him with an excited yes.

Their kiss and embrace were filled with love and emotions. Just four weeks ago, two lives had been separated by one wooden door. Now Lance had found the door to Ari's heart, and they would soon begin a life together. They sat down and began to discuss their future together. The most important item on Lance's list was buying an engagement ring.

Lance said, "I would like to take you to Tipton Jewelry store on Cache Road. I've heard it's the best place in town to buy a ring."

He then told her about his impending deployment so they could make their plans before it happened. Deployment is a normal part of Army life and she understood.

Neither of them wanted this night to end. The rush of feelings for each other was paramount. The night was summed up with one word—joy.

# Forty-Two

As they passed through the Bentley Gate, Lance saluted the guard. Today was the second happiest day of his life. Crossing over Route 62, driving on Sheridan Avenue, he passed NW Cache Road. As he approached W Gore, he turned on his left signal. They were nearly there. Two blocks down, he parallel parked right in front of Tipton's Jewelry Store.

Arielle waited for Lance to open her door. Tipton's was the newest jewelry store in Lawton, and it sparkled. Stepping through the glass door, they could see elegant showcases inside. An impeccably dressed store clerk approached them and asked, "How can I help you today?"

And so the shopping began. From her earliest days, Ari had thought of this moment. She remembered her daydreams of being a bride. Not in her wildest dreams did she foresee being a part of this decision. Lance told the clerk they wanted to see some engagement-wedding band combinations. Buying the set seemed logical.

"Come this way," he said.

They walked past several glass counters with lights shining on the diamonds and their brilliant colors sparkling in the light.

The clerk reached for a black velvet pad and placed it on top of the glass surface. He slid open a wooden panel, reached in, and brought out a sample box of rings. Taking out a set, he placed it on the black velvet pad where the diamonds' luster sparkled in the bright light. True to the mark of a fine salesmanship, he started them out with the high-end rings.

"Here is a one-carat diamond with fine clarity, preset with six prongs and a pure-white gold band." Reaching for Ari's hand, he slipped the ring on her finger for effect. Emotions surged in Ari's heart. *This is for real!* As she looked at the ring, she knew it symbolized their love for each other. It was more than a ring; it represented their future and commitment to each other. Her cheeks were flushed, and she felt warm as she contemplated the beginning of her time to be a bride. Lance loved watching his future wife's gentle, loving expression.

Thrilled for the moment, inwardly she knew this ring set was not the one. Even though Lance had cautioned her not to worry about the cost, she was shaping her options. As Lance watched Ari, his heart filled with joy. He had watched other men choose engagement rings, so he had determined to let his future wife choose her own. In his heart he knew he had made the right choice. Watching her face and seeing the sparkle in her eyes as bright as the sparkles in the diamond was truly a rare gift.

Leaving this showcase for the one next to it, the clerk produced another box of rings, allowing them to look over all the sets as he told about them.

"In this box are half-carat diamonds. The clarity of each stone has been rated." Arielle pointed to a grouping of rings, and the clerk pulled them from the box and placed them on the pad. "This is a four-prong diamond. The band has four smaller diamonds—two on each side."

Ari picked up the ring with a pleased look on her face. Placing it on her finger, she extended her arm in front of her to get a good look. She looked at her hand from all positions and decided she liked it. The bands needed to complement each other. Her band was a very petite ring—a good match. Turning to Lance she looked for his input on the husband's band. It was a two-tone gold band with white gold on the outer edge and a rich golden color in the middle stripe of the band.

When Ari asked him to try it on, Lance responded, "It reminds me of you—rare and elegant."

In the midst of this joyous occasion, Ari was balancing need over wants, expenses over costs, and not over the top but not shortchanging herself in this purchase. In her heart, this set was the perfect one for them. The clerk complimented them on their choice and reached for the sizing gauges. He took down their ring sizes and completed the receipt.

In just one hour, their lives had taken another step toward converging. It would be a few days before Ari could subtly hold out her hand for Natalie and the girls to notice. The next event on the list would be to tell Lance's parents.

Both of Lance's parents had inspired him to continue his education. They were both professional people who had been working for decades building a life together. Saturday would be the day they would share their happy news; they had a dinner date with them. In Lance's opinion, nothing was like a home-cooked meal!

On the way to his parents' home, they stopped at Tipton's and picked up their rings. Carefully, the clerk polished the diamond one last time and slid it on Ari's finger. The next stop was home. Right on time, Lance and Ari arrived at the house.

As Lance opened the front door, he called, "Knock, knock! We're here!"

Kate wiped her hands on her apron and walked toward the front door to greet them. Andy was already in the front room and left the comfort of his comfortable chair to hug each of them. Ari liked the warmth they extended toward her.

The house was filled with the aroma of food being cooked. The table was set for an informal meal, and everyone took a seat. Holding hands, they prayed over the food, and Andy included a blessing for the cook. Lance could hardly wait for his mother's mouth-watering pork chops because of the special way she prepared them. Other serving bowls on the table contained mashed potatoes, broccoli, and bread sticks.

Andy wanted to know how the car was running. "Where have you taken it? Have you been over to Wayne's Drive-In?" The conversation moved on to his deployment and the preparations for it. Andy wondered if he would need to store the car and his other things in the garage.

What was it about eating food that made you naturally discuss your experiences of eating out at other places? The subject of Meer's Restaurant came up, and everyone joined in talking about the place and its history. After sharing their wonderful memories of being there, Lance's parents wanted to know what Ari thought, seeing it was her first time to visit.

She replied, "I love a good cheeseburger, but Meer's cheeseburger is phenomenal. When it was placed in front of me, my eyes could not believe what I saw! It was huge, juicy, and loaded. I've never seen or eaten anything like it." They all agreed.

Kate cleared the table and brought out the coffee, and Lance knew the time had come. Both were somewhat nervous—more so for Ari. Lance said, "Mom, Dad, we have news."

Kate took a deep breath and held it. Andy could see the announcement coming and was glad.

Lance continued, "We're getting married."

Pushing her chair back, Kate stood and moved to hug Arielle. She whispered in her ear, "I'm so happy to have a daughter." Her voice was choked up with emotions.

Excitement filled the air. Lance's parents were totally accepting of their engagement. The normal questions followed. "Have you set a date yet? Do you have any details?"

Their first announcement had gone wonderfully well. They sat and talked; Kate and Andy both wanted to know their soon-to-be daughter-in-law better.

This was one of those times when no one wanted the night to end. Lance simply could not make himself return to base—not just yet. They drove to Wayne's Drive-In, ordered shakes and then began to make plans. Lance had only a few weeks before he left the country. Together they agreed to put in for a few days leave to go see her parents and tell them the news. First things first meant filling out the proper paperwork, having it approved by their commanding officer, and making the 670-mile trip. They were young and in love; being together was all that mattered.

Outside the nurses' lounge, up and down the corridor, people and patients heard screams of excitement. Natalie, Barbara, and Joan were on break with a few other nurses. Even though Ari was being obvious, Natalie hadn't spotted the ring. When she finally did, a room full of excited women surrounded her to see the ring, get the details, fuss over her, and find out the date. She wasn't sure she would show them the ring in a group setting because she was so reserved, but nevertheless she enjoyed all the attention surrounding her ring.

# Forty-Three

When Lance and Ari left the base early Friday morning several hours before reveille sounded, the crisp morning air greeted them. They made a right turn on Route 62 and headed toward Amarillo. They had decided to take Ari's car because the trunk was bigger, and the cooler was on the back seat for drinks and snacks. Theirs would be a gas and restroom stops only trip. Now on the road, they saw the firing range on the right and open fields on the left. Traffic was very light. Shortly before Amarillo, they took the entrance ramp onto I 40. Ari was trying to plan their arrival so they'd be on the west side of Amarillo in daylight.

It was now her turn to be the tour guide. Slowing a little, she directed Lance's attention to the left side of the car. She asked, "Do you see them set back off the road?"

"Are those cars? The front ends are buried in the dirt!"

They were passing Cadillac Ranch in Texas. The owner, an artist of sorts, had buried the front end of the cars in the dirt, leaving the remainder of the cars to extend from the ground at a slight angle. It was a graveyard of caddies from 1949 to 1963. In a nice neat row, the cars pointed their tail fins into the air. Each car had been adorned with the owner's artistic paint job until tourists took it upon themselves to redecorate for him. As they drove by, all Lance could do was shake his head.

They approached a sign that read "Santa Rosa—60 miles." It would be a good place to stop. A little further down the road was Ari's welcome home sign—"Welcome to New Mexico." When they crossed into her home state, she was that much closer to her parents' home. Taking one of the exit ramps into Santa Rosa, the time had come to refuel and change drivers. While Lance pumped the gas, Ari prepared some food to snack on. Theirs was like a well-timed pit stop. In just a few minutes, they were pulling on to the entrance ramp and back on to the interstate racetrack.

While on the interstate, they traveled at a good speed. However, when they pulled on US 550, they would be traveling hundreds of miles on a two-lane road. Merging into light traffic, they settled in.

Albuquerque rose up in the horizon and to the north were mountains. Ari grabbed the map to make sure before she said, "We're looking for I 25 heading north."

"Got it. What's the next good sized town north?" he asked. Folding back the map to look, she said, "It looks like that will be Bernalillo, and our next turn is right there—US 550."

"Let's look for a McDonald's to grab a quick burger."

Ari smiled at the suggestion; they would like more than a snack, but she was in a hurry to get home. She was bursting at the seams to show Mom her ring. Ari had been on drives home before; this one was different. She was with Lance, and he was bringing out the best of life. She wondered, *What is it about love? The way I feel about life has changed. Being with Lance brings to me a freedom to live as never before.*

As they entered the city, the tall buildings marked the downtown area where many corporations had their offices. Just ahead was I 25. Moving into the far-right lane, Lance took the exit ramp north. In the rearview mirror, he saw the tall buildings, and out the front window, they saw the beautiful mountains ahead.

With Lance back at the wheel, they were swiftly conquering the road. They were in and out of Bernalillo in no time. Route 550 started out as a four-lane road until they were outside of town. He was happy they had gassed up there because they were now traveling in a desolate country. Up ahead was a sign that read "Los Alamos National Laboratory—Exit CR 4."

"Ari, I have heard guys talking about Los Alamos; it's top secret and requires the highest security. I think seeing it would be intriguing. But I like being out in the field with my men. You might like this; I also heard it's where they built the first starship, Enterprise."

"Oh, stop! I love those movies."

They laughed together as Lance continued, "There's something about the science of firing a projectile with precision. Those guys are all about future weapons. Artillery is my thing. Guess we all have our niche."

Ari liked long drives, and she rejoiced that Lance was enjoying the journey too. Yellow warnings sign appeared often with the squiggly arrows alerting the driver to a section of dangerous curves ahead. Her car hugged the road with each curve. Then she spotted the sign for Angel Peak Park. A series of flashbacks enter Ari's mind.

"Lance, Angel Peak! I love the day my dad took us to Angel Peak, and we hiked several trails. I have to tell you that seeing Angel Peak at the viewing area was breathtaking. You know what my dad did?"

Lance shook his head.

"He planned for us to have our Saturday family devotional out there in the beauty of nature. I treasure that memory."

For the next few minutes, Ari recapped the family outing—the rattlesnake in the road, the rules for hiking. Her mouth became like a fountain as her childhood memories bubbled up and out. Lance loved hearing all about those times. He was getting to know her and his future in-laws better every day.

Bloomfield and Route 64 were just ahead; in 30 minutes she would be home. She began to fill Lance in on more of the family details. He already knew her parents owned an insurance agency. Mike wrote the policies and kept in contact with their clients while Judy answered the phone, took care of the books, and everything else.

"Joey is married and living in Arizona with a busy one year old who is crawling and pulling herself up. Sammy is married and living in Kentucky. Neither of them will be here today." She added pertinent details to help with small talk at the dinner table. Just outside of Bloomfield was another sign that caused Ari to bubble up inwardly—Farmington Lake. In an excited tone of voice she told Lance all about her times of being there and how one of the best days of her life was when she learned to water ski.

On their left, running parallel to the road, was the San Juan River. Just as they came into Farmington, on the left was the Anamis River and then they were on E. Main Street. The feeling of being home rushed into Ari's heart.

Home is the state of being with peace and the profound sense of belonging. As 5:00 p.m. approached, the drive was nearing an end. A somewhat choked-up Ari told Lance to turn left. In two blocks, she would be coming home for the first time with the love of her life.

# Forty-Four

Judy was delighted to have Ari coming home. Her firstborn would be the last one to be married. In her mind, she was running through her to-do list. Mike was on his own today. When they first began to operate the agency together after she quit the photography business, she had wondered how it would be spending so much time with one another. She realized now that the business had just brought them closer together.

In this time-crunched day of making preparations for Ari and Lance, she needed to get the food bought, flowers for the table, and the house and bedrooms cleaned. Her mind drifted to Mike. These days they were not often apart. In the next instant, her heart filled with an unexplainable good feeling—Ari will be home! The absence of her baby girl was like a missing piece in her soul. For years she had known they would eventually have a permanent empty nest. But the reality hadn't set in until now. A family of five began with two and returned to two.

Her enthusiasm showed in Judy's step as she walked through the grocery store. In aisle three she spotted Grace from church. She stopped to greet her and mentioned that Ari was coming home and would be at church on Sunday with her fiancé, an Army captain. They chatted until they realized they were blocking the aisle. At the checkout counter, Mary the checkout girl, asked how she was doing, and Judy recanted that Ari was coming home. As Mary entered the prices, she got the scoop. With her groceries packed in brown-paper bags, Judy walked to the car. Her last stop was the flower shop where she greeted Marge.

"I need a bouquet of flowers today," she said.

"Do you have something in mind, Judy?" she asked.

"Yes, all bright colors."

"Take a look at the groupings I have here in the cooler. The ones on the left are $15, and the ones on the right are $25." Judy pointed to the bouquet on the left, middle shelf, on the end. Marge casually enquired if anything special was going on. She knew that Mike and Judy often hosted dinners for clients and company coworkers and friends.

"Yes, Martha, Ari is coming home for us to meet her fiancé."

Marge excitedly asked for details as she wrapped the flowers, and Judy bubbled over as she shared them.

Finally arriving home from her errands, she quickly brought the bags into the kitchen. First, she needed to put the flowers in water. Pulling out her crystal vase, she carried it over to the sink to fill. With care she arranged the bright blossoms in the vase and stepped back to look. Satisfied, she carried the arrangement into the dining room and placed it on the table.

Judy needed to begin cooking. The phone rang, interrupting her plans. Mike wanted to know where the Pearson's file could be found. Over the next few hours, food was being cooked, rooms cleaned, and clothes laid out.

Mike closed up shop early and headed home. He helped with the last minute details and got cleaned up and dressed in the casual clothes that Judy had set out for him. Everything was ready, there was no time left, when they heard car a door close. They were here!

Judy was the first one out the door with Mike close behind. As soon as Lance opened the car door for Ari, the happy reunion began. Mother and daughter hugged in a new kind of embrace. Judy took Ari's left hand and lifted it up to get a good look at her ring.

"Oh, Ari, it's beautiful. When we have time, I want to know all about the trip to the jeweler!"

Mike too took a look at her hand to see her ring and smiled at Ari with approval. Mike shook Lance's hand, and excited chatter filled the air. Mike motioned for them to head toward the house. As they stepped inside, they smelled the scent of flowers, a clean house, and the aroma of Mom's home cooking. Some serious spoiling was going to take place. Even though Ari was 26, Judy had stepped back in time to when she had taken care of her as a child. The feeling was good then, and it felt wonderful now. Mike and Judy's hearts were blessed that for just a few days, the nest would no longer be empty.

Ari's small overnight bag went into her old room, and Lance would stay in Sammy's and Joey's room. The time had come to talk. Ari and Lance sat side by side on the couch as Mike and Judy sat in the chairs across from them. Judy wanted to know about the pursuit and the romance. Ari looked into Lance's smiling face and began to detail their first date. The embarrassing miscommunication about what would have been their first date was not mentioned, although it would make a great anniversary story someday.

She left out the chemistry and the description of his eyes that first night. She focused on the Patriot Officers' Club, knowing her dad with his military experience would like to hear about it. Just as they began to talk about going places together, a noise in the kitchen demanded Judy's attention. Both Judy and Ari went into the kitchen together. As she was about to round the corner, she gave Lance a sweet smile.

A pot was beginning to boil over, and the lid was about to come off. Reaching for her stove mitten, Judy quickly took action. She asked Ari to bring out the dinner rolls and butter as they entered the world of girl talk. "Ari, Lance is a handsome man!" They shared some highlights of the romance before returning to the men.

Mike changed the subject from the pursuit to their spiritual lives. He said, "Ari tells me you were raised Baptist. Were you and your parents in the same church in Lawton while you grew up?" Mike wanted to hear that Lance was saved. *She might be twenty-six, but she's still my baby girl,* his father's heart thought. Mike was delighted when Lance opened up and told him about his family's rich spiritual heritage. They began swapping God stories until the girls came back in to say that it was time to go into the dining room and eat.

Steam rose from several platters of food as they held hands to say grace. Mike led them in prayer. "Father God, we thank You for Your abundance this day. Bless this food, our time together, and be in our midst. In Jesus' name I pray. Amen."

Judy squeezed Mike's hand before letting go. Ari's time to glow had come. Laughter filled the air when they told them about the best cheeseburger in the world in a building that looked like it was about to fall apart. Time paused as hearts were renewed, and a new relationship began. Love and laughter filled the air.

Saturday passed in a flash. The unity in the spirit that everyone was feeling enabled them relax. Mike needed to go to the office, so Ari took that opportunity to let Lance see it before showing him around Farmington. Judy kept busy at home being Mom again. It was a long, but short day; in other words, the day was full but flew by. Again at the evening meal, hearts were connected as stories were shared. At the end of the meal, Mike asked them to go into the front room where they took time to honor God together. In so doing, they entered into another dimension of relationship. Before ending the night, Lance wanted to have some time alone with Ari, so they walked down the block in the crisp night air. For Ari, being home felt good. When they returned to the house, they retired for the night.

As Ari turned out her bedroom light, she saw the breeze move the curtains in the window. Slipping into bed brought back fond memories. She thought about life and how being in love could be so wonderful. As sleep began to come, she could hear the train whistle blowing off in the distance as it rolled thru the countryside.

On Sunday morning, Mike drove them all to church. Ari was excited to be in her house of God. It had been such a long time. She had told

Lance awesome stories of God's being there and touching people's lives. Now he was going to feel the atmosphere, and she wanted them to experience it together. Ari's church family made a huge fuss when they came in the door. Hugs and handshakes happened with every step.

Grace had the church ready to welcome them home. The sound of the organ turning on prompted people to come into the sanctuary. Mike led them in, letting Judy enter the pew first and then following her as Ari and Lance sat on the end. The organist began the service with the song "What a Friend We Have in Jesus." When the church erupted into worship, it was lively, and Lance noticed.

Pastor Smith took the podium and everyone sat down, but the woman in front of Lance was feeling the Spirit. Boldly she spoke in her heaveny language for the church to hear. The way she spoke brought alarm to Lance. In a loud manner, she started to peel off a litany of odd sounds that were words in a foreign language.

Ari knew Lance was about to step out into the foyer and even before his first move, she placed her hand on his leg conveying her assurance it would be all right. He turned to face her, eye to eye. His expression showed that he was not pleased. In that moment, the first time since they had met, he closed his heart. He made a quick exit to the foyer where he paced back and forth. Running through his mind was the thought, *What is that scripture about testing the spirits?* It would not come to mind when Ari appeared.

"Lance, what is the matter?"

"That woman was out of control. She made no sense at all." He turned and walked away from her, trying to figure out if they could be a two denominational marriage because right now he had serious concerns.

"Lance, the apostle Paul guides us about speaking in tongues. Right after you stepped out, another person interpreted for her. The message expressed God's love for each of us. That is exactly what the gift of tongues is for—the edification of the church."

"I have been in discussions about tongues. It seems too radical for me."

A gathering went unnoticed when the foursome had entered the church. Angels who had not seen each other in years embraced and blessed each other. The new angel, who was the guardian to Lance, was introduced and welcomed and soon was needed.

Rushing over to Lance in the middle of his struggle to accept the idea of the gift of tongues, he lifted his head towards heaven as if asking for advice. Moving his left hand just over Lance's head, a beam emanated from his palm. For a split second, Lance had a vision. As in a movie, he suddenly saw the instant the Holy Spirit had entered the upper room in the book of Acts. He saw the look upon their faces, the tongues of fire over each person, and heard them speaking in other languages. In an instant he felt and saw all they had experienced that day.

Ari interrupted him. "Lance, please can we talk about this later? Please come back into the service with me."

If it were not for the new experience of seeing Pentecost in a vision, he would have told her no. Now, his bedrock foundation had been shaken. Although his theology was in question, he agreed to go back in the service. His angel drifted back into conversation with the other angels, and they swapped God stories.

Ari's angel burst out laughing. He said, "You had to see it. There was Ari in her quarters in her seeking-God posture, praying God would bring a godly man into her life. So God released His plan to bring the two them together, and Ari at first refused. God was using her friend Natalie to bring them together, and Ari was balking.

"Now get this—they had a first date planned, and she forgot! Well, we—referring to Lance's angel and I—we put grace into motion, and it came to a time when only one wooden door separated them. Then Ari opened her life to meet Lance, and it was all over. We high-fived, gave praises to God, and the rest is history. Truly a match made in heaven!"

One of the angels, who had known Arielle and her God destiny in life, approached her angel. He wanted to know, so he asked, "Has she discovered it yet?"

"No, not yet," he responded.

Mike and Judy were praying in the spirit while Ari and Lance were out talking. Holding hand, heads bowed quietly, they petitioned God for His help. They were relieved and thankful when Ari and Lance soon entered and took their places once again.

At the conclusion of the service, finishing the meet and greet, they all returned home for a Sunday meal. Ari's heart had sensed a deep spiritual and emotional disconnect with Lance, and quietly she felt panic. Things were not going the way she had hoped or so she thought. They needed time alone together, and it came after the lavish meal Judy cooked. The couple's pressing need to talk was understood by her parents.

Reaching for Lance's hand, Ari said, "Let's take a walk."

No words were spoken between them for awhile. As if retracing a childhood path, they stopped in front of her elementary school and sat on a wooden bench in the shade of the trees. Lance was at a loss for words. He went into the Old Pentecostal church one person and came out another. His rational, articulate, and analytical mind had experienced the supernatural. Although he could do the geometry to fire ordnance more than a mile and have it hit with precision, he was now struggling to not only understand what he saw in the vision, but how to explain it to Ari.

As she tried to speak, he put his hand up to her lips and stopped her. He said, "I have something to tell you." Her heart sank. "I don't know what to say so I just might as well blurt it out."

Although Ari had seen difficult medical emergencies, stopped arteries from bleed outs, and dealt with a person dying, she had never felt like she was dying before.

He took a breath and said, "I saw something while we were in the foyer." Since she wore her emotions on her face when she was with him, he quickly saw her deep concern turn into sheer confusion. He shared with her in detail his view of the upper room the instant the Holy Spirit arrived.

Ari was stunned. With each detail he shared, she wondered how he could have seen and experienced all of it during the time he was in the foyer when to her it was but a blink of an eye.

He shared for more than an hour, and at the end, she explained to Lance that God had given him an open eyed vision where your eyes can be open and yet you are seeing something happening beyond your current circumstances. It had all happened in the foyer where they had been suddenly divided and with one experience from God they were cemented back together.

It was up to Lance to embrace the supernatural, and that question would be answered another day. However, Lance made Ari promise not to share his experience with anyone. If he outranked her, it would have been an order. But for now Lance had passed his first and second evaluation tests. Soon would come his third and final test.

Ari had arranged for them to have lunch with her pastor, seeing he would be performing the ceremony. For the sake of time and being considerate of the pastor, they met in a restaurant near the church. Sitting down at a table, they enjoyed some small talk, ordered lunch, and then moved into serious conversation about their steps to stay pure and guidance on how to handle their time while they were separated when Lance was in Korea.

Pastor Smith gently asked the hard questions and was confident in them as an engaged Christian couple. A time was discussed for their wedding day, and seeing it would take place the following year, they understood they had plenty of time for the details. Their food arrived, a blessing was prayed, and rich fellowship was enjoyed.

Leaving the restaurant, they looked into each other's eyes, feeling they were on the right path. Now the rush was on to get home, pack their bags, and return to base. It was hard for Judy to say goodbye; she cried. Mike had already said his goodbyes that morning before leaving for work. What comforted Judy was knowing that in a short time, Ari would be home to stay; her enlistment was up soon, and she would be coming home.

At first, Ari and Lance were quiet in the car as they left Farmington. Near Farmington Lake Lance remarked, "Pastor Smith is tough; he pulled no punches. Seems to me, he would have been a good Marine."

# FORTY-FIVE

The race was on. Lance had just over two weeks to get ready to deploy to Korea. He had to put in his papers, finish his advanced training, and pack up his belonging for storage. The whole process was hard for him; all he wanted to do was spend time with Arielle. Thankfully, there were still the opportunity for a wonderful evening together. In the armory building, an Officers Gala event would be held for all the advanced artillery graduates.

Generals, colonel, majors, and captains took part in the officers' dinner. Catering trucks brought in the needed equipment, including lavish decorations. The Army's military band was present for a night of musical entertainment. Lance was in his dress blues, and Ari wore an attractive gown. This official function evolved into a romantic evening for the couple. The tables and chairs took up most of the space. A two-foot-high platform would stage the ceremonies and directly behind the platform were several of the newest artillery cannons. It would be a night to remember.

Walking up to the receiving line, the couple entered as if they owned the room. They were poised, elegant, and confident. Tonight Lance and others would be acknowledged for finishing their training. Their first priority was to work the room and meet superior officers—part of the official etiquette in this type of dinner. Work it well, and you meet the standard. Fail and scrutiny may follow you. Ari and Lance passed with flying colors.

The lights dimmed, signaling the attendees to take their seats; the meal was about to be served. Taking the microphone, tonight's host welcomed everyone. Visiting dignitaries were recognized and applauded. A short speech was given, ending with the cue to begin the meal. From the rear area, waiters came out to serve each table. Everything was top notch—the food, the service, and the music. As the meal ended, a general was introduced who took the podium.

"I am commending the artillery commanders on their completing their training. America stays strong with our military strength. You men have proved our ability to defend our country's interest." He continued to give an inspiring speech.

When formal duties were completed, the time had come to break off and dance. On the dance floor, it was only the two of them. Moving across the floor as one, the scope of the room narrowed down to just them. Dancing is done in unity and is an intimacy shared by two people who are moved by the music. No words were needed. They were grabbing every minute together, knowing Lance would soon be deployed.

When love is thriving, the last thing new lovers want is to be apart. They had reconciled with the fact by knowing that in six months Lance would return on leave. Letters would be shared to keep the flames of love ignited, and the occasional phone calls would keep the two hearts connected. How do you prepare to be apart once love has made life great? You don't.

Ari rose early; she put on the dress she wore for their first date. After making sure her hair was just right, she did her makeup to look her best and grabbed a padded envelope by the door. She was on a mission to see Lance off at the airport. The government charters planes to take soldiers to their new assignments. Soon Lance would be boarding a 737 on its way to Anchorage and then on to Korea.

The time had come to board, and Lance was taking one last look for her. He was third in line to pass through the gate when he heard her calling him. They met in a deep kiss and embrace. "I thought I was too late. Here, I have a surprise for you. Don't open it until you're in your new quarters."

"I love you, Ari." He had to leave, but the tug on his heart was heavy, and he wanted to stay with her. She wanted him to stay. Ari stood at the window to see if she might get one more glimpse of him through a plane window until the plane taxied away.

The soldier at the gate stepped up to the car and asked for his papers. Lance handed them to him, and the guard went inside the gatehouse. Through the window he could see him pick up the phone. Returning, he said, "Here are your papers, Commander. You're expected at the Turtle Farm." The soldier saluted Lance as he entered Camp Stanley, a short drive to the north from Seoul. Walking into the building known as the Turtle Farm, Lance was directed to the major's office. During this tour of duty, Lance would be part of the 1st Battalion, 31st Division FA. Camp Stanley was one of the many artillery units defending South Korea in a time of fragile peace.

Camp Stanley was at first a tent city in 1955. The construction of the first buildings began in 1969. Not much had changed since then. Lance pulled up to his assigned quarters—one of the first erected Quonset huts in the rear of the camp. As he stepped out of the car, he took a moment to look at the towering hills right outside the camp. From his previous tour, he had hiked to the top of the hill. From the top he could see the sprawling city of Uijeongbu on the opposite side of camp. Beyond that, not far to the north was the DMZ.

To say his quarters were modest would be accurate. The hut was not built for comfort but function. In the fifteen years since its construction, upgrading the environmental needs, specifically the heating systems, would have been a welcome improvement to the officers staying there. In January and February, it would be cold. Grabbing his duffle bag, he entered the door and stepped into his room.

*Now I can open my gift from Ari.* Ripping open the envelope, he found two items—a 5x7 picture of the two of them and her red scarf. He could smell her perfume. A gift with memories! Refocusing on why he was there at sixteen hundred hours, he had a briefing at HQ and then chow. He had just enough time to write Ari a letter and thank her for the gifts.

The common area had a table and chairs. The afternoon sunlight was coming through the window to illuminate the room. He was alone as he wrote.

> Dear Ari,
> I am settled in to my quarters; it makes Fort Sill look like the Ritz. I miss you. As I am writing, an image of us driving to Meer's comes into my mind. Your red scarf was flowing in the wind with the top down. Your brown hair was about your face. Riding in my car was never so enjoyable until you came into my life. As I am looking ahead, this tour is different. I know time will pass quickly, and we will soon begin our lives together. My heart aches to be with you.

Lance detailed what his life was now like in Korea. He was sharing his heart in ways he had not done with anyone before. After addressing and sealing the envelope, he had a little time to get ready for the briefing. A schedule was given out to commanders for training in the live firing range. Lance's first assigned time would be in two weeks. It was a trial run of men and equipment. The second exercise scheduled was in January when he would have a full week of exercises.

Ari's life with Lance had been filled with love, adventure, and fun, and she reluctantly returned to the routine she had before she had met him. Natalie and her other friends filled her social gaps. When the four of them were together at the Patriot Club, they all talked about Ari's upcoming wedding. Her time to shine as the bride-to–be had arrived. Topics of discussion including color schemes for the dresses, and whether there would be traditional vows or would they recite their own. They wanted to hear about her church and the type of ceremony they were planning. They wanted to know as many details as possible and enjoyed fussing over the future bride.

The wedding was being planned a year in advance, but Ari's enlistment was up in just four months, and she had decided to leave the Army. Knowing she would be leaving soon, she let the girl talk swirl around her. At the end of each daytime shift, she hurried to her quarters and bounded up a few steps to her mailbox in hopes of finding a letter. She knew time was a premium for Lance, and that is why each letter was precious to her. She could never hear enough about the ways he conveyed to her that she was loved.

He wrote, "Ari, I'm going to the Air Force Base in Seoul on the third Saturday of the month. I'll call you from there at ten hundred hours your time. It will be twenty-two hundred hours in Seoul."

In their excitement to talk to each other, it took a few moments for them to hear the sound of their voices and make the adjustment of calling halfway around the world since there was a time lag of five seconds. In the beginning they each kept talking over the other. Although it would have been easier if they would say Roger when each of them was finished, in reality that was too rigid. In future calls they would become accustomed to the lag and focus on the details of Lance's leave. Their first phone call was driven by the need of lovers to reconnect.

Outside of Ari's quarters, she listened for the last time as an Army captain to the sharp, clear notes of the trumpet playing reveille at six hundred hours. Tears filled her eyes. The Army had brought many changes and challenges into her life—education, discipline, experience, and Lance. She planned to savor this day; it was the end to a season of her life. She wanted to remember the time she had given to taking care of the needs of her patients. Ari's education, training, and experience had been used to bring healing to others. Coming into the Army, she was building a life for herself. Leaving the Army, she would be building a life with Lance.

The girls had planned a small party for her on this night. She came to Fort Sill alone and on assignment. She would be leaving alone, but richer than when she had arrived. In the morning, she would be a civilian once again as she loaded up her car with the same amount of clothing and belongings as the first day she drove out of Farmington three years ago.

Approaching Bentley Gate, she saluted the soldier on guard duty for the last time. Exiting the gate, she turned her car toward home and reflected on her drive with Lance to meet her parents. She even laughed when she thought about Lance's implying the starship Enterprise had been built at Los Alamos. At home, she had already secured a job at the local hospital as an ICU nurse. She would be moving into her old bedroom and becoming part of a family of three. The nest would no longer be empty for a little while, and Mike and Judy welcomed her home.

Nightmare Range was true to its name. Stepping beyond the camouflage flap, Lance walked toward his unit. Camp Stanley's artillery unit was filled with new recruits. This joint exercise would bring him needed training. January had a way of hardening men against the toughest elements in the country. Captain Lance had just been given the firing coordinates. Shouting orders, men and the weapon came alive. Wearing communication gear, he was listening to commands from the Div. Tach. Op Center. In the next few days, he would see the proficiency these men had learned in their basic training. They stood to the ready, and the command was given.

Lance shouted, "Fire!"

A puff of smoke belched from the muzzle of the cannon as the projectile flew to hit the mark. With the recoil of the cannon, the shell was ejected, and in a fluid motion, the men reloaded. The recruits were learning to work as one to aid in their efficiency with the goal of scoring high marks.

The hillsides were marked with numbers to easily see where the shells had exploded. Loading shells into cannons offered the men warmth from the bitter cold. On both sides of the DMZ were artillery units in a constant state of readiness. Tension was very high most of the time. The live exercise was for the benefit of North Korea to see America's resolve. They would practice until they were battle ready.

Returning to Camp Stanley at the end of a weeklong training was Lance's first opportunity to rest. Opening the Quonset hut door, he realized the temperature was not much warmer, but at least he didn't see his breath. When he removed his boots and socks, he saw the frostbite. He could feel his feet were cold, but he had no time to deal with it until now. He was grateful that he only had a mild case and could treat it himself. This round of training at Nightmare Range had been some of the coldest days of his life—a price he would gladly pay to be part of this unit and keep America strong.

Weary, he had time to think of Ari and wanted to write a letter to connect with her, but knew it would have to wait. He had reports to do and briefings to attend.

# Forty-Six

For twenty-six weeks, Lance and Ari lived separate lives building toward a life together. On Lance's leave, he flew into Farmington Airport. As his plane came to a stop on the tarmac, stairs were rolled up to the front door of the plane. Ari intently watched each person deplane as she looked for her loved one. When she saw the best specimen of a man walk down the stairs, she knew it was Lance. Passing through the gate doors, Ari ran to embrace him. A passionate kiss brought an end to their time of separation.

Back at the house, Judy left Mike to fend for himself at the agency while she prepared to welcome Lance home. Sammy's room was ready for him, and a hot meal was on the stove. On Ari's desk in her bedroom was a list of details to go over for the wedding. In the next two weeks, all the planning would have to get done. At the top of their list, however, was whitewater rafting—fun first, planning second.

In the evening at the kitchen table, Mike wanted to hear all about Korea. Lance's stories brought back memories to Mike's time in the service. When he came to the frostbite on Nightmare Range, Mike shook his head, recounting a night when he was in a foxhole during the Korean Conflict, pinned down by crossfire. When he peeked above the lip of dirt, he would hear the sound of bullets whizzing by as the enemy took shots at him.

"Lance, it was coldest right before sunrise. My foxhole was half-filled with water, and the top of it had frozen. I wanted to run to safety, but each time I peeked out, the bullets would fly past me. God watched over me those two nights. Can you believe I didn't get frostbite? After that, nothing could be as dangerous."

Neither Judy nor Ari had ever heard that story. It was just three soldiers sharing life in the military. Pride for her husband welled up in Judy's heart; she had never known the real price he had paid.

Each day had its own joy. Ari took Lance to the lookout at the Plateau. "Lance, did you know that on the Gemini mission the astronauts could see two manmade things from space?"

Lance enjoyed Ari's sharing her childhood memories. "No, what did they see?"

"They could see the Great Wall in China and the steam plume from the Four Corners generating station right out there. Can you see it?"

As she pointed northwest, he said, "Yes, I do."

"My dad worked as a boilermaker for over twenty years at the plant. Then Mom and Dad opened the insurance agency in town."

They both talked until sunset as they watched the sun drop beyond the horizon. Then they double-timed it back to the car before it was dark.

Their time together had started with an embrace and kiss; now it was ending with the same. Lance was returning to his post at Camp Stanley, and Ari was returning to work in her favorite part of ICU—coronary care. In the days ahead, she would continue to prepare for the wedding.

What would Arielle do without her mother and best friend? They teamed up to get all the preparations for the wedding finished. The amount of work required for a single event for one day was utterly amazing. One of the biggest events in a girl's life was her wedding day. How Ari dreamed of this day, and now that was nearing, it was totally different than she had imagined. It was even better! Judy now had two jobs—secretary in the insurance office with Mike and wedding planner with her daughter. She relished both of her jobs, working for two of the loves in her life.

The flowers and wedding cake were now ordered. The hall in the basement of the church had been reserved. The time of the wedding had been set for three in the afternoon, and the printed invitations had now arrived. Seated at the kitchen table, Judy and Ari began to address the invitations. Judy could write in a beautiful script style, so she was appointed to address the envelopes. One hundred invitations would be mailed out to family and friends, and a verbal invitation would be extended to her church family. Ari was in charge of writing an invitation to the family to come a week early. Years had passed since the entire family had time together. Rafting, horseback riding, hiking, and skiing on Farmington Lake were all on the table to be enjoyed. Between family, friends, and church family, they expected 250 people to help them celebrate their marriage.

# Forty-Seven

Joey's family arrived, and the house erupted into chaos. Voices were raised and hugs were shared. Clinging to Joey's leg was his daughter, who was not quite sure about this fanfare. Mike and Cindy, Joey's wife, gave each other a quick hug. Sammy and his wife were soon to arrive. The house would be full of life for the next week. They went into the front room to talk and catch up. An hour later, Sammy's car pulled into the drive, and the greetings started all over again. Lance was due in tomorrow, but for now, it was all hands on deck; the party had started.

In the days ahead, aunts and uncles and cousins would be pouring into Farmington. Each day's activities were open to everyone. Mike and Judy would hold down the fort to babysit and attend to details.

Ari and several of her family members met Lance at the airport. What a warm reception to an Army captain who had just finished his tour in Korea! His new assignment would be in the states, and his top priority was becoming a husband.

Even though his role in their lives had changed, Mike's fathering role returned to him, and it felt really good. All his children were under his roof again. Is there ever enough time once you find love? At each day's end, the room filled with the excitement of telling stories of that day's adventures.

The mood changed on Friday as things turned serious. The time had come for the last fitting on Ari's beautiful wedding dress. Tuxedos were picked up in town. The florist and bakery were contacted with schedule times of when to arrive at church. Women at the church had volunteered to decorate the hall in the basement. The rehearsal was at hand.

When the church doors opened, fifty people entered, surprising Pastor Smith. He had never had so many attend a rehearsal. He brought the group to attention and began walking them through the ceremony step by step. Afterwards, the attendees were invited to dinner at the local BBQ diner in town.

As for Lance, his parents and family escorted him out, explaining that he need not see Arielle after the dinner until the next day. Just as Ari was about to leave, she turned to look into the sanctuary. She reflected on exactly how much this church had contributed to her life. Since the day the fire broke out, this church had seen the power of God touch the lives of many families. People danced in the Spirit, and lives were restored by the healing power of God. People were delivered from the strongholds of evil. She remembered the day she was baptized in the Holy Spirit. This place was the only place for her to be married—before the God she loved so much.

It was Saturday morning, and all the women were up early because they had appointments to have their hair done in town. Judy had a friend coming to do Ari's makeup. Lance was staying in a hotel room with the men until the time when he needed to be at the church. Everyone would be dressed in their finest clothing for this special day—the last day Arielle and Lance would be single.

The phone was ringing and someone needed questions answered regarding problems that were popping up. Mike was assigned to handle the last-minute details. Today was Arielle's day; she was the focus of attention. Today the world revolved around her. Today was the day that every bride looks forward to.

In a panic, someone asked, "Where are the wedding bands?"

Someone reassuringly answered, "In the trusted care of the best man."

The church was nearly full as the organist began to play and quiet everyone. With joy she played a combination of keys to let people know it was time and then began to play the wedding processional. From the side of the church, Lance, his best man, and two others standing up with him, entered and walked to the center aisle and turned toward the back. In the back of the church, the ushers pulled open the doors for everyone to get a glimpse of Mike and Arielle standing in the foyer. A very beautiful bouquet of flowers was in Ari's right hand as she held onto her father's arm.

The first night Lance had seen her came back to him in a rush; she was stunning! In this moment, she was the most beautiful woman he had ever seen. Arielle's wedding dress brought out the very best in her. The sight of her took his breath away. The bridesmaids came into view from behind the doors to begin their walk down the aisle. Following them up the aisle came Mike with Arielle on his arm to do his last act as the predominant man in his daughter's life. As tough as he was, his eyes began to fill with tears.

Everyone stood to look at the beautiful bride. Upon reaching the wedding party, Mike kissed his daughter on the cheek, extended her hand to Lance's and stepped alongside of Judy in the first pew. A bridesmaid adjusted Ari's gown and took her flowers as they turned to face Pastor Smith. The organist slowly stopped the music.

Pastor Smith began by sharing Scripture about the joining of a man and woman. He challenged them to make God first in their hearts and then to hold each other in the second position. He shared that living out their faith would build for them a strong foundation upon Jesus Christ.

When the storms of life came, their marriage would survive. He directed them to face each other.

Pastor Smith asked, "Arielle, do you take Lance to be your lawful wedded husband through good times and bad, in sickness and health for as long as you shall live?"

"I do," she said as she looked into Lance's eyes as if the world had disappeared, and it was only the two of them. Her gentle, loving expression was a gift to only him. Judy grabbed Mike's arm and squeezed it hard.

Pastor Smith turned to Lance and said, "Lance, do you take Arielle to be your lawful wedded wife through good times and bad, in sickness and in health for as long as you shall live?"

"I do," he replied confidently. The best man stepped up to Lance and handed him the wedding bands. He handed his band to Ari, and Pastor Smith motioned for him to place the ring on Arielle's finger. She in kind placed her ring upon his finger as a burst of emotions filled her heart. She felt the elation held within wedding vows. Lance's joy was evident in his watery eyes.

Pastor Smith announced, "You may now kiss the bride!"

In an act of tenderness, Lance kissed Arielle for the first time as husband and wife. Pastor Smith asked them to turn toward the people, and in a loud, booming voice, he said, "I present to you Lance and Arielle, husband and wife!" Applause filled the room, and the organist loudly played music as the newlyweds walked down the aisle together.

In the foyer they exchanged hugs with the bridal party and lined up in the receiving line. The ushers escorted the parents first, and then pew by pew family and friends met the newlyweds. The ladies from the church headed directly downstairs to bring out the cake, appetizers, and drinks. Everyone rejoiced and entered into the celebration of this blessed event. Pictures were taken, the cake was cut, and as the center of attention, Lance and Ari talked to everyone.

Lance's parents embraced Arielle, welcoming her into the family. Seeing their son find a godly woman brought great joy to them. In their hearts they feel God's blessings today.

A celebration was taking place beyond human sight too. Angels were present to partake in the joys of this day. They knew that God had begun a good work. One couple joined together was destined to touch the lives of many. In these last days of church history, God would mold them for His divine purpose.

In a flash, several hours had passed. If time could have been suspended, they would have done it. The next phase of their plans was to begin right here. Everyone gathered at the front door of the church as they hurried to the decorated car. In the loving nucleus of their families and friends, they drove to their secret place. As they stood before their hotel room door, two lives would become one.

# FORTY-EIGHT

A day later, holding hands, they strolled onto the famous Fisherman's Wharf in San Francisco. For those growing up in small towns, this was like being on another planet. An endless line of restaurants offered mouth-watering specialty dishes. On one side of the boardwalk were all the buildings; on the other was an open marina with so many boats they couldn't be numbered.

Today, life was different. For the first time, they knew what it means to be one. Even if they stepped apart, they felt the other's immediate absence. At a glance into their partner's eyes, they knew each other.

The wharf was so big, they spent the day here, and the next day would be another one filled with sightseeing. Lance asked, "How do we choose which restaurant to eat in? I guess we'll have to stay longer and try them all."

There was no way for a person to be prepared to cross the Golden Gate Bridge. To them, it was clearly the most spectacular bridge in the world. Lance headed across the bridge to Golden Gate Bridge Park. He had heard the best view of the bridge was there.

Walking up to the viewing area, Ari said to Lance, "It's beautiful! To think men made this; it has to be one of the wonders of the world." Near them was a park service board with information on it. Lance drifted there and began to read.

He called to Ari, "You're not going to believe this!" He pointed to a post on the board. At first glance, she was stunned. "Future filming site of Star Trek IV: The Journey Home"! Looking at each other, they laughed.

Ari glibly replied, "I guess they'll have to fly the ship over from Los Alamos."

If it had not been for the time crunch, they would have stayed longer. This place felt good—just sitting for a while and taking it all in. The next thing on their must-do list was riding the cable cars. Their goal was to see all the sights they could squeeze in, ending with an excursion to Alcatraz Island.

Being in the military meant that moving was a constant requirement. Lance's assignment in the state was to be part of the ROTC Department at

Lamar University in Texas. The couple would be residing there for the next three years. Living close to campus, they busied themselves making a home. They had rented a furnished condominium. Not having furniture helped them keep things light with the knowledge they would eventually be relocating to their next assignment. They were also keeping their options open-ended. With her experience and training, Ari easily secured a job in a nearby hospital, working in the coronary care unit—a delight to her since the third love of her life was caring for heart patients.

A few blocks away from their condo was their new church home—an Assembly of God church with a good mix of young people and college students. The core of the membership was comprised of the local families. Ari enjoyed the active spiritual atmosphere at the church.

They lived the best of life there in Beaumont, Texas. When they weren't working, they were exploring. What better place? They had a huge national forest to the north. To the south was the Sabine National Wildlife Refuge where they went kayaking. To the west was Houston and to the southwest was the city of Galveston. A must-see on their sightseeing list was the place where General Sam Houston won the battle for the state of Texas. On the site is a monument ten feet taller than the Washington Monument because everything was bigger in Texas. Visitors to the site could read the history in the visitor center at the base of the monument and then take a tour of the infamous battleship Texas that is moored in the park.

Their next assignment was in Germany. At this point, it only seemed logical for Ari to request to have her commission reinstated as an Army nurse while Lance was assigned there. She put on a uniform again but this time in a foreign land. Medical cases were brought in from other parts of the world. If a soldier were injured and in serious condition, he would be airlifted to the base hospital in Germany.

Lance and Ari grew deeper in love. Because of their love, they felt they could take on the world. On leave they visited the beautiful sights of Europe, making the most of their time there.

Lance and Arielle both had an unquenchable thirst for knowledge. Taking courses and earning degrees were a part of their lives. Whatever they put their minds to, they achieved until there was a surprise.

One day Ari walked into the bedroom looking at Lance, although he did not notice her expression at first. She cleared her throat. Finally he realized she wanted him to ask a question.

"What's on your mind this morning, darling?"

"I'm late."

"No, honey. You can still make it to work on time."

Sweetening her smile, she repeated it again. "No, Lance, I'm late."

Confusion crossed into understanding, and he stated in a joyous voice, "You're late!"

In a slow nod, she confirmed his suspicions.

Now he was pumped and shouted loudly, "She's late!" He was jumping up and down on the inside. *I'm going to be a father! What wonderful news!* He took her in his arms as they embraced and hugged. They kept this news private from their friends at the base until her second trimester. Together, they made calls home to tell their parents of the news.

"Mom, ask Dad to come by the phone; I have news."

Judy yelled into the front room, "Mike, I need you to come to the phone." He eased up and out of the chair and came to stand in the kitchen.

Judy said, "Ari, he's here." Once they put the receiver where they both could hear, Judy said, "Okay, Ari, we can both hear you now."

"Mom, Dad, we're going to have a baby!"

Tears filled Judy's eyes; Mike shouted, "Congratulations!" Hearts were filled with joy upon hearing their news.

Now it was Lance's turn; the call was made. He made sure both his parents were at the phone when he said, "Mom, Dad, we're having a baby!" Happy voices could be heard; they wanted to know the due date.

"Will the baby be born there or will you be home by then?

Life suddenly began to evolve around the newest member of the family. Bethany would be born in the local hospital in Germany not far from base. Together, in the act of love, a baby was conceived. They started it together, and they were going to finish it together. Lance was by Ari's side; together as a team they labored to bring her into the world. She was their beautiful baby girl, born with hair long enough for the nurses to put a little pink bow in it. All they could do was look at their daughter in awe of God's miracle of birth. They were now a family of three.

Ari and Lance moved from being a couple to becoming parents. They had hoped for this day and welcomed the experience. What is it about becoming a family? It is when the things you lived and experienced as a child bubble up in you that you work to recreate for your child. In just a few months, they would be returning to Fort Sill.

Soon back home in the Lawton area, they were beginning to grow roots. In the following year, Raphael became the newest addition to the family. Theirs was now a family of four. This time, a support network surrounded them. Grandparents and friends helped fill in needed times as Ari and Lance continued to advance their lives. Ari, using her master's degree in nursing, would be teaching in the university while Lance entered Command General Staff College.

In the coming years, Ari would finish more classes and enter hospital administration employment. It would be the beginning of the end to the healthcare role in her life.

Like sliding tectonic plates, one sliding under the other creates a subduction zone. Ari was entering the administrative phase of her career as this part of her tectonic plate was sliding under her spiritual plate that was riding higher. Within her heart came the clashing of the two. Grinding slowly, one over the other, intense friction and heat began to accumulate until something had to give.

Ignoring her call to ministry, no longer allowing it to rise in her conscious mind, she would eventually find that it contributed to her feeling of unrest in her position in life. She thought if only she could bring change to the administration, she would meet her internal goal to see people healed. However, the feelings and desires we harbor within our subconscious might as well be invisible. It was as though there was an internal engine moving her forward in her blind attempts to meet the driving needs inside.

The defining day in her life—the day young Sammy had come home from the hospital in Colorado—set her life on a course to help people with health needs. The next significant fork in her path was hearing the argument in Pastor Billings' office. Her parents had been hurt deeply by the words he said to them that miracles ceased after the apostle died. They were sharp, hurtful words especially when they knew beyond a shadow of a doubt that God had healed Sammy. The final decision for her came in the betrayal of her close friend Susan. Ari's only fault was loving God and believing He healed the sick like her brother. The common denominator with all of these was the supernatural that brought joy to her family with Sammy's healing. Unfortunately, the aftereffects were too hard to handle for one young girl.

As a result she had made choice and created a mind set to do all she could in the medical profession. God had another plan for her. He will call us, give us prodding in the direction of His calling, but not overrule our free will. Arielle had seen hundreds of instantaneous healings in the Old Pentecostal Church, and yet she stepped into the medical profession and began to be used of God to bring healing to others while in school and in the marketplace.

Having a busy life is a good way of not dealing with internal baggage. Ari and Lance and their deep love for each other was enhanced with children. Their lives modeled God's plan for the family. He was first in their lives and their spouse was second with their children a close third. Discovering the joy of parenting, seeing the children's first steps, hearing their first words, and watching their children grow held a joy they gladly embraced.

Time passed by quickly—too quickly sometimes. Getting involved in hospital administration was not like hands-on healthcare as a nurse. The posturing for provision to benefit departments within the hospital structure began to grate on her. Right now, she would deal with it, but what was happening at work was like a mild infection within her.

Ari focused inwardly, and it was consuming her. Her dissatisfaction with her job was rising. She was used to succeeding in everything she attempted. With higher elements at work, a tug of war was being waged inside of her. She wanted to make things right, but the hospital politics were revolving around finances and not the care of patients. And so she set her sights on becoming the hospitals CEO.

# Forty-Nine

The proverbial corner office was only one step away for Ari. Being in administration, that office would be the culmination to all her hard work and goals to be the CEO.

The phone on her desk rang, bringing her out of a daydream. She was needed right away in the conference room down the hall where the annual budget meeting was taking place. When she walked in, all eyes were on her. She asked, "What is the problem?"

The accountant replied, "We're projecting being a million dollars over our proposed budget for next year. ICU, Surgery, and ER are saying they cannot cut any more resources in their departments."

Looking at the department directors while seeing their stony expressions, she said, "Give me their proposed budgets, and I'll go over them and make my final decision."

Ari turned and walked back to her office. Quibbling between the department heads continued for a few more minutes, and then they all left for their offices, determined they would not be the ones to make the cuts. Placing the binders on her desk, Ari returned to the work at hand.

The phone rang; it was the corner office. She listened to her boss dictate how the budget problem was going to go. She was left to tell the people how and where their budget had been cut. The emergency room had lost the battle this time and would have to find new ways of saving money.

Over the last few months, Lance had been watching Ari retreat inward. It is not like her to do this! Being blessed with natural instincts and wisdom to handle most everything life had thrown at her, she now hit a brick wall. The immovable forces before her consumed all her internal resources and wore her down. Lance wanted to fix it for her, even if he knew that it was her struggle to win not his. As she came to the tipping point, her ability to look at the clues and see the cause and effect was no longer working.

Right now her relief valve was her joy in being with the children. Bethany and Raphael were thriving in the loving care of the family nucleus. The years had been rolling by. Although Ari and Lance had the best life had to offer; unfortunately, in some ways, life was becoming more difficult. Sleepless nights, loss of appetite, and not being able to do the things she enjoyed to lift her spirits had taken a toll on her.

But tonight, it was time to attend the Wednesday night service at church. The children had their groups, and Lance and Ari fed on the spiritual life released in the worship and praise. During the worship, Ari's heart and spirit felt the burden of work lift off, and it felt good.

"Go to Brownsville!" she heard. Ari stopped singing and looked around. She had heard someone speak in her left ear. But no one was near her; Lance was on the other side. It had been a long time since she had experienced the supernatural. The voice caused her to be taken aback. She told no one, but something began within her. People in church had been talking about the revival taking place there. The stories reminded her of the activities in the early days of her life.

She weighed the possibilities of taking the 850-mile trip to Brownsville. *It's time to talk with Lance,* she decided.

On Saturday morning, the coffee was ready. When it was just the two of them, she said, "Lance, I've been thinking about going to the Brownsville revival. I've heard God is really on the move down there. What do you think about my taking off a few days, and Beth and I attending a few meetings?"

Lance didn't need time to think. He had always known the supernatural was a huge part of her life. She had been fully invested in their education, his career in the military, and fulfilling her work obligation. She was a wonderful, loving mother and wife, and she thought of everyone else before herself. This decision was a no-brainer for him.

"I think it would be a wonderful idea!" he agreed.

Funny how generational things can be triggered; Beth was nearly the same age as Ari was when she first attended the Old Pentecostal Church and witnessed firsthand the Holy Spirit being manifested. Now Ari was excited for her own daughter to experience Brownsville. The plans were made for a mother and daughter adventure in God.

Talking with people who had been there, Ari heard that lines formed early, and so they planned their schedules accordingly. Beth would need reading materials while they stood in line. Ari was going to bring a big purse to hold water bottles and snacks and a book. She seldom had time to read for pleasure. An older woman at church had given her a book about Kathryn Kuhlman's miracle ministry, and standing in line would be a good time to read it.

Experience is a great teacher. Standing in line directly in front of the church were hundreds of people. Filled with excitement, they began waiting for the doors to open. It was hot in the sun, and Ari and Bethany could have used hats and sunscreen. The people in line with them were all talkative. The two of them listened to stories and experiences of those around them. People would offer pointers when others revealed that this was their first visit. A number of people came in a group from a church. The people behind them had come from eastern Texas. They had ridden in a 12-passenger van through the night to get there. The pastor asked Ari how she had decided to come to the revival.

Reluctantly, she said in a low voice, "I was in our Wednesday night service when I heard a voice telling me to go to Brownsville."

The pastor's mouth dropped open in disbelief. "Last month, I was riding my mower cutting the grass, telling God I wanted my own stories to tell. I heard a voice say the same words as you did. I knew it was God. Now we come back weekly to get another filling just by being in the atmosphere. When you get close to the doors, you'll feel it."

Beth looked like she was reading; however, she was taking it all in, wondering what they were talking about. *How could this church be so different than ours at home?* she wondered.

Finally there was forward movement in the line. The doors would be opened soon, and an orderly rush would be on to get a seat before the church was full. Just before they entered the door, an atmosphere of love washed over the two of them, and they locked eyes for barely a moment. Once inside they were directed to the left, and they simply followed their leader. They were able to get seats on the far left side, three rows from the back. At least, they were in. Now they would wait together until the service began.

Beth leaned over to whisper, "Mom, it feels really good in here. It feels like love. I know it says in the Bible that God is love. Is what I'm feeling mean He is here with us now?"

"Does it feel refreshing?"

"Yes."

"This is what it was like for me and your grandparents every time we went to church. It's why they would stay so late; it was hard to leave when you felt Father God's love on you."

Ari was disappointed they didn't have a better view. If things went as she had heard they did, the Holy Spirit would be flowing tonight, and there would be much to see.

From the first note played by the worship team, things got lively in the Spirit. Beth couldn't see what was happening up front. Ari switched with people in her row to be at the end. Then Beth could kneel on the pew to see. The church was filled with people worshipping God, and the atmosphere increased. The pastor took the podium, the worship team went quiet, and church business was conducted. News was shared, the collection was taken, people greeted each other, and then it was time for the message.

Beth was intent on listening tonight. If something was different and new, she didn't want to miss it. As the pastor began his message, it felt spiritually alive to her. Spiritual life was flowing directly into her emotional heart. As the pastor spoke, she could grasp the biblical illustration in her mind. She was learning and being fed. The message went an hour but felt like five minutes. The worship team returned, praise songs were sung, and the prayer team walked to the front.

The pastors announced, "All those seeking prayer, come forward now." People flowed from their pews and went forward. The pastor moved as freely as he could, reaching out, placing his hand on a person's head and down they went on the floor under the power of the Holy Spirit. Beth would not be denied; she stood on the pew to see over the people. In her heart, she was trying to decide if she should walk up the aisle to see what was going on. She leaned over and whispered into Ari's ear, "Mom, we need better seats tomorrow."

The night was over; they lingered before leaving the church. Beth walked up the aisle to be able to see around the adults. People were laid out all over the front of the church. The prayer team ministered to them, praying over them. Assistants covered the women with cloths to keep things modest. Quietly walking out, they left to find a late-night restaurant. Sitting at the table, Beth recognized people from the church at other tables. The restaurant was alive with conversation about what God was doing and how the Holy Spirit had touched them during the service. At their table, Ari would try and answer all Beth's questions.

Each service was building on the previous one; miracle after miracle happened. On their last night when the altar call was given, they went forward together. That night an evangelist had spoken, and as he moved closer to them, the spiritual atmosphere was electrified. He placed his hand upon Beth, and power shot into her body with a jolt. She staggered. As he placed his hand upon Ari, a wind swept across her.

In the unseen realm, an angel stepped up alongside of Ari. He placed his hand upon her shoulder, and she felt it. Within her welled up an inner witness. Her eyes looked back and forth across the altar area. Many healings were happening. In a nonverbal manner, a message was understood. "Ari, you are a lioness of God; you are to begin a revival and healing ministry. It is what you are being called to do."

On the long ride home, mother and daughter talked about the meetings. Beth described what she felt when she was prayed for on the last night. She said, "Mom, it happened so fast! All he did was place his hand on my head, and I felt like lighting shot through me. Then a peace washed down over me. If I hadn't fought it, Mom, I would have been down on the floor like all those other people. I feel different on the inside, but I can't tell you why."

Ari talked to her about her experiences when she was her age. They had shared the trip, the experience, and the Holy Spirit together.

Knowing his wife, Lance wasn't surprised when she began to talk about ministering in the supernatural. In hindsight, since Brownsville, she understood that God was closing the door to her work in the Health Care System. Knowing this took a huge weight off her back. She let it go and was looking for God to direct her path. Ari dove into researching the ministries that were seeing the most miracles happen. One was chosen that had a schedule of missionary trips in the coming year. She had a list of pro's and con's ready to have the conversation with Lance and the children when the time was right. This decision would affect them all. Her first step would be to ask for the support of the family.

Meanwhile they all needed to have some fun together. Ari made plans for the family to spend time together hiking. She talked with Lance and he agreed to do a day hike to Wichita Mountains, a prescription for adventure. Come Saturday morning she would have loved to yell, "Hey kids, get your hiking gear out" just like her dad had done. But Bethany and Raphael were older, and scheduling the hike was important. Soon they had the date set and were all looking forward to it.

Before they knew it, the date arrived. Backpacks, water bottles, snacks, sunglasses, sun screen, towels, books to read, and of course binoculars were all put into the trunk of the car. It was a short ride on I 44 to the Route 49 turn off. On the road, Lance had flashbacks of a beautiful woman wearing a bright red scarf around her neck. The wind had moved her hair as it curled over the windshield. She remembered, *Oh how he had loved that convertible!*

Pulling off the road and onto the parking area they came across a sign that read, "Bison Trail." Ari and Lance were older now, but still in good physical shape. They were ready for a day of surprises. It had been years since they had the kids up here. Back then, Lance had carried Raphael on his back so they could finish the hike before dark set in.

He popped the trunk open and the kids eagerly reached in to grab their gear. Together they walked over to the trailhead board. Bethany read the warning: "Stay on marked trail" when Lance and Arielle burst out laughing, remembering one of their first hikes together years earlier.

Raphael and Bethany led the way. The worn trail was easy to follow, but as they made their way around the boulder, it was harder to determine which way to go. The hike turned into pure adventure. Breaking out of their rocky path, they all scurried up on top of a huge boulder. Raphael got the binoculars out of his backpack and looked down onto Fort Sill.

"Dad, I can see puffs of dust in the target range. How far do you think that is from here?"

"We're about seven miles from the range. The ordnance you saw explode traveled 1.2 miles from the cannon firing line."

Ari and Beth brought out some snacks, and they all ate and soaked up the warm sunshine. The thought on Ari's mind, *I'm hoping for no close encounters with a buffalo today. One is enough for a lifetime.*

Finishing their hike without any buffalo surprises, they stowed their gear in the car and set off for Meer's Restaurant. The kids had a surprise in store for them.

Lance and Ari were not surprised to see that Meer's Restaurant had not changed in the last twenty years, although it was a marvel it was still standing. Lance and Ari thought the kids' eyes would pop out of their heads when the legendary cheeseburger arrived. It was total food and visual overload. The family laughed and talked their way through the meal.

Ari pointed to the window table and told the kids that was where she had her first Meer's burger with Lance. She shared how the crowd always gathered outside and about the ride home in the convertible with the top down. They were all fond memories for the two of them.

The time had come, however, to change the focus from the past to the future. Ari began, "I have some new ideas I want to run by you all."

Of course Lance already had a preview and was interested to see the children's reaction. She continued, "I have a month of vacation time built up at the hospital. What I have been praying about is going on a mission trip. Ever since going to Brownsville I have this burden to give it a try. What are your thoughts?"

Bethany was first, "Mom, where would you go? Near here or out of the country?"

"I'm thinking about traveling to Africa."

Raphael quickly spoke up, "How long would you be gone?"

"Adding the time I need for training and traveling to the place where the meetings will be held, it will be three and half weeks."

Silence. They were all thinking. Beth knew it would be better than Brownsville and she had seen how alive Ari became there—the joy was evident on her face. She said, "I think it would be good for you."

Raphael wanted to know who was going to cook while she was gone, and Lance objected to it by saying, "Hey buddy, I cook mean barbeque beans and franks." They laughed because they knew Dad would order out a lot.

Lance asked, "Hon, can you just sign up for one of the trips or do you have to get some type of training first?" From there Arielle laid out all the plans and preparations needed for taking the mission trip. They were all swept into her doing this as if they were all going.

The waitress came by, and they ordered ice cream. Where they were going to put it in their already full stomachs was yet to be seen. They fell into all the details in planning Ari's trip. Lance sat back and smiled, knowing she would be in her element.

The last hurdle on her list was getting the time off from work that would correspond with the ministry's scheduled trip. The hand of God was on all the details. It was if He had planned for her to go all along. All that was needed was for her to take that first step.

# FIFTY

Stepping out of the Crusade's van, she took three steps and paused. Despite all the activity around her, she was in her own world within her own thoughts. The awareness of what had brought her to this moment came flooding back—unexpected and emotionally powerful. Unlike her normal self, calm and in control, a sense of being overwhelmed rushed over her—not a sense of "What have I done?" Hers was instead a sense of "It has begun!"

Just in front of Arielle stood her guardian angel. The expression on his face was one of pure joy. He wanted to savor this moment. Year after year, event after event, he had hoped for this time to come—the apex of her destiny, the beginning of becoming the meaning of her name, "Lioness of God."

He stepped up to her left ear and spoke into her heart and mind. "Arielle, Lioness of God, welcome to your destiny. Walk in humility and release the power of God."

He wanted to say much more. But in the spiritual realm during times of divine interactions with humans, only what is needed is given. He knew that day she was a vessel of the healing power of God. He was proud.

"Ari! Arielle! We need to follow the group." Sandy, her roommate, startled her back into the present. The day was warm with a cloudless sky and a mild breeze. In a short time, everyone would be engulfed with the full heat of the day. The time had come to put into action all their prerequisite class time. Ari knew the drill of following laid-out procedures; she had acquired this skill while in the military.

Today was activations time. Following Sandy, she climbed the ten steps up to the platform. The wind caught her dress, and it swayed in the wind. The breeze was a welcome relief in the Tanzanian heat. At the rear of the platform, three rows of folding chairs were arranged in fifteen chairs per row. The last two rows had been reserved for all thirty volunteers. The row of chairs in front of the volunteers was for the local pastors and dignitaries.

Arielle took in her surroundings. Being in the back row, she and Sandy were directly under the aluminum structure that held the monitors and sound equipment. The platform was rectangular, thirty feet deep by fifty feet wide. Three foot high handrails were at each end of the platform for safety. They didn't want any person missing a step and falling from the stage—one of those lessons the team had learned along the way.

A tall black curtain was directly behind Ari and Sandy and ran the length of the stage as a backdrop to make it easier for the people to see those conducting the service. Careful planning of the event placed the stage on the north end of an expansive field to ensure no one had to deal with the blinding sun affecting their ability to watch and be involved in the service. This event had been very well conceived. All the minute details were taken care of so Jesus could be the focus. This service was going to be all about Him.

It was the final step up onto the stage that took Arielle's breath away. In all her life's experiences, nothing could have prepared her for what she was seeing. Thousands upon thousands, if not ten thousand people, were standing in the midday sun for this crusade. She was filled with wonder and joy. Emotions filled her heart that all of them came to be part of what God was doing in this nation. Dressed in their finest clothing, a sea of colors was in fluid motion as the crowd moved and swayed in anticipation. They had heard of the signs and wonders, the healings and deliverance happening in the crusades. They heard the Christian God was alive. She thought, *I have to remember all these details and commit them to memory; my husband and children will not believe this.* Our most meaningful events in our lives are the ones we share with our loved ones.

On the other side of the stage, people started coming up the stairs. The members of the choir were taking their positions. Three rows of believers were ready to worship God and help bring everyone into praising the Trinity. Minister David was dressed in casual apparel; his general appearance was not the typical type of a church person attendees would expect to see. However, there was no doubt on anyone's mind; they knew he was an anointed man of God. In order for the large crowd to hear him speak, sets of speakers ran the length of the field every two hundred feet.

A hush fell as he walked to the center of the stage and began to speak to the crowd. In a loud commanding voice, he said, "Jesus Christ is Lord of lords and King of kings!" His interpreter, standing right beside him, translated the message into Swahili, their national language: *Yesu Kristo ni bwana wa bwana na mfalme wa wafalme.* All the people started praising God. Again he spoke, "Let us all worship our King Jesus." Turning to the choir, he gave them their cue. In a burst of energy and beautiful voices, they sang a cappella.

The sky above the crusade opened in the spiritual realm, and the air was filled with electricity. The power of the Holy Spirit responded to the unity of praise. A dome of the glory of God covered the area. What everyone had come to experience was the tangible presence of God! Unseen to the human eye, a sea of angels swept into the crowd and took up their positions. An intersection of heaven and earth had begun.

Ari and Sandy looked at each other in awe. Never in their life had they experienced anything like this at home. The magnitude of the presence of God was beyond comprehension. The choir finished their final song in what seemed to be only minutes. Minister David again walked to the center of the stage as the choir left quietly. He began his message about God's plan of salvation for the human race. He showed them why they must be born again spiritually by Father God.

"Through the finished work of Jesus' sacrifice on the cross, we today can accept Him as a personal gift," he proclaimed. As he spoke, a spirit of repentance swept across the gathering. People wept. Hearts were softened. Faith rose up. As in a crescendo, he challenged them to invite Jesus into their hearts and lives. A call was given to pray to receive Jesus as their Savior and Lord. Minister David led them in the prayer to declare Jesus as Lord, to commit fully to His authority, and to follow Him the rest of their lives. Thousands of people opened up their hearts to Jesus. As it was a few decades ago in a small town in New Mexico, the roaring wind of the Holy Spirit could be heard. It sounded like superheated steam rushing through the pipes in the Four Corners generating plant. As the Holy Spirit reached the people, He circled above the crowd. Thousands of separate streams entered human hearts and changed them forever.

Through their faith, the Holy Spirit entered into their spirits, and they became a new creation. They were born spiritually and had entered into eternity with Father God. They were now adopted children of God. Running parallel in front of the platform was a myriad of angels, darting into the crowd and administering God's blessing.

Now it was time. Minister David, with a twirl, spun around, and pointed to the volunteers. "You are released!" Ari's heart began to beat within her chest. With a quick look at Sandy, they stood and headed for the stairs. Stepping down to the dry parched dirt, they turned toward the crowd and walked forward. Each volunteer would enter the sea of humanity with an interpreter.

Ari said a quick prayer, "Father God, let Your Holy Spirit flow through me. Use me, Lord." She thought, *This is why I came all this way. If not for my little brother's illness, this journey may never have happened.*

Thirty faces looked into a dense sea of humanity. In an instant, they gained the understanding of how Jesus felt when He had crowds gathered around Him. It would be different today; some would be healed and delivered. In the Scriptures, it often is said, "and He [Jesus] healed them all."

Again words came from the platform, "You are released." The crowd began to press forward, making it hard for the volunteers to walk among the people. They were packed so tightly now, it was body rubbing against body to make any headway into the sea.

An interpreter was to be with each volunteer but some quickly got lost in the crowd, so they had to adapt. Ari selected her first person for prayer. She placed her hand upon his head, not knowing his needs and said, "In the name of Jesus, be healed." Instantly the man responded to the healing. Ari heard him speaking in English.

He said, "I can hear again!" and began shouting, "I can hear again!" A bit stunned that a miracle has actually happened, she asked him, "How long have you been unable to hear?"

He responded, "For over a decade."

People were pressing against her now to receive from God. In her mind, a revelation was birthed. She moved on. This was why she had come here and what she had hoped to experience. Compassion for the people welled up within her heart. Seeing God move in power, she took her place as a lioness of God.

Ari placed her hand on top of heads and prayed in a strong commanding voice, "Be healed in the name of Jesus!" Many would have fallen under the power of God if there had been room to fall. The angel with Ari began to move, opening a circle for her to minister in. No longer being able to go deeper into the crowd, she walked in the created circle and became one with God's activities.

Arielle quickened her pace. The prayer time was nearing an end, and she was racing to touch as many people as possible when a mother got her attention. Her little boy had two locked wrists that were bent inward, making the use of his hands very limited. Taking his hands in hers, she began to pray until she felt movement. Startled, she looked at his wrists as they stretched out and went into a normal position. The woman screamed, and tears flooded her eyes as she began to praise God. Ari took his hands; his wrists were normal. Smiling in delight, she moved on.

From the platform came the call: "Volunteers, return to the stage." Ari had her orders. As the circle around her closed, she pushed her way toward the front. Leaving the sea of people, she was directed toward the bus in back of the platform. For their safety, the crowd would be dismissed to return to their homes before darkness fell. However, on this first day, a few of the volunteers felt unable to return. Seeing God's power in action, they felt compelled that more people needed healing and delayed the ending of today's crusade. They had been told in no uncertain terms in their training that once the return call was given, they needed to stop immediately. It took an additional thirty minutes to retrieve the stragglers. The bus exploded with God stories of healings.

With the last volunteer aboard, they returned to the hotel to eat and have their first after-the-Crusade meeting. The first item at the meeting was to establish order. Warnings were given: if a person did not return when called, that person would be restricted from the volunteer team. They moved on to outlining the details for tomorrow's meeting. Concluding for the night, they were dismissed, and Ari went to her room.

After she and her roommate talked, Ari rested in bed, placing her hands behind her head, and began to examine the clues. Running through her mind was the thought that she had never before been a part of something like this. Because of her years of nursing and medical experience, she knew the human body and its working parts. *But what happened today?* she wondered. In her childhood, she had watched the miracles of healing happen in a void of comprehension. In this movement she had another void of understanding—a piece was missing. In her mind she reran the prayer time until she fell asleep.

As if reveille were being played, Ari awakened early. She began the motions of the day with her heart and mind, waiting to hear four words being spoken: "Volunteers, you are released." When that moment came, she again waded into the sea of humanity. Knowing her role, she began to release the healing power of God upon people. Moving from person to person and seeing them respond to God, it happened. As she placed her hand upon a young girl's head, she felt electricity leave the palm of her hand and flow into the girl. The emotion was powerful and shocking. Her mind made a note to think about it later, and she moved on. Miracle after miracle was taking place. Whatever they needed God was releasing to heal them. Just like yesterday, it flowed with ease.

Loud chatter filled the air on the bus with what God did in the prayer time. Testimonies were shared one with another. For the volunteers, being used of God had brought fresh significance into their lives and hearts. Co-laboring with the Holy Spirit in the supernatural had heightened their spirits and new godly esteem was felt. They were really making a difference with their lives, and it mattered to those for whom they were praying.

During her time of reflection, Ari contemplated the power she felt leave her hand earlier. She had seen damaged bodies. Some needed medicine and care to recover. Others needed surgery to continue life. Then there were those who died. Today she saw something in the spirit she had not understood to this depth. In the Bible story of the woman with the issue of blood, virtue left Jesus, and she was healed. Today, what Ari felt was virtue. Virtue was targeted power to heal. It had left her hand, entered the girl, flowed to the unhealthy area, and regenerated the bad tissue and functions so they were healthy. As always, one question led to another. It would take time for her to know the power was the Holy Spirit—one of His elements to be freely given in the world.

Each day for Arielle was the same—God healed as she prayed for those she could touch in the sea of humanity. No wonder the people would travel hours to attend a meeting. God showed up and touched their broken bodies and gave them back their lives. They returned to normal. Why here and how is God moving were the questions.

Ari knew the American health care systems from the bottom to the top. Having been a nurse and working her way up in hospital administration, she had firsthand experience. She knew the best man could do in the healthcare system paled in comparison to the power of God. She was not discounting the system because professional caregivers were generally moved by compassion and were only working from their knowledge base and within the scope of practice—but without God. Generally, people wanted to help hurting people; however, compassion has its limits. What she was witnessing was what she thought America needed. In this rush of new information, she had to remember God still used doctors and medicine, but she experienced a twinge of pain in thinking how many more could be blessed at home if God were free to heal supernaturally.

In an overview of the crusade, Ari's administrative learning came into play. She laughed when it was brought down to a single point. It was like the movie *Field of Dreams*. It all came down to the single phrase in the movie where Kevin Costner hears, "Build it, and they will come." Similarly, "Invite the Holy Spirit to come and make Jesus the focus. He will come."

Here in Africa, in the people's day-to-day living, faith was required just to survive. Arielle thought, *How does this level of faith, revelation, and intimacy with Jesus enter the American society?*

The ministry team hopscotched across the globe as they made their way home. During the long hours in the air, most of them caught up on their sleep. In all the excitement during the crusade, the one thing that was in short supply was sleep. Ari was too full of all that she had recently seen, so she lowered her tray table to write in her notebook. Although it was nearly full at this point, she made entries to examine later. The obvious issue on her mind was leaving the healthcare industry.

In a flash, she looked back on her life and for the first time could see some things she had overlooked. God had knocked on this door before and perhaps now was calling her to step through. She rolled this thought around in her mind until she drifted off to sleep. She had a dream. . .

> A toddler took a square block and look at a large plastic ball with various shaped holes in it, knowing she could slip the square through the proper hole and let it drop inside. The toddler just needed to learn which hole on the toy was a square one in order to drop the right block through it. Sitting next to the child was the mother, watching and allowing her child to learn. The scene shifted until she was viewing her own life. In front of her, watching through her own eyes, she saw the progression of her training to be a nurse. When she looked beyond, there was a wall with a wide open door.
>
> She watched as she grew in knowledge. In her spiritual journey, God looked on at her progress. Ari was taking the event of Sammy's healing and transferring it upon the medical profession. In her hands were the tools of healing, trying to fit them through an invisible barrier of supernatural healing. Within her heart, faith arose and she saw the tools of the medical profession pass through the barrier of faith where broken human bodies were restored. Looking beyond this scene and to the wall, she saw the door swing close and shut. The sound of the door hitting the jamb startled Ari awake.

She got it. A new door had opened in her life when she heard the voice say, "Go to Brownsville."

Landing at JFK New York, the team would begin to scatter. They entered the immigration room and showed their passports. It was the last leg home and a tearful goodbye for Ari and Sandy. They had shared something unique, and that bond would keep them in contact for many years. Ari, feeling the jet lag, wearily viewed the arrival and departure monitors. She did not expect anyone else from the team to be going to the Will Rogers Airport in Oklahoma.

In the air once again, she brought out her notebook and began her to do list: 1) Contact Global University for the Pastoral Degree Program. 2) Search local areas that are experiencing supernatural healings. 3) Build a ministry team? Is there a stand alone ministry in my future? She couldn't even begin to imagine what God was going to lead her to do in this new season of adventure.

In the scheme of airport rankings, Will Rogers is ranked number one in cuteness. Twenty-four gates were ready to meet new arrivals. After she passed through the door and into the gate area, Lance, Bethany, and Raphael were waiting for her. In Beth's hand was a bouquet of flowers welcoming her home. Ari picked up her pace and rushed to embrace them. She dropped her carryon bag and gathered them all in her arms. Tears filled her eyes; it seemed like an age since she had been with them.

While she was gone, her life had changed and she needed to tell them all about it. But right now, even if she wanted to talk, she couldn't. Her emotions were overwhelming her. How deeply she had missed them. She had relished her time of being in Africa, but her family was her life and love. When she could say a word, she merely shared, "You will not believe what happened!" It would take weeks to tell them about all the miracles and wonders she had seen and how she had the pleasure of being part of God's work.

Off to the side, Ari's guardian angel was greeting his new arrivals. They had a conversation, aligning days and times of God's divine appointments. There would be a convergence of people and resources to build God's supernatural ministry. America was in a season of comfort, a time of blessings given to the Body of Christ. However, Matthew 24 clearly tells us hard times would be in the future. God always has a remnant at His disposal. Ari would be part of building a ministry, and "They will come."

# About the Author

Tom Donnan was pronounced clinically dead of a heart attack in February 2006. But God wasn't done with him. He brought Tom back to the land of the living with a burden to see revival come to America.

He frequently travels and ministers with Pastor Phillip Corbett, as well as to churches for speaking engagements on his own. He has also written a book entitled *Healing the Nation*. He has five grandchildren.

## Contact Information

You can email Tom at: Healingthenation1776@gmail.com